Worth
Waiting
For

BOOKS BY TILLY TENNANT

Hopelessly Devoted to Holden Finn
Mishaps and Mistletoe
The Summer of Secrets
The Summer Getaway
The Christmas Wish
The Mill on Magnolia Lane
Hattie's Home for Broken Hearts
The Garden on Sparrow Street
The Break Up
The Waffle House on the Pier
Cathy's Christmas Kitchen

AN UNFORGETTABLE CHRISTMAS SERIES
A Very Vintage Christmas
A Cosy Candlelit Christmas

FROM ITALY WITH LOVE SERIES
Rome is Where the Heart Is
A Wedding in Italy

HONEYBOURNE SERIES
The Little Village Bakery
Christmas at the Little Village Bakery

MISHAPS IN MILLRISE SERIES
Little Acts of Love
Just Like Rebecca
The Parent Trap
And Baby Makes Four

ONCE UPON A WINTER SERIES
The Accidental Guest
I'm Not in Love
Ways to Say Goodbye
One Starry Night

TILLY TENNANT

Worth Waiting For

bookouture

Published by Bookouture in 2020

An imprint of Storyfire Ltd.
Carmelite House
50 Victoria Embankment
London EC4Y 0DZ

www.bookouture.com

ISBN: 978-1-80019-213-3
eBook ISBN: 978-1-80019-212-6

Chapter One

Ellie slammed on her brakes. Distracted by what she had just heard, she hadn't noticed the lights change to red until she was almost on top of them. Through the rear view mirror, she noted the man in the car behind purse his lips.

'You did what?' she squeaked. She listened, phone clamped to her ear, her frown deepening. 'I'm coming over now. It doesn't matter if I'm at work – this is more important. Stop arguing, Mum, I can't leave it now…. Yes, I realise it's illegal to answer my phone while I'm driving but you're not giving me much choice…' She ended the call and tossed the phone onto the passenger seat. It seemed churlish to blame her mum for driving and talking, but she felt churlish right now.

At the next roundabout, Ellie swung her Mini around.

As she drove up the other side of the dual carriageway, back in the direction she had just come from, the phone rang again.

'Dad? What's up?' She listened, a new and deeper frown forming. 'You did *what*?!' she squeaked again in a voice so high it was possible that dolphins off the coast of Scotland would hear it. 'Well, how the hell did you manage to set fire to one of those?' She listened for a moment and then sighed. 'I could come over in an hour or so…' She narrowed her eyes as a thought occurred to her. 'You did phone the fire service before you called me, didn't you? Don't get upset, I'm just checking… no, I don't think you're stupid… yes, of course that doesn't mean I don't want to come over and help… no, it *does* matter! Of course it does, it's just that I told mum…. yes, I've spoken to her… no, she didn't ask about you… no, I can't give her a message; you know she won't listen anyway… I have to go to her first because she needs help at Hazel's place. OK, I'll be an hour.'

At the next set of lights, Ellie rang one of her speed dial numbers. 'Patrick… yeah, I'm good… I'm going to be late for this school thing, can you cover it?' She listened for a moment and then grinned. 'It's only some crappy local author, just listen to her, get the gist of what she says to the kids and tell me later. If I can get there I will… I'm really sorry to ask again… you know I'll love you forever… Yep, it's both of them this time… No, they're still not speaking. I know, I owe you big style.' Ellie ended the call and tossed the phone back to the seat. She chewed her lip as a double-decker lumbered from the bus lane onto the dual carriageway ahead of her, and with a grey haired old man driving the car in the parallel lane, blocking her progress, it was as much as she could do not to jam her fist onto the car horn.

'Bloody hell, shift it, will you!' she muttered savagely.

The phone rang again. 'Jethro…' she screwed up her face as there was an irritated beep from the car behind, 'you know I love you but whatever it is, can it wait?' She listened for a moment. 'I'm gutted for you, but she wasn't right for you, I always said so… I will phone you later, I promise… I told you I fell asleep that time… OK, hang in there… if in doubt, just go to default setting: as we know, copious amounts of whisky helps to mend broken hearts.'

Just as she had tossed the phone back onto the seat the screen flashed again to signal another call. She really needed to get some sort of apparatus to answer her phone safely in the car if every day was going to be this mental.

KASUMI

Ellie sighed. This one would simply have to wait.

*

Ellie knocked at the sleek black front door. From within, she could hear what sounded suspiciously like voices filled with hysterical panic, but she tried not to let the idea send her spiralling into a state of panic too. Instead, she waited patiently, aware that it might take a while. After a few moments, however, she decided that her mum and aunt probably hadn't heard her knock, and had just raised her fist to try again when the door swung open. Her aunt Hazel appeared.

'Has she managed to stop the water?' Ellie asked, stepping in as Hazel stood aside. She frowned as her aunt let out a wheezy laugh. 'And what are you doing exerting yourself?' Ellie added.

Hazel's chortle became even louder and wheezier. 'Your mother couldn't very well answer the door *and* keep the towel over the hole, could she?'

Ellie watched as her aunt took wobbly steps down the hall into the kitchen, every so often a hand reaching out for the support of a wall. 'Did you ring the plumber?'

'Yes,' Hazel said without looking round. 'He said he'd be about an hour, but you know that means he's going home to have his dinner first and he'll be over when he feels like it.'

'Probably charge you an arm and a leg too,' Ellie said.

Ellie entered the kitchen to find her mum looking virtually suicidal as she desperately pressed a soaking towel against the wall. A large puddle had formed at her feet and water ran down the wall in a steady stream, despite her best efforts to stem the flow. On the worktop sat a rust-bitten old electric drill and an assorted and very random looking selection of screws. Leaning against the wall was a large Monet print in a wooden frame. Ellie shook her head wonderingly.

'What the hell were you thinking of? You could have electrocuted yourself if you'd hit a wire. There must be wiring and water pipes all over the walls here… it is a kitchen, after all. I think springing a leak is actually the best outcome we could have hoped for in this scenario.'

'I bought this lovely print for Hazel and I was putting it up. The kitchen was the room it suited best,' her mum said in a defensive tone.

'Mum… you've never used a drill in your life. Couldn't you have got a man in?'

'This is the new Miranda Newton you're talking to. I don't need men anymore, not for anything.'

'You bloody well do for my kitchen,' Hazel cut in.

Ellie sighed and turned to her aunt. 'Couldn't you have talked some sense into her?'

Hazel held up her hands and shrugged. 'You think I've ever been able to tell my baby sister what to do? Besides, it's cheered me up.'

'Mum turns your kitchen into a scene from *Titanic* and it cheers you up?'

'Well, it's exciting. It gets boring sitting here day after day waiting for those bloody scans.' Hazel made her way slowly to the kettle. 'At least we've got water in here,' she said, shaking it. 'So we can have a cuppa while we wait for the plumber.'

Ellie glanced at Miranda. 'What about Mum?'

'She'll have to drink hers over there, one-handed,' Hazel said serenely. 'You could write a story about her heroism and personal sacrifice as she struggles to stem the tide of water threatening to engulf our street, even at the expense of biscuits with her tea.'

'Very funny,' Miranda snapped.

Ellie paused thoughtfully. 'Has anyone actually considered shutting the water off at the mains?'

Miranda glanced at Hazel with a sheepish expression. 'I didn't think of that.'

Ellie rolled her eyes heavenwards as if seeking divine strength.

'I just panicked, that's all,' Miranda added in a defensive tone.

'I did think of it,' Hazel said with a smirk. 'But I was having too much fun watching your mum panic to say anything.'

'Thank you,' Miranda said. 'Just wait until I get my hands on you...'

'I'm ill,' Hazel fired back. 'You're supposed to be caring for me. I'll have you up for assault.'

'You'll have me up for more than that,' Miranda growled. 'There's no point in doing things by halves.'

'OK, ladies...' Ellie said, trying not to laugh as the situation seemed to grow more absurd by the second. 'Hazel, is the stopcock under the sink?'

Hazel nodded. 'If you're determined to spoil my fun then yes, it is.'

*

As Ellie and Miranda mopped up, Hazel made a pot of tea and brought it to the table. Ellie's phone buzzed a text. Hazel picked it up and peered at the screen. She glanced at Miranda briefly before passing it to Ellie, who was on her way over, wiping her hands on her jeans. Hazel raised her eyebrows in a sign of collusion as Ellie looked at the screen. She nodded briefly at her aunt before locking the phone again and stuffing it in her pocket.

'Is it someone important?' Ellie's mum asked vaguely.

'No,' Ellie said, wringing a teacloth out into a bucket. 'It can wait for a while.'

'But if it's work…' Miranda pressed.

'It's not work. When I've done here I'll reply.'

Miranda looked up with a hint of suspicion in her expression, but then seemed to let whatever argument she was brewing up pass. 'Have you seen anything of your dad?' she asked instead in a carefully neutral tone.

Ellie was spared a reply by the sound of a knock at the front door echoing through the house. She sprang up with far more enthusiasm than was necessary. 'I'll get it,' she chirruped.

Out in the hallway she heaved a sigh of relief. The situation between her mum and dad was getting stickier by the day. Anyone else would simply have taken them both by an ear and smacked their heads together to knock some sense into them. Because that was how they were behaving – like a couple of toddlers. But Ellie couldn't risk upsetting either of them; the emotional trauma would be too much to bear on top of everything else going on in her life.

'Plumber,' a beefy, bristle-haired man announced as Ellie opened the door.

'Brilliant… through here.'

There was no need to tell him where the hole was: the man audibly sniggered as he walked into the kitchen and saw the mess. Miranda shot him a hate-filled glare but he seemed oblivious as he wandered over to inspect the damaged wall.

*

Fifteen minutes, a great deal of broken plaster and two hundred pounds later, the plumber had packed up and gone. As all the excitement had clearly worn Hazel out, the three women had moved into the living room so she could rest.

'I'm in the wrong profession,' Ellie remarked as she pulled on her jacket to leave. 'Emergency plumbing is the job to be in; he must be rolling in it.'

'The house insurance will cover it and I really can't be bothered to care,' Hazel said, lowering herself into an armchair.

Ellie bent to kiss her on the forehead. 'Have a nap. Mum's going to clear up, aren't you?'

Miranda nodded.

'It's the least she can do,' Hazel said, stifling a tired grin.

'I'll call tomorrow, bring some cookie dough ice-cream,' Ellie added.

Her aunt's appetite had disappeared a few weeks back, and her weight had become dangerously low. Ellie and her mum had tried food after food to tempt her, until they had been delighted to discover her penchant for cookie dough ice-cream, raspberry jelly and custard. Since they had introduced those things regularly into her diet, blatantly against the advice of Hazel's oncologist, her weight had steadily increased again and she had felt much better.

'Sounds lovely,' Hazel said in a voice that was already becoming sleepy. 'How about you bring that film over too... you know, that funny one you were telling me about the other day...'

'Funny film... check. Ice-cream... check.' Ellie kissed her mum. 'Try not to blow Hazel's roof off or anything while you're both home alone.'

'Very funny. When are you coming for tea next?'

'I'm not sure, I have –' Ellie's reply was cut short by her phone ringing. She pulled it from her pocket and frowned at the screen before she answered. 'Hey... yes, I'm coming over now... Ok, see you shortly.'

'Who was that?' Miranda asked, narrowing her eyes slightly.

'Nobody,' Ellie said brightly as she headed for the door. 'Got to run. Catch you later.'

*

Ellie pulled up outside a block of flats near the outskirts of town. Getting out of the car, she glanced up at the immaculate frontage. The building was a renovated psychiatric hospital, now restored to its former Victorian glory (minus the inmates and barbarism, of course) and furnished with brand new trendy apartments. But Ellie knew that the particular apartment she was going to visit would be anything but trendy and well-kept.

At the main doors, she buzzed and waited. A tinny voice crackled through the intercom.

'Yes?'

'It's me.'

Another buzz and a click and Ellie pushed open the doors into the main atrium.

The door had been left open for her when she arrived at the flat, and she let it swing shut behind her.

'Dad?' she called as she wandered into the living room. There was no reply. 'OK, Dad…' Ellie said quietly through pursed lips as she surveyed the debris. 'Either you've climbed out of the window to avoid talking to me or you're buried under dirty crockery.' She pulled the heavy curtains open, releasing a little cloud of dust as she did so. 'Bloody hell, it's like Miss Havisham's gaff in here… Dad!' Ellie employed the full capacity of her lungs this time.

Her dad shuffled through from the kitchen, glasses abandoned on top of his head, his greying hair sticking out at odd angles and black smudges across his nose and cheeks.

'Since the building is not a smouldering ruin, you appear to be alive, and the four horsemen of the apocalypse are conspicuously absent, I take it everything is under control,' Ellie asked, doing her best Roger Moore eyebrow.

Her dad grinned sheepishly. 'It was only a tiny fire after all. I just panicked.'

Ellie was getting used to hearing that phrase from one or other of her parents. When together, they had argued like the proverbial cat and dog, but apart they were totally lost. It was the third time her dad had called her that week over a domestic disaster. Either his estrangement from her mum was turning him into some bizarre Frank Spencer clone or it was a cry for attention. Ellie couldn't be sure – he had been known, on occasion during her childhood, to electrocute himself whilst changing a light bulb and had once fallen through the open loft hatch – so the former was worryingly possible.

'I still don't know how you managed to set fire to a toilet roll,' Ellie said. On the drive over she had considered several whacky theories. The truth was oddly disappointing.

'It just happened to be on the side when I lit the stove and I knocked it over with my arm.' He shrugged apologetically.

'Right...' Ellie glanced at her watch. She had been far longer than she had anticipated and was already pushing her colleague, Patrick, for more favours than she could ever repay in this lifetime and probably quite a few reincarnations to come. 'Do you need help clearing up the damage?'

'It wasn't that much really.'

'So you'll be OK?'

'I'm sorry,' her dad said. 'I suppose you should be at work.'

'Yes, I should.' She could have mentioned that he'd been fully aware of her work commitments when he phoned her earlier but she didn't. 'I'll pop over later if you like,' she added, seeing the shadow of melancholy that crossed his features. He brightened instantly.

'That would be nice... if you're sure it's no trouble. I could show you the new pan pipes I had delivered today.'

Ellie could think of a million things she ought to be doing, quite a lot of them involving people her own age and none of them involving painfully out-of-tune pan pipe playing, but she simply smiled. 'Of course it isn't. I'll bring you some shopping.'

'How do you know I need shopping?'

'Dad... you *always* need shopping. You can't eat musical instruments, you know, so why do you insist on buying all this crap instead of feeding yourself?' She glanced around. 'And do you think we can have less of the jumble sale vibe around here when I get back?'

'I know... I've been meaning to clean up.'

'When was that, exactly? 1982?'

He pouted like a sullen schoolboy.

'Sorry,' Ellie said, her heart lurching at the sadness in his expression. He was having a hard time without her mum, but with all the chaos in her own life it was easy for Ellie to forget that he needed things to take his mind off that. She reached to kiss him on the cheek. 'I would stay now but I really have to meet Patrick to cover a story.'

Her dad forced a smile. 'Say hello to him for me.'

'I will,' Ellie called as she headed for the door.

*

Ellie pulled into the open gates of Millrise Academy of Excellence, formerly known as plain old Millrise High School before the government had decided that every school needed to sound as though it trained kids in the arts of espionage, astrophysics and ninja assassination. Grabbing her phone and favourite polka-dot satchel from the passenger seat, she leapt out of the car and hurried to the school reception.

'Hi, I'm Ellie Newton, from the *Millrise Echo*,' she announced breathlessly to the impossibly perky looking woman on the reception desk.

The woman gave a faint look of surprise. 'I thought you were all finished here...' She pulled the visitor book around to read the entries. 'Yes, Patrick Morgan from the *Echo* signed out an hour ago and the lady author, Suzy Salford, signed out a few minutes later.'

'Shit... sorry, I mean, I was supposed to meet Patrick here.'

'I'm afraid they've both gone.'

Ellie chewed her lip for a moment. 'OK, thanks,' she said finally. As she walked back to her car she dialled Patrick.

'I'm so sorry,' she said as he picked up. There was a chuckle from the other end of the line.

'You're racking these favours up,' he said. 'I actually think I did a pretty good job of passing myself off as a real live journalist today. I really don't think I need you anymore, *partner.*'

'Yeah, yeah, but who would you wind up all day if you didn't have me?' Ellie grinned as a wave of relief washed over her. She hadn't really thought for a minute that Patrick would be angry with her, but she was beginning to wonder if she was pushing her luck.

'You should thank your lucky stars that you didn't get there in time anyway. That author was the most boring woman on the planet. She could have died half way through the question and answer session and nobody would have noticed. God, I'd hate to read one of her books.'

'You'd hate to read *anyone's* book,' Ellie quipped as she unlocked her car.

'Seriously, though...' Patrick added. Ellie stopped dead.

'What?'

'You need to stop running around after your parents. They're adults and they need to stop leaning on you all the time. In fact, aren't they supposed to do this sort of thing for *you*, not the other way around? They know you have an actual job and a life of your own, right?'

Ellie sighed. 'Vernon understands how things are and he said he was OK with me popping off from time to time as long as my work got done and I managed to stick to deadlines. Things are just a mess now. They'll calm down when Mum and Dad work things out and get back together.'

'It's been months. Have you considered that they might never get back together?'

'Of course they will,' Ellie said in a voice that suggested nothing was more certain. 'I'm on my way into the office now. Are you heading back too?'

'Yeah. You bring the coffees, I'll bring the Jammy Dodgers and my notes, and we'll meet in the kitchen for *Operation Snorefest*.'

Ellie giggled. 'OK, I'll see you in half an hour.'

Chapter Two

Ellie swung round on her chair with a jerk. There were only so many ways you could make a story about shopping trolleys stolen from a local superstore interesting, and Ellie had been smothered into a sleepy haze by the office's central heating as she tried vainly to do just that. It wasn't helping that she had fallen asleep in front of her dad's TV the previous evening when she popped back to see him. After throwing a pizza in the oven, they had watched reruns of *Bergerac* together and Ellie had woken just after one in the morning with a stiff neck and the TV still murmuring in the corner. Her dad had fallen asleep too and barely even opened his eyes as she nudged him in the direction of his bedroom. Ellie could have stayed over, but faced with the prospect of going to the toilet in the night and being sucked beneath her dad's washing pile as if it was some kind of fabric-based quick-sand, she decided that she'd rather drive home. Back at her house, it had taken another hour and two cups of Horlicks before she felt sleepy enough to go back to bed. At Vernon's announcement, however, she was suddenly wide awake again.

'Seriously?'

Vernon nodded and stretched into a huge yawn, obviously suffering from the heating and the effects of a slow news morning as much as Ellie. 'Bloody nutter.' He glanced at Ellie with a wry smile. 'I suppose you want this one?'

'I do! I swear if I have to visit another school dress-up day I'm going to jump from the nearest motorway bridge.'

'That's because you keep getting mistaken for one of the kids and ending up in detention,' Ange called over her shoulder as she stared intently at a photo of an escaped armed robber spotted in a local branch of Toys 'R' Us that morning perusing the Barbie stand.

'Ha ha,' Ellie shot back.

Ellie looked much younger than her twenty-seven years on account of her petite stature and huge brown eyes in a heart-shaped face. She had styled her hair into a short, elfin cut in the hope that it might age her, but it had only made her look younger still and a little like a pixie from an Enid Blyton book, much to her annoyance and to the hilarity of the rest of her office at the newspaper. Ange whizzed around and gave her a huge grin.

'You know I'm just jealous, right? It's been about thirty years since I got mistaken for anyone below retirement age.'

Ellie laughed. 'I don't know what you're worried about, you always look super glam.'

'Yeah, like a glamorous granny.' Ange raised her eyebrows.

'Noooo, like Joan Collins.'

'I rest my case.'

'Back to this story then...' Vernon chuckled. 'You might want to get a move on with this one, Ellie. If the police get a sniff he'll be gone before you arrive.'

Ellie frowned. 'Aren't there human rights laws about things like that? If he wants to sit on a street corner, can they stop him?'

'Depends how much of a nuisance he is, I suppose,' Vernon mused. 'I'm not really *au fait* with that area of the law.'

'No...' Ange cut in, 'kerb crawling is your speciality...'

'Oi! Only as part of news stories!' Vernon laughed.

Ellie turned to him. 'So let me get this straight… this guy has decided to camp out on the corner of Constance Street because he wants to win back his girlfriend?'

'It would seem so.'

'Wouldn't it be easier to text her like normal people do?'

'One would imagine that he has tried all the usual methods and failed.'

'It's a bit odd.'

'A bit romantic,' Ange offered.

'Romantic?' Ellie repeated.

'Don't you think so?'

'It sounds like attention seeking to me.'

'Of course it is. He's seeking the attention of the woman he loves.'

'Romantic or not,' Ellie said, shaking herself and grabbing her polka-dot satchel from under the desk, 'this is the first decent story I've had in months.' She leapt from her chair and rushed for the door. 'Catch you guys later.'

*

Ellie searched her brain as she drove, trying to remember the exact location of Constance Street. She had a vague idea that it was one long row of terraced houses amongst a labyrinth of other terraced rows on the outskirts of Millrise. But as her sat nav had reset itself to *confuse* rather than *navigate*, she had yanked it from the dashboard in a fit of temper. It now lay stuffed under the passenger seat and Ellie had to rely on memory alone.

Just as she turned into a side street, her mobile rang.

'Hey Mum, what have you done this time?' She clamped the phone between her ear and shoulder as she changed gear.

Her mum's tight voice came down the line. 'Are you driving… *again*?'

'Yeah, it's OK though; I'm always driving when you phone and you don't usually snap at me. What's up?'

'I bloody do! I've told you time and time again. Phone me back when you've stopped.'

'No… hang on, Mum,' Ellie sighed as she swerved towards the kerb and pulled on the handbrake. 'Is everything OK? You sound a bit tense.'

'I'm bound to be tense when you insist on doing everything while you're trying to drive. You'll kill yourself one of these days.'

Ellie frowned. It was on the tip of her tongue to remind her mum that the reason she did everything whilst trying to drive was that there was so much to do. 'OK, I won't do it anymore if it bothers you that much… what's really wrong?'

There was a loud exhale at the end of the line, and then silence for a moment. 'It's your aunt Hazel.'

'The latest scans are back?'

'They're… they're…'

'Mum?'

Ellie's mother sniffed hard. 'You're at work; this should probably wait until later.'

'Mum, you can't call me with half a story and then expect it to wait all day. I know it's bad, so just tell me.' Ellie cut the engine. 'The cancer has spread, hasn't it?'

'Oh Ellie…' her mum began in a choked voice, 'it's in her lungs, her glands… it's everywhere.'

'Oh God. Poor Hazel…' Ellie murmured. 'You want me to come over?'

'No, love, there's no point. You've skipped work enough for me as it is and you can't do anything here anyway except mope.'

'But... what about you?'

'I'm fine; it's Hazel we need to worry about.'

Ellie watched absently as a little old lady dragged a disgruntled looking dog past on a lead. 'I should call to see her when I finish work. Do you want me to pick you up first?'

'If you don't mind, that would be good.'

'OK, see you later...' Ellie went for the call end button but her mother's voice came through again.

'Ellie...'

'Yeah, still here.'

'Please be careful when you're out on the road...'

'Of course, Mum. Love you.'

'Love you too. More than you can ever imagine.'

Ellie ended the call and let her head fall to the steering wheel. She screwed her eyes shut tight. Though they had all been expecting it, this was not the news she had wanted to hear about her aunt. Drying her eyes, she took a deep breath and steadied herself. There would be time to dwell on the sorrows that were coming, but right now she had a lead to follow. Her aunt Hazel would be furious if she thought for a moment that people's lives had been put on hold for her illness – an illness with a path that was now headed for only one destination, no matter how many tears were shed.

*

As soon as Ellie turned into Constance Street, she saw the figure of a man sitting on a striped, fold-up chair. He had a piece of card bearing some writing and a photo of a girl leaning against the wall by his side, a thermos flask down on the pavement at his other side. Other than the black, well-cut reefer coat and his immaculate grooming, he could have been a tramp begging for change. The day was the usual sort of winter's day in Britain – grey and heavy with a damp chill in the air that seemed to find a way through clothing to seep into bones and joints. Ellie felt cold just looking at him huddled there. Avoiding the nearby double yellow lines, she pulled up a few feet away and grabbed her notebook from the passenger seat of her Mini.

'Hi!' she called in the brightest voice she could muster as she made her way over.

Covering all sorts of stories and meeting all sorts of people, Ellie was always prepared for all sorts of receptions when she approached someone for the first time, but he looked up with a smile so warm and genuine that for a moment it threw her off-guard.

'I'm Ellie Newton,' she said, quickly recovering her wits and sticking out her hand. 'From the *Millrise Echo*.'

He reached out and shook hands. Ellie couldn't help but notice the strong warmth of his grip – not in the over-masculine way that some men she went to visit grabbed her hand, but in a way that suggested a certain ease with himself. 'I wondered who would get here first,' he said, 'police or newspaper.'

'Police?'

'I'm sure some mean-spirited busy-body will call them sooner or later to move me on.'

'Right,' Ellie smiled. 'Don't worry; I don't want to move you on. In fact, I want you to stay right there until my photographer gets here.'

He unfolded a second seat from against the wall and patted it for her. 'Want to get comfy while you wait?'

'Thanks.' Ellie sat and opened her notepad. 'Prepared for visitors, eh?'

'For one in particular… if she ever shows up…' he said, his expression suddenly melancholy.

Ellie watched him carefully. He was undoubtedly good looking: caramel skin, huge dark eyes and closely cropped black hair, the sort of smile that could light up cities. For the second time that day, she was wrong-footed and had to shake herself. 'I'd like to do a piece about you for the paper – well, about the reasons you've decided to sit here – if that's OK.'

He nodded. 'Sure, why not. If it gets Gemma to notice then I'm game for anything.'

'That's her name?'

'Gemma Fox.'

'Is this her?' Ellie nodded her head in the direction of the photo on the card. He picked it up and gazed at it.

'Yeah. She's gorgeous, eh?'

Ellie examined the photo. The girl had blonde locks tumbling over her shoulders in perfectly formed waves, huge green eyes and a full mouth. She looked like supermodel material. Ellie suddenly felt very plain, but she pushed the thought to the back of her mind. 'She's lovely.'

'I know. I should have told her that more often…'

Ellie glanced at the picture again. This woman didn't look as if she needed people to tell her she was beautiful – the certainty of that knowledge seemed to shine from every fibre of her being. 'Can I ask your name?' Ellie said, steering the conversation away from this annoyingly perfect specimen of womanhood.

'Ben Kelly.'

'Ben short for Benjamin or just plain Ben?' Ellie asked as she scribbled down the details.

'Benvolio, actually.'

Ellie glanced up and he met her questioning look with a grin. 'Nothing to do with me – all my mum's idea.'

'It's… unusual. I'm jealous. I wish I had a more imaginative name,' Ellie replied, noting it down.

'What's wrong with Ellie? It's nice.'

She looked up and shrugged. 'It's nice. And also very common.'

'If you leave off the *Volio* bit, mine's quite common too.' He flashed her another disarming grin.

Ellie bit back one of her own and bent her head to her notes again. 'How long have you been here?'

'Since this morning. I didn't call the newspaper, by the way, a woman who lives on the street did.'

'Does it matter?'

'I'm just explaining, in case it looks like I'm out to gain notoriety or some sort of fame by proxy. The only attention I really want is Gemma's.'

'I didn't think that, and I don't mind who called us – a story is a story.' Ellie glanced along the street. It was an unremarkable row of red-brick terraced houses, much like many rows in the north of England – some crumbling, some decked out with the latest mod cons – all unique and quirky despite the uniformity of their build. 'Have many of the residents been out to see you?'

'Not yet. But it's early and people haven't got in from work. I expect somebody will have something to say when they do.'

'That doesn't bother you?'

He shrugged. 'If I chose an easy task that wouldn't really prove anything to Gemma, would it?'

'Why Constance Street?'

'Because this is where we first met. She dropped a tenner as she walked along. I picked it up and ran after her…' He grinned at the memory. 'Got her number while I was at it.'

'Cute. Does she live on this street?'

'Across town.'

'Do you think she'll notice you're even here then?'

His grin returned. 'She will now you're reporting it. And it just feels like the right place, y'know?'

'Not really. But this is your party.' Ellie paused as she held him in a carefully measured gaze. 'So, what's so special about her? Why all this?'

'What's so special about anyone? We can't help who we fall in love with.'

'How long do you plan to wait here for her?'

'Until she comes to me.' His expression was deadly serious for the first time during that meeting. Ellie had no doubt at all that he meant it.

'So...' Ellie chewed her pen thoughtfully. 'What about the practicalities?'

'I have my flask here,' he said, shaking his thermos with a grin. 'Isn't that all a boy needs?'

'You're going to need more than that if you're here overnight.'

'There's a lovely lady at number ten, she said I could use her toilet if I needed to.'

'But if Gemma doesn't come straight away, you're going to need a lot more than a flask and a quick pit stop.'

'Yeah, I know that. I was just joking about the tea. A mate of mine does bushcrafting...' Ellie gave a confused frown and he smiled. 'Wild camping... survival skills... eating berries and road-kill, that sort of thing,' he explained, though Ellie didn't really look any more enlightened at this. 'Anyway, he has loads of kit that he says will see me through if I have to stay for any length of time. He's bringing some of the less invasive stuff over... don't want to annoy the residents by stringing a tarpaulin up between their houses, but an arctic grade sleeping bag wouldn't go amiss.'

'You really intend to stay here for days then… weeks even?'

'I hope not. She'll come for me before long.'

'You sound certain of that.'

'I am.'

Ellie gazed at him for a moment. 'Why did she leave you in the first place? I presume she did the leaving?'

'Yeah…' he replied with a heavy sigh. 'I suppose I just got lazy and she got bored. I know now that I should have done more, been maybe a little bit more exciting, more what she wanted.'

'How long had you been together?'

'Two years. We shared a flat for a year – one of those new ones where the Queen's Head pub used to be. Only rented, but nice. We did the usual couple stuff: take-outs on Friday nights, going to the cinema, weekends away in the Lakes. Sometimes she came and watched when I had band practise and at first she came to all my gigs. I'm not loaded – I pick up the odd fifty quid for a gig every now and again and I have a bar job… and I'm starting to do guitar lessons, which pays some…' For a moment he seemed to sit a little taller. 'I'm going to get my own music school eventually: singing lessons, guitar lessons, employ other people to teach other instruments – a proper legit business.'

'That's cool,' Ellie commented as she scribbled it down. 'We don't have anything like that in Millrise, do we?'

'Not yet,' he grinned again. 'But I'm going to put this town on the musical map like Liverpool or Manchester – somewhere that produces loads of great music.'

'It's about time someone did,' Ellie agreed. 'I've often thought we need more creativity around here.'

He smiled at her, and Ellie found herself caught up in the bright intensity of his gaze, fired by all the hopes and dreams of his future.

She mentally shook herself as he spoke again. 'Anyway, Gemma's job wasn't brilliantly paid either but we got by. Nothing that would rock the world but I thought… I thought she was happy. Turns out she wasn't.'

'Didn't she talk to you about it?'

'We had rows, like any couple. I never realised that they were more than that. She never said a word about being fundamentally unhappy until she left.'

'Perhaps she thought she would hurt your feelings.'

He shrugged. 'Yeah, because leaving me didn't do that at all.'

Ellie's next question was cut short as they were hailed from a few feet away. From a car parked next to Ellie's a man emerged: mid-thirties, slim and good-looking, hair already greying but swept up into a trendy quiff, camera on a strap slung around his neck.

'Alright, Ellie?' he grinned as he made his way towards them.

'Patrick!' Ellie smiled, 'you're just in time. Ben and I were about to get a coffee.'

'We were?' Ben asked with a faint look of surprise.

'Yeah, I was just going to suggest a Starbucks… my treat, of course. I don't know about you, but I'm freezing already and I've only been out here half an hour. You must be perishing; you need a hot drink inside you.'

'I have my flask.'

'Rubbish. I've been on enough folk festival road trips with my dad to know that flask tea tastes bloody awful. We need a proper coffee with foam and chocolate bits.' She turned to the new arrival. 'How about I let you two get on with the photos and I'll bob around the corner for the drinks?'

Ben gave an uncertain smile and Patrick nodded as he undid the case of his camera.

'Sounds good to me,' Patrick said airily. 'Mine's an Americano.'

'Who said I was buying *you* one?'

Patrick laughed. 'Because, Ellie Newton, you owe me coffee every day for the rest of your life!'

'Go on then,' Ellie said with an indulgent smile. 'I suppose I could stretch to one more.'

'Nice one. Now get lost so me and Ben can talk about cars and football and things that girls don't know about.'

Ellie glanced at Ben, biting back a wry smile. Somehow, she didn't think cars or football were his thing.

*

It seemed that the coffee shop was entirely staffed by new starters, and as Ellie waited for what felt like an eternity to be served, the warm scents of coffee and cinnamon filling her head, her phone flashed up a message.

I drank a whole hip flask of whisky last night and my heart still hurts. Do we have a plan B for this scenario?

Ellie couldn't help a smile. She was used to Jethro's antics. When they were at university together, Jethro had fallen in love with practically any girl who would snog him, so she wasn't overly worried about his mental state. Together with the incredibly glamorous and slightly wealthy Kasumi (whom every red-blooded male within a ten mile radius fancied), the three had simply become rather unlikely best friends. But right now she did feel guilty that she still hadn't found the time to go and visit him to offer a friendly shoulder to cry on.

I'll try to find time to visit soon, promise.

You'd better, if only to help speed up my alcohol-related demise.

Ellie slipped the phone into her pocket. She would have to answer him properly later, somehow, in between all the other things she had to do. But right now, she had a story to get to.

*

When Ellie arrived back at Constance Street, Patrick and Ben were giggling like a couple of schoolgirls.

'What's so funny?' Ellie asked in a slightly bemused voice.

'Oh, Ben was just telling me about the time he fell off the stage and broke his arm at one of his gigs.'

Ellie raised her eyebrows. 'Sounds hilarious.'

Ben chortled. 'I was writhing on the floor in agony with my guitar still strapped to me. The crowd thought it was part of the act, like I was trying to be Jimi Hendrix or something. So they just picked me up and crowd-surfed me around the venue for about twenty minutes before I could make anyone understand that I was actually hurt.'

Patrick let out a guffaw. 'Bloody brilliant.'

'I think it sounds awful,' Ellie replied, handing them both a coffee.

'You did have to be there,' Ben admitted. He lifted his cup slightly with a grateful smile. 'And thank you, it's very kind of you to get me one.'

Patrick slid an arm around Ellie. 'That's Ellie all over. When she's not beating me up she's actually quite nice.'

'Shut up,' Ellie laughed, nudging him in the ribs. 'So, have you done your photos?'

'Yep,' Patrick replied, peeling the lid from his cup and taking a sip. 'Oooh, that's a spanking cup o' Joe.'

'Great.' Ellie handed Patrick her cup. 'Hold that for a minute while I finish up with a few last questions.'

*

'If he could sit this out until Valentine's Day, it would make a bloody brilliant feature,' Patrick said in a low voice as he and Ellie walked back to their cars.

'That's a month away. There's no way he can stay out here for a month.'

'I don't know… he seems pretty determined.'

'*A whole month*, though?' Ellie glanced back as Ben lifted his hand in farewell. They had left him with the lady resident who had previously offered the use of her toilet, the same one who had called them to cover the story. She seemed to be quite attached to her unconventional neighbour already and was now trying to force a plate of shepherd's pie on him, despite his polite protests that he was a vegetarian. 'He'll be back in his flat by tomorrow night.'

'Tenner says he isn't.' Patrick turned to her with a mischievous wink.

Chapter Three

Miranda Newton opened the front door with the most utterly defeated expression that Ellie had ever seen. She swept a stray blonde lock behind her ear. Her hair needed washing, Ellie mused vaguely, and it wasn't like her mum not to be perfectly groomed at all times. Though she had not given birth to Ellie until her thirties, Miranda had always looked youthful and vivacious and could easily pass for a woman ten years younger than she was, even now. People often commented that it was her mother who had passed on the wrinkle-resistant genes Ellie seemed to have inherited. They looked uncannily alike too, aside from their very different hairstyles: Miranda's was usually smoothed into a neat bob where Ellie wore hers short and tousled. They both had huge brown eyes and pert noses with more than a sprinkling of freckles across them. Ellie's mother had always covered hers with foundation, but Ellie had learned to love hers. Today, however, Ellie's mum didn't look like that woman at all.

'I got away as early as I could,' Ellie said as she stepped over the threshold and followed her mum into the hallway.

'I told you not to worry.'

'Yes, you did. But your voice said otherwise.'

Miranda let out a heavy sigh as she entered the living room and sank into an armchair. 'I can't believe after everything she went through to get well the damn disease came back like this. And so quickly too. It doesn't seem right.' She had clearly been crying for most of the day and now her eyes filled with new tears. 'If there is a God up there who loves us, he has a funny way of showing it.'

'It's pure and simple bad luck, Mum. Some people get ill, some people don't. Just like some people fall in love forever and some don't, or some people can have children and some can't. A sad fact of life.'

'Your aunt Hazel must be very unlucky indeed then, as she couldn't get pregnant, lost the love of her life and then got ill.'

'Yeah…' Ellie kicked her shoes off before flopping down on the sofa across from her mum, 'Life sucks for some people more than others.' She let her head fall back and stared up at the ceiling. 'Shall we go over now?'

'You've only just finished work; don't you want a cup of tea or something to eat first?'

Ellie looked at her mum and shook her head. 'I've got this story to write up for tomorrow so I need to do that as soon as I get home. The earlier the better.'

'You can't keep skipping meals, you'll be ill.'

'I don't skip meals.'

'Don't lie to me, Ellie. Remember, I brought you up. The moment you fixate on a task, you always skip meals.' Her jaw tightened. 'You get that from your dad.'

Ellie smiled. Being fixated on a task wasn't the only reason she was skipping meals at the moment, but to point out the extra pressure her parents' estrangement was causing her didn't seem the best way to soothe her mum at present. 'I have to prove myself in this job, Mum. I love it. I can't make four years of student loans count for nothing and I can't go back to that tedious job that I had before university. If I have to skip the odd meal then so be it.'

Miranda folded her arms. 'I'm glad you've found something you want to do, but that doesn't mean the rest of your life has to suffer.'

'Vernon didn't get to be deputy editor by finishing at five on the dot every evening and snuggling down to watch *Antiques Roadshow* with the missus. He worked bloody long hours to get to where he is and if I want to do the same then I have to do that too.' She stretched and ran a hand through her hair. 'You worry too much.'

Miranda pouted. 'It's hardly surprising with the luck our family has had over the past few years.'

'I know.' Ellie leaned forward and squeezed her mum's hand. 'Shall we get going?'

'We might as well. Delaying it won't make things any easier.'

*

'I'm going into the hospice,' Hazel said flatly.

Ellie and her mother both stared at her.

'Why?' Miranda asked. 'I thought you were happy to stay at home.'

'I won't be a burden to anyone,' Hazel replied. She was doing her best to retain the air of someone who was completely in control, but Ellie could see beneath the determined set of her aunt's jaw that her heart was breaking. At this moment, the statement Ellie had made only half an hour earlier about life being unfair had never seemed truer.

'We can look after you,' Miranda pleaded.

Hazel cut her short with a hand in the air. 'You can't even drive, Mi. How are you going to get over here two or three times a day? And Ellie has her job. It's either the hospice or getting care to come to the house every day, and that would cost a fortune.'

'If it's money —' Ellie began.

'I have enough money,' Hazel cut in. 'But, I'm not spending it on that.'

'We talked about this already,' Ellie replied firmly. 'I don't want anything when you… well, I don't want money left to me… not like this. I want you to get the best care for what time you have left.'

'I've made my decision.'

Ellie sighed and exchanged an exasperated look with her mum.

'I could move in for a while,' Miranda offered. 'I'd be here all the time then.'

Hazel rolled her eyes. 'That sounds bloody brilliant. I've always wanted my house demolishing by a crazed, middle-aged DIY novice. And I'm even more excited about the prospect of cohabiting with a perpetually sulking clean-freak.'

Miranda folded her arms and scowled at her sister. 'Sarcasm won't throw me off the scent.'

'I know. I'm sorry. I just don't want you giving up your life for me. I'm nobody's millstone.'

'You wouldn't be a millstone,' Miranda insisted. 'You're my sister. I can't just abandon you to the care of strangers when you need me most.'

'Ellie needs you.'

'I'm old enough to take care of myself,' Ellie said. 'Remember?'

'I don't doubt that for a moment,' Hazel replied in a level voice. 'I never had the children I wanted and you're the nearest I have to a daughter. I want to leave you what I would have left my own.'

'I don't want it…' Ellie winced as she caught a hurt look from her aunt. 'I didn't mean it like that. I just want the same as Mum does – I don't want you to spend the rest of your time being looked after by strangers. Mum and I can do it.' Despite the purpose of her tone, Ellie wasn't entirely sure the last bit of her argument was true. With the hours she spent working these days, she suspected that most of the looking after would be done by her mum. But knowing how much it mattered to her mum that Hazel stayed at home for her final days, she would back her to the hilt, no matter how many white lies it took.

Ellie's gaze swept the room they now sat in. It had once been Hazel's pride and joy, decked out with all the latest interior design trends: bright colours, sumptuous furnishings, every ornament perfectly positioned for maximum aesthetic effect. Now the detritus of illness was everywhere. The chunky corduroy sofa that Hazel was draped across was piled high with blankets and cushions, the coffee table littered with packs of tablets and water bottles, a sick bowl within easy reach. The weak January sun had broken through the clouds and showed the dust on the windowsill where a few years previously not the tiniest speck would have rested. Now that Ellie thought about it, perhaps her aunt would be better in the hospice. Perhaps the house only served as a reminder of all she had lost, even before the cancer struck. At least in the hospice she'd have constant supervision and care, and relief from the painful memories. She glanced at her mum, wondering whether to voice her thoughts. Miranda met her gaze and Ellie saw it at once – the stubborn refusal to give in. Just like she would stubbornly refuse to forgive Ellie's dad, no matter how much he pleaded and how lonely she was without him.

'Maybe…' Ellie began slowly, looking at her aunt, 'you should give it a few weeks before you do anything about the hospice, see how you get on here first.'

Miranda nodded her approval. 'I think that's a good idea.'

'I know what you're trying to do,' Hazel countered, 'but it won't work. You think by then I'll be too weak and useless to organise it and you'll refuse to so I'll just have to stay here.'

'God!' Ellie squealed. 'Would you listen to yourself? We're just trying to do the best we can for you.'

Hazel pouted as she shot Ellie a defiant look. But then her expression softened. She sighed. 'Right... I won't phone straight away. Happy?'

Ellie nodded vigorously. She gave her mum a cautious glance and saw that she seemed happier. 'Right,' she said briskly before the argument could be reopened, 'who's for jelly and ice-cream?'

*

Ellie closed the front door behind her and let out a sigh. She glanced at her watch. It had just gone ten. She and her mum had left Hazel sleeping and Ellie had dropped Miranda off, excusing herself from going into her mum's house to continue a discussion about family problems that seemed to go around in ever-decreasing circles, by feigning tiredness and an early start. Not that she needed to feign anything now as she let out a huge yawn that took her completely by surprise. She had been running on adrenaline the whole day and now she was alone it had subsided, leaving her exhausted. Bed most definitely called, but she stopped mid-way along the hall and clapped a hand to her head.

Jethro. She had promised to call him. He never went to bed until midnight at least, even though he started work at a ridiculously early hour. Ellie had often wondered how he did it, and imagined he was probably still running off all the sleep he'd accumulated during university when he missed almost every pre-noon lecture by still being in bed. She pulled out her phone and dialled as she clicked the light on in her living room and flopped on the sofa.

'So... what happened?' she asked as his soft voice came through, the merest hint of a mid-Welsh accent betraying his origins.

'I thought you'd been kidnapped by aliens or Richard Branson or something,' Jethro said jauntily.

'Richard Branson?' Ellie laughed. 'You're never right; you know that, don't you?'

'That's what Aleksandra said.'

Ellie was serious again. 'Oh, Jeth. Are you very upset about her?'

There was a pause, a pregnant hiss of static on the line. 'I'm OK. It was probably never going anywhere.'

'I never thought she was right for you,' Ellie said. 'Far too boring and stuck up.'

'She wasn't boring!'

'But she was a little bit stuck up… Kasumi said it too and Aleksandra must have been stuck up if the poshest person we know thought so. I mean, she was one of those people who called tea *dinner*.'

Jethro laughed. 'OK, maybe a little bit stuck up. Although *I* keep telling you that tea is something you drink and dinner is your evening meal. Honestly, you northern wenches.'

'Right, boyo,' Ellie quipped.

'Oi! Less of the *boyo*!'

Ellie giggled.

'So, when are you coming down to London to see me?'

'I want to, I really do, but everything is crazy here right now. Mum and Dad still aren't speaking and my aunt Hazel is… well, she's not good. And then there's work, of course, which is as busy as ever.'

She had often envied Jethro his move to London – sometimes more than others – and this was definitely one of those times. It seemed like the perfect escape from all the pressures that weighed on her daily until it felt like she might implode. The decision to stay in Millrise whilst her best friend took off for a bright and sparkly life in London wasn't made lightly. Many times since their graduation, Ellie had wondered whether it had been the right one. And then, to make matters worse, shortly afterwards, Kasumi went to work for the same TV company and moved too. But Jethro and Kasumi both had wonderful, supportive, complete and definitely-not-dysfunctional families. There was nobody who needed them at home like there was for Ellie. Besides that, while her friends had been aiming for TV jobs from the start, Ellie had always harboured a secret and probably not very glamorous ambition to work for her local newspaper. She had grown up with it documenting the news events that shaped her life and the town she loved and had been thrilled beyond measure when Vernon offered her the position. Her life looked set to be perfect. But that was before her parents split up and Hazel had been diagnosed. That was back in the days when everything seemed as simple as deciding on her new work wardrobe and which car she would put a deposit on with her first paycheque.

'If you're not careful I'll be thinking you've gone off me,' Jethro said, breaking in on her morose thoughts.

'You've got girls queuing up so I wouldn't let a little thing like that worry you.'

'None of them can play drunken Trivial Pursuit like you, though.'

'Yup. Queen of Triv, that's me.'

'You promise you will come soon? I'm a boy nursing a broken heart and I need someone to make me laugh.'

'You've got Kasumi.'

'Yeah, but she just lectures me. It doesn't help that she's generally fondling Sam at the time.'

Ellie laughed. 'Lucky Sam. So that's still going strong?'

'Unfortunately. They're so happy it's sickening.'

'I will come soon, I promise. Just let me get things straight here.'

'I'll hold you to that,' Jethro said. 'How's work anyway? What counts as news these days in Millrise?'

Ellie laughed. 'No more Holden Finn sightings, if that's what you mean.'

'Damn, I could go mad for being on holiday in Turkey when that little gem broke. A megastar from the biggest boyband on the planet makes the news in Millrise and I'm not even in the country. I was with a bloody useless girlfriend that time too.'

'See, that's the trouble girls cause,' Ellie continued with a chuckle. 'If it's any consolation I'm still gutted that I didn't get to cover it either. But I had quite an interesting one today.'

'Yeah?'

'This local guy has camped out on a street corner. He says he's going to stay there until the girl who dumped him comes back.'

There was a derisive snort from the end of the line. 'He can have one of my exes if he wants. What a cock…'

'Jethro!' Ellie squeaked, half laughing and half shocked. 'You can't say that.'

'I can and I just have.'

Ellie giggled. 'I happen to think he's quite sweet.'

'Uh-oh…'

'What?'

'Could it be that someone has melted my ice princess?'

'Don't be ridiculous!'

Even though she couldn't see Jethro's quick grin, she could almost hear it in his voice. But then he was serious again. 'You sound tired, Ellie.'

'That obvious, eh?'

'Yeah. I'll let you get some sleep.'

'Thanks. Goodnight.'

'Goodnight, Ell. Thanks for calling, I feel better already.'

Ellie locked the phone screen. It would be so easy to let her eyes close, but she pushed herself wearily up from the sofa and headed upstairs.

*

'Cracking story,' Ange called as Ellie came into the office balancing three instant coffees on a tray. Ange had that morning's newspaper spread out in front of her and was poring over a large and very flattering photo of Ben that sat alongside Ellie's text.

'Almost as good as that story *you* got last year about that woman who was seeing Holden Finn… what was her name again?'

Ange screwed up her forehead in concentration. 'Blimey, I think that was a bit more than a year ago. What was her name… Bonnie? That was it, Bonnie Cartwright. That was a corker of a story. It's hard to believe it was true, though, and she denied it even when the nationals got involved. You've got to hand it to her, she could have made a fortune off the back of that affair but she didn't.' Ange turned her attention back to the photo of Ben. 'Holden Finn might be super famous but he doesn't do much for me. Now this boy…' she tapped a finger on the newspaper, 'he's a complete dish. His girlfriend must want her head examining.'

'Looks aren't everything,' Ellie said as she placed Ange's mug in front of her.

'No… but they certainly make it easier to forgive a lot of misdeeds.'

Ellie laughed lightly. 'I bet you were a right tiger once upon a time.'

'*Once upon a time?* Cheeky! What makes you think I'm not still one?'

Ellie laughed louder this time. 'Of that I have no doubt.'

Vernon pushed open the office door just as Ellie was putting a mug on his desk. 'Ellie… loved the story about the nutter on the street corner.'

'Thanks,' Ellie smiled. But after a pause it turned into a frown. 'I didn't make him sound like a nutter, did I?'

'Of course you didn't,' Ange replied, throwing Vernon an exasperated look.

Vernon simply grinned. 'He did that all by himself, there was no need for Ellie to embellish it.'

'He wasn't a nutter,' Ellie said. 'A bit of a dreamer maybe, but not mad.'

'Aren't they the same thing?' Vernon took a huge bite of a bacon and egg sandwich.

Ellie shrugged. 'I might drive down to Constance Street in a bit; see if he's still there.'

'Oh he's there alright.' Ange looked up from the paper. 'Newsroom have had two or three reports this morning from residents who say he spent the night out there, despite a couple of grumpy old men from further down the road trying to move him on.'

'Did they threaten him?' Ellie asked sharply.

Ange laughed. 'By all accounts they were too busy being threatened by their own wives to threaten him.'

'Why?'

'Apparently, the women of Constance Street thought it was the most romantic thing they had ever seen and decided to take your Romeo under their protection. So they were feeding him tomato soup and allsorts. You can imagine what most cranky old husbands would make of that. So when they tried to move him on, the *Wife SAS* sprang into action.'

Ellie looked at Ange thoughtfully. 'That's got to be worth a follow-up story then, don't you think?'

'Too right. I would have gone myself but I knew you'd want it.'

Ellie smiled as she sat at her desk and took a sip of her coffee. 'Thanks, Ange. I'll sort out my loose ends here and head over.'

'Patrick said he'd go with you if you wanted,' Ange added.

'Oh? Where is he?'

'Out at some WI event I think this morning. But he said to phone if anyone was going and wanted him, otherwise he'd head off to some pool jobs.'

'He's such a good boy, always looks out for me.'

'He is. Fiona is a lucky girl.' Ange let out a long sigh and closed the newspaper. 'All the good ones are taken.'

Vernon spun around. 'What about me?' he cried. At least, that was what it sounded like, although it was hard to tell through his mouthful of sandwich.

Ange tutted. 'As I said, all the good ones are taken…'

Ellie smiled as Vernon turned back to his PC monitor in a mock huff. 'Somehow I don't see you and Patrick being suited,' she said.

'Is that your not-so-subtle way of saying I'm far too old for him?'

'No, you're far too glamorous and sophisticated for him.'

'Oh, Ellie, you always say the right thing.'

'Really? It seems like a rare occurrence these days.'

Ange tried to catch Ellie's eye but she was already engrossed in her own computer screen.

'Things still bad family-wise?' Ange asked gently.

Ellie didn't reply, and an awkward silence descended on the office. Finally, she spoke without looking round. 'I'd rather not talk about it if it's all the same to you.'

*

A brisk breeze rattled the bare trees as Ellie made her way to the corner of Constance Street. The day was milder than those of the previous few weeks and she couldn't help but feel relieved that Ben would be in for a slightly more comfortable night if he was here again tonight. In the tiny terraced gardens along the row, the occasional snowdrop could be seen poking up from the otherwise empty flowerbeds. There was a definite promise of spring – early, but there all the same.

Surrounding Ben were four women, ranging from around forty to sixty years old at a guess, all chatting animatedly to him and to each other. The sounds of girlish and slightly hysterical laughter rang out down the street. As Ellie passed, she saw male faces scowling out from a couple of windows – the husbands of the members of Ben's new fan club? It didn't take a genius to work out that their disgruntled looks meant they probably were. Ellie couldn't help a wry smile to herself. She could imagine the conversations in their homes later. Ben was managing to make them all look much less than satisfactory in the dreamy male stakes.

The echo of a car door slamming on the almost empty road caught Ellie's attention and she spun around to see Patrick jogging towards her.

'Morning!'

Ellie glanced at her watch. 'Afternoon, actually.'

'Doesn't time fly when you're having fun?' Patrick grinned.

Ellie nodded in the direction of the little crowd at the corner. 'They certainly look as though they are.'

'I'll bet it's the most excitement this street has seen since the Blitz.'

'They didn't have the Blitz here.'

'Well…' Patrick shrugged. 'Some other exciting thing then.'

Ellie frowned. 'I'm not sure *exciting* is the word you're actually looking for in that context…'

'And that's why you write the words and I take the photos.'

Ellie couldn't help a broad smile. Patrick had this infectious way of lifting people's moods – they just looked at him and felt instantly better.

'I thought maybe we could get some photos of Ben and his harem,' Ellie said in a low voice.

'Not exactly The Spice Girls, are they?' Patrick replied as he glanced towards the little group.

'They seem like a lot of fun though,' Ellie mused. 'Should be good for a story and a mad photo or two.'

And in the middle of them was Ben. Far from being troubled by his vigil, he seemed to be thoroughly enjoying his spot of socialising. His smile grew even wider and brighter as he spotted Ellie and Patrick approaching.

'Long time no see,' he hailed as they approached.

Ellie smiled. 'Still here then?'

'As Gemma didn't show, it looks like another night al fresco for me.'

The four women had now stopped talking and were all watching Ellie and Patrick with interest. Patrick aimed his most disarming smile at them.

'Are you ladies his bodyguards?'

One of them giggled. 'You could say that.' She glanced at Patrick's camera. 'Are you going to do photos?'

Patrick nodded. 'If you don't mind I thought I could take some of you as well as Ben. It might be nice for people to see that you're behind him in his quest.'

'Oooh,' another one squeaked, 'do you think we could nip home and put some slap on first?'

Ellie looked them over in turn. As far as she could tell, they all looked as if they had full war-paint on, along with their best clothes, already.

'Of course,' Patrick said with a gallant sweep of his arm. 'You go and make yourselves *more* beautiful whilst Ellie here has another chat with Ben. I'll wait for you.'

The women giggled in unison and hurried off while Ben shot Patrick a knowing look.

'You've done that before, mate.'

'Comes with the territory. People like to look their best if they think they'll be in the paper.'

'So, how was your night?' Ellie turned to Ben.

'Cold,' he smiled.

'No sign of Gemma at all?'

'Not yet.'

'Don't you have mutual friends or anyone who has let her know you're here?'

'My mate, Darryl, texted her.'

'And?'

'She didn't reply.'

'Maybe she hasn't seen the text yet?'

Ben shook his head. 'I know her; she's stubborn. She'll make me sweat for a while before she comes.'

'Sweating is one thing you won't be doing out here in January,' Patrick cut in as he rubbed a cloth over his camera lens.

Ellie frowned. It was none of her business, of course, but she was beginning to form some strong opinions of Gemma Fox and none of them was complimentary. If a man was going to such lengths to win *her* back, despite what her feelings on the subject might be, Ellie would at least go and talk to him, if only to persuade him that getting hypothermia wasn't a very sensible thing to do. Not Gemma Fox, it seemed. But that wasn't the only thing troubling her. How could Ben be so relaxed and cheerful in the face of the task he had set himself? Was there really a man in the world so determined to get his girl that he would go to these lengths? Or, despite his protestations the previous day, was there another motive for Ben's camp-out? The more she thought about it, the more intrigued Ellie was. Now if she could get to the truth of it, *there* was a story to be had.

'You're not a little tempted to buy a bunch of flowers and head over to her flat?' Ellie asked. 'It would be a lot simpler, not to mention warmer.'

'*Our* flat,' Ben corrected. 'Not that she's there now. Gone back to her parents.' He frowned slightly. 'It won't be my flat either if I don't make this month's rent,' he added in a quieter voice.

'You're risking your flat?' Ellie asked, glancing at Patrick with a barely disguised look of disapproval.

Ben shrugged. 'I suppose it sounds stupid. It's a sacrifice I'm willing to make if I have to… I'll do whatever it takes. I have a little bit of money saved, though – funds to start the business that I guess I'll just have to save all over again – and I'm hoping it will be enough to see this through. When Gemma does come for me I'm sure she'd be happier still having a flat to go back to at the end of it.'

Ellie resisted the urge to shake him. She had never heard anything so reckless in her life. But then she thought about her parents for a moment and realised that she probably had. 'You're still certain she's going to come for you even though a newspaper report still hasn't brought her here?'

'Yes. Because I won't give up until she does.'

Ellie frowned. 'And you can't go to her parents' house to talk to her because…'

'I told you yesterday,' Ben said, 'it's not enough. You don't know Gemma like I do. She wants big gestures. A bunch of flowers won't cut it. I have to prove my love to her, and my proof has to be massive.'

'Other couples talk it through, work it out.'

'Not us.'

'So you're still determined to stay out here?'

Ben nodded.

'What about the police?'

'They won't come unless someone puts in a serious complaint,' Ben said with what Ellie suspected was forced confidence. 'They've got bigger fish to fry than me.'

Ellie raised her eyebrows. 'You're quite a public fish right now though. Or at least you will be, come tonight's edition.'

'Oh, my ladies will look after me.' Ben smiled as he looked beyond Ellie to see the group of female residents returning. To Ellie they looked just as they had done a few moments ago. One of them carried a clear plastic tub containing a large fruit cake and the other had a tray with a teapot.

'Here they come,' Patrick said to Ellie in a low voice, 'Charlie's Angels...'

Ellie bit back a grin and smoothed her face into a professional smile. 'All sorted?'

One of the women, with wild white hair, nodded vigorously. 'Are you putting us in the story too?'

'If you'd like to be,' Ellie said.

They all murmured their enthusiastic agreement.

Ellie whipped a spiral-bound notepad and a pen from her satchel. 'I'll start by taking your names...'

White haired lady spoke first. 'Annette Shufflebotham,' she announced. 'I called you yesterday,' she added with obvious pride.

'Thank you Annette, we do appreciate it,' Ellie said amiably.

'Sonia,' a taller woman in her forties, with a bob so smooth you could almost mistake it for a crash-helmet put in. 'Sonia Hurd – H-U-R-D. I live next door to Annette and I saw him out of the window too. I just didn't phone the paper quite as quickly as *she* did.'

Ellie detected the faintest hint of competition as Sonia glanced across at her neighbour. Ellie looked inquiringly at the other two.

'Janet Smith.' She had a long, gaunt face and fluffy blonde hair pulled into a huge pony-tail – Sonia's worst hair nightmare, Ellie imagined. Which just left a lady with a mousey, short-back-and-sides that any fifties barber would have been proud of.

'Lena… I know, just like the singer,' she laughed.

Ellie frowned and looked to Ben and Patrick for help but they seemed as lost as she was.

'Never mind,' Lena sighed. 'Surname is Smith too… but Janet and I are not related in case you were wondering.'

'Great,' Ellie said as she scribbled the last name down. 'Not great that you're not related,' she added quickly, looking up. 'I mean that we have all that down.' She turned her attention to Patrick. 'Have you got to rush off anywhere? I could do the interviews after you've taken photos if you like?'

Patrick grinned a bit too enthusiastically for Ellie's liking. 'No, no, I have nowhere to be. I'll just listen in if that's alright with you.' This was Patrick-speak for: *I'm going to let you deal with these nutters and then laugh hysterically as soon as I get to the car.*

Ellie tactfully avoided a reply and went back to her questioning. 'So…' she said to the assembled women, 'what made you want to get involved? You saw Ben outside and what went through your minds?'

'At first I wondered whether he was in some sort of trouble,' Annette said. 'You know, homeless or on drugs or something. But then I came out to see if he needed any of the emergency services and he told me that he didn't want to move from the corner in case Gemma came back for him.' She seemed to flush slightly at the memory. 'It was such a lovely thing for a young man to do. Especially these days when the world is full of churlish unemployed thugs in their damned hooded sweaters.'

'Technically I'm sort of unemployed now,' Ben put in tentatively. 'At least I don't imagine my job will be there now as I haven't turned in for my shifts.'

'He does his best not to be churlish and thuggish though…' Patrick grinned.

'But you're not the same,' Annette said to Ben in a soothing tone. 'You lost your job through no fault of your own.'

Ellie silently wondered whether his employers would agree with Annette's view of the situation but she kept her opinions to herself.

'I saw Ben through my window too, like I said before,' Sonia put in. 'Then Annette told me why he was there and, naturally, I wanted to help. It was me who drafted in Lena and Janet.'

The two women in question murmured agreement.

'Why would you do this for a complete stranger?' Ellie asked. Her professional curiosity was beginning to give way to something much more personal. She glanced at Ben as he watched the exchange with a placid and amiable expression. There was something undeniably attractive about him. Perhaps it was that little bit of the dreamer in her that recognised a fellow dreamer in him, the bit of her that she had always tried to stamp out for fear it would distract her from pursuing her career goals if she let it get a firm hold. He was good-looking, charming and likeable – she could see why a bunch of older women who looked to be settled into a rigid domestic routine might view him as a wildly exciting and romantic figure. Ellie was beginning to feel the attraction herself, but pushed such thoughts to the back of her mind. They were far too dangerous to think about for more than a second.

'Men aren't like Ben anymore,' sighed Sonia as she looked fondly at him. Clearly she didn't share any of Ellie's concerns and was pondering the possibility of installing Ben at home in place of her own husband.

'I know,' agreed Annette with equal longing in her voice. 'I can't imagine my Geoff standing on a street corner waiting for me. If I left he'd be straight down the pub drinking himself stupid with the housekeeping.'

'I'm sure that's not true,' Ben said modestly. 'Loads of blokes would do this for the girl of their dreams.'

The collective sigh from the four women as they gazed at him with almost comically soppy expressions was loud enough to be heard in the next street.

'Gemma's a very lucky girl,' Ellie commented, ignoring the lovelorn musings and trying hard to keep the cynicism and dislike for a girl she had never met out of her voice.

'I think so too,' Lena said. 'I can't believe she hasn't come running already.'

'We need to make more of a splash,' Janet said with such conviction in her tone that it seemed she had never been more certain of anything in her entire life.

'You mean more publicity?' Lena asked.

Janet nodded vigorously, her ponytail flailing madly behind her.

'We're running another piece in the paper tomorrow,' Ellie reminded her.

'No offence, love, but we need something much bigger than the *Echo* for this story.'

Ellie frowned. 'Are you suggesting it could go national?' she asked doubtfully.

'Of course it could! It's nearly Valentine's Day and this is a perfect story.' Janet rolled her eyes. 'Honestly, I thought you were a reporter.'

Ellie bit back the offended retort that sprang into her mouth. 'I *am* a reporter,' she replied coldly. But perhaps going national wasn't such a bad idea, she thought, as long as she could keep ownership of the scoop. The last thing she wanted was some slimy City tabloid boy claiming it. She began to wonder why the idea hadn't occurred to her before. This was exactly the sort of story to set the internet on fire and get the big boys running to Millrise, as well as increasing her own profile. It couldn't hurt to try.

Chapter Four

'Full page, early right – you have been a busy girl.' Ange tossed the first edition of the day's *Echo* across the office to Ellie.

Ellie opened the paper and flicked through. 'Page five. Brilliant.' Her gaze ran quickly down the text and over the accompanying photos – one of Ben in an earnest, beseeching pose down on one knee holding his notice board, one with him, grinning, surrounded by his bevy of local guardians and another, smaller inset of the incomparable Gemma. Ellie was particularly proud of the headline:

THE MAN WHO CAN'T BE MOVED

'Patrick's photos are fab,' Ellie commented graciously.

'As always,' Ange replied. 'He's wasted here.'

Ellie looked up. 'Roll your tongue in; you're drooling again. And Patrick is happily married.'

Ange grinned. 'Just because you're on a diet, it doesn't mean you can't look at the cakes.'

'Look at the cake any harder and you'll melt it into a pool of icing and mush.'

Ange let out a huge laugh as Ellie spread the paper across her desk to get a better look.

'Ange…' she began slowly as she read the page.

'Ellie…'

'Do you know anyone on the nationals who might be interested in this story?'

Ange appraised her colleague thoughtfully for a moment. 'As your scoop?'

Ellie nodded.

'I'm not sure. Vernon would, I expect.'

'I think this story has some real mileage in it.'

Ange swung idly from side to side on her chair. 'As long as the lovely Gemma doesn't make a premature appearance and take him back to her bosom.'

Ellie glanced back at the paper. 'That's one hell of a bosom,' she mused as she gazed at the photo of Ben's ex-girlfriend. 'You'd need a sturdy crowbar to prise him free from those.'

'Fake, I'll bet,' Ange said as she ambled across to look over Ellie's shoulder. 'She obviously likes to show them off though – it's a wonder she doesn't get pneumonia in that top.'

Ellie laughed as she folded the paper up. 'I'll ask Vernon when he gets in… where is he this morning anyway?'

'Football scandal. Some local player was discovered with the tube of a vacuum cleaner stuck in an orifice where vacuum cleaner tubes don't belong. Vernon's gone to see if he can get the player's side of the story.'

Ellie winced. 'That's not going to end well, is it?'

'Nope. I keep telling him that he doesn't need to go out on stories now he's editor but you know, once a journo, always a journo. Last time he went out on a job like this he came back with a black eye.' Ange grinned. 'I've already been out to Tesco and picked up some steak, a tub of Vaseline and a bottle of whiskey so we're covered for any eventuality.'

'And that's why you're such a great colleague,' Ellie laughed.

Ange nodded with mock solemnity. 'Every office should have a me.'

'I suppose I should check that Gemma Fox hasn't stolen my scoop away in the night, shouldn't I?' Ellie said, reaching for her satchel. 'I'm guessing Vernon will be missing for some time yet so I might as well nip out.'

'You might as well, my dear. If Romeo is still out there, give his pert bottom a squeeze from me, won't you?'

'You're so disgusting,' Ellie laughed.

'I know. But when you get to my age you stop caring about it.'

*

Ellie flung her satchel onto the passenger seat of her car and climbed in. As she always did, she fished around and pulled out her mobile phone, leaving it on the seat for ease of access. Ellie couldn't bear to miss a single call, even whilst driving – after all, that call might be the story that would change her career. Besides which, with the way her aunt was fading daily and her mum increasingly unable to cope, Ellie needed to be on standby for them too.

She was just about to start the engine when her phone screen flashed up a name.

KASUMI

Ellie snatched it back from the seat. 'Hey, Kas! Long time no hear. I thought that boyfriend of yours had locked you in a dungeon somewhere.'

There was a musical laugh from the other end of the line. 'He tried but we lost the gimp suit and it all seemed so pointless after that.'

Ellie grinned. 'Still enjoying life in the Big Smoke?'

'It's unbelievable here,' Kasumi replied in a dreamy voice. 'There's so much going on and so many opportunities... you should move down, it's not too late, you know. I'm sure I could put in a word at the station. You go on about how much you love the newspaper, but TV is where it's at, my lovely little friend. Anyway, Jethro says you're coming down to see us soon.'

'Not just yet. But as soon as I can.' Ellie's mind flitted briefly to the hundreds of reasons why she couldn't leave Millrise in the immediate future and all of them seemed to be problems without resolution.

'That's good, because the station is sending me to Florida on location next week so I won't be around.'

'Ooh! Sounds gorgeous.'

'It's for a travel programme on the kids' channel. I have to fly out with a load of brats, though, so there is a price to pay for this glamorous life.'

Ellie checked her watch. 'Aren't you supposed to be at work?'

'Catherine just left the office to go on a location scout and I was bored.'

'Honestly, I don't know how you get away with it.'

'Charm, my dear,' Kasumi purred. 'Pure and simple.'

'Sadly, I am bereft of the kind of charm that lets me run circles around my boss, and I have a story to get to so, fun as this has been, I really need to get on. Shall I call you later? You can tell me all about which type of waxing you've had done for Florida.'

'Perfect. See ya, sexy.'

Ellie couldn't help grinning down the phone. She could just picture her friend's perfectly formed lips in a mocking pout, her dark, almond shaped eyes – keen and fiercely intelligent – shining with mischief. At university, Kasumi was the girl whom every boy wanted to date (including Jethro, Ellie suspected, though he knew better than to try) but her proud beauty and razor sharp wit somehow made her too terrifying to ask. Once she had arrived in London where beauty like hers was on every street corner, it became diluted to something less remarkable. But to Ellie she would always be Kas, the girl who loved nothing better than to get drunk with her on Stella Artois and play pointless board games until they both fell asleep across one another. Life had seemed so much simpler then.

'See you later, Kas,' she replied, barely able to keep the wistful sigh at bay.

*

When Ellie arrived at Constance Street she was relieved to find Ben still in what had now become *his* spot, flanked by his four angels.

He greeted Ellie with a broad smile.

'Here she is, my favourite reporter.'

'How many do you know?' Ellie asked with a wry smile twitching at the corners of her mouth.

'Just you,' Ben said airily. 'But if I knew any more, you'd still be my favourite.'

Lena whipped out a coffee pot, seemingly from nowhere, and held it up to Ellie.

'I've just made coffee if you'd like one.'

Ellie dragged a hand through her hair. 'Why not?' she said. 'That sounds lovely.'

As Lena turned her attention to a makeshift little kitchen set up on the pavement, Ben shot Ellie a quick glance and mouthed something that she couldn't quite make out, holding his own mug slightly aloft. Before Ellie could make sense of it, Lena had presented her with a steaming drink.

'Thanks.' Ellie took the mug and sipped. It was warm and comforting in her hands, but as soon as she tasted it she realised that Ben's signal had been a warning. It was undoubtedly the foulest cup of coffee Ellie had ever had the misfortune to be handed, and now she would have to drink it if she wasn't going to offend Lena. With a barely perceptible grimace, she placed the mug on the ground and hoped that if she kept everyone talking long enough they might not notice she had left without finishing it.

'No sign of Gemma then?' Ellie asked.

Ben shook his head, the carefree charm he usually wore so well replaced with the look of melancholy that the mention of Gemma's absence always seemed to elicit in him. He put down his own mug and folded his arms across his chest, as if he was trying to hug his heart. The gesture showed a vulnerability that pulled at some deep emotion in Ellie, something so hidden she had yet to name it. She felt the strangest urge to throw her own arms around him as if, perhaps, their combined power could somehow mend what he could not do alone.

'Have you considered that she won't come back to you, no matter what you do?' Ellie asked gently.

'Of course she will,' a voice cut in.

Ellie spun around to see that Sonia was red-faced and her nostrils were flaring in a vaguely disturbing manner. 'What kind of idiot woman would leave him sitting here forever?'

Ellie privately thought that Ben was as much of an idiot for thinking that sitting on a street corner would bring Gemma running, but she resisted the impulse to say so to Sonia.

'Someone has to be practical.'

'You just cover the story, lovie, and we'll worry about whether Gemma comes back,' Sonia said.

Lena bent down to retrieve Ellie's cup and clasped her hands around it. 'It's already getting cold – best to drink it up,' she interrupted in an effort to soothe the conversation.

Ellie tried to give a grateful smile as she took the mug and gulped back as much as she could manage in one go. 'What did you think of today's spread?' she asked, glancing at each of the group in turn.

'Not big enough,' Janet said.

Ellie raised her eyebrows.

'It did have some lovely photos,' Lena added. 'I offered to go to Gemma's house and take a copy of the paper but Ben didn't want me to.'

'I didn't think it would be such a good idea,' Ben said. 'The plan is to stay here and wait for her to come. If Lena had gone there Gemma would have shut the door in her face and refused to listen.'

Ellie frowned. She had never heard such misguided logic in her entire life. 'She's really that stubborn?'

'No… well, yes. I just don't think she would have appreciated a strange woman turning up on my behalf.'

'But if Lena had come directly from you…' Ellie frowned.

Ben sighed. 'I'm not really explaining myself very well.'

'I'm afraid you're not,' Ellie replied before swigging back the rest of her coffee and handing the cup to Lena with a forced smile.

'I took Gemma for granted,' Ben said patiently. 'That's why she left me. If I'm going to show her that I can change, then I have to make amends in a way that shows her just how much I care. Like I said before, if it's not tough, then it's no proof at all. So I can't have a third party going to fetch her on my behalf. I have to wait and she has to come – it's that simple.'

At that moment as she gazed at him, Ellie couldn't decide whether he was the most kissable man in Millrise or the most stupid. The other women in her company had clearly plumped for the former as they released a collective sigh. What Ellie wanted to do, more than ever, was to tell Ben exactly what she thought of Gemma Fox and how he would be much better off without her. But it was none of her business. Her job was to report events, not interfere in them. She forced a bright smile.

'If you're determined to stick it out then you can count on me to check in every now and again – report in the *Echo* on your progress. Would that help?'

'That would be amazing,' Ben said.

'I still think it needs bigger coverage,' Janet said.

'I'm working on that too,' Ellie replied.

Ben's eyes widened. 'You are?'

'Is that OK?'

He scratched his chin slowly. 'I suppose so. I'm not great at making an exhibition of myself but I suppose this is worth it.'

Ellie raised her eyebrows. 'You're not good at making an exhibition of yourself?' She swept her hand over his little campsite and he grinned.

'This is different. I'm OK with this, and when I play with my band that's OK too because I just stand at the back with my guitar and it's like doing a job. I don't have to talk sitting here and I don't have to talk on stage. It's the talking that's a problem – I always seem to say the wrong thing.'

'I don't know about that,' Ellie said. 'From what I've seen you seem very articulate.'

'That's because you're not pointing a TV camera or radio microphone at me. It's kinda why we scaled down the band, to be honest.'

'Stage fright?'

'Not exactly,' he laughed. 'I just don't think straight in those situations. I'm afraid I'll get myself into trouble.'

'I know that feeling,' Ellie smiled. 'I'm sure you'd be fine. If it helped, we could run over some scenarios that might crop up during an interview and you could have some answers prepared. I expect that *Radio Millrise* will be round here any day now so you might as well be ready.'

'What, like a practise run?'

Ellie nodded. 'I suppose so, yeah. Just like a practise run.'

'I'd like that.'

'Oooh!' Lena squeaked. 'I'll go and get fresh coffee if you're staying a while.' She looked at the others. 'We can pretend to be the audience!'

Ellie threw Ben a loaded glance. 'Maybe we should have tea this time… if that's OK? I don't know about you, Ben, but too much caffeine for me and I'll be like a budgie on a pylon.'

'Oh yeah, me too,' Ben said with exaggerated earnestness. 'Tea would be a much better idea.'

Lena clapped her hands together and gathered her cups. 'Great! I'll be back shortly.'

As she walked away, Sonia eyed Ellie and Ben with a knowing look. 'Her tea's worse than her coffee. That woman could ruin the taste of water just by looking at it.'

*

Ellie longed for a lazy supper and a hot bath. The day had been a very trying one, with problems over deadlines, and copy with last minute mistakes spotted, not to mention Vernon turning up with a burning ear after being hit by a coke can thrown from a first floor window by a disgruntled footballer's wife. But home was still a distant dream. She had promised her dad she would visit and it was a promise she had to keep.

She arrived at her dad's building and buzzed for entry. As always, when she got to the flat she found the door already open for her.

'Hey, Dad!' she called. Glancing around the room she noted socks and boxer shorts hanging over the radiator, days of newspapers piled on the coffee table alongside takeaway cartons and sweet wrappers, a banjo (just one of the musical instruments he owned but couldn't actually play) and, bizarrely, a box of assorted screws and a screwdriver. The last object filled her with particular trepidation. As for the rest of the mess, she had seen better kept digs during her student days.

Just as she was about to collect some dirty mugs, her dad shuffled through from the kitchen, still in his dressing gown despite the fact that it was teatime.

'You've lost weight again. I only saw you a week ago and I can tell.' Ellie looked him up and down with a critical eye. 'And you were skinny enough to start with. I thought you were getting your hair cut too.'

'What's the point?'

'Because you make the guy who sells the *Big Issue* outside M&S look like Gok Wan, that's the point.'

'Have you talked to your Mum yet?' he asked, ignoring her scolding.

'It's not a good time, Dad. You know that.'

'It's never a good time,' he mumbled like a petulant toddler.

Ellie sighed. 'You and Mum are as bad as each other.'

'I'm the one willing to give things a try... it's your mum being stubborn.' He looked at his hands. 'And I didn't even do anything wrong...'

Ellie threw her satchel down on the sofa and sidled past him with a handful of dirty cups. He followed her into the kitchen.

'That's not how Mum sees things,' Ellie said, letting the mugs fall into the washing up bowl with a clatter and turning on the hot tap.

'Do you think she's right?'

Ellie turned to face him. 'It doesn't matter what I think. It's Mum you need to talk round, not me.'

'But do *you* think I was wrong?'

'I don't want to discuss it.' Ellie squeezed the washing-up-liquid bottle. The last dregs came out with a wheeze and a cloud of tiny bubbles. Her dad went over and laid a hand on her arm.

'Don't wash up, Ell. It makes me feel guilty when you clean up after me.'

'Then clean up after yourself and I won't have to!'

He dropped his hand and stepped away. 'Does she know you're here?' he asked quietly.

'No,' Ellie said, 'and you'd better not tell her either.'

'She can't begrudge you seeing your own father!' A defensive note crept into his voice.

'No, but she isn't strong enough right now to be rational about it. I don't want to stress her out any more than she already is.'

He dropped into a chair at the table. 'How is your aunt?'

'Not good. The cancer is worse and she's not going to make it.'

Her dad stared into space as he digested this news. 'That's too bad,' he said finally. 'I always liked Hazel; she's a good girl.'

Ellie sniffed hard and nodded. 'I know.' She took a deep breath.

'I miss you both,' Ellie's dad said into the pause.

Ellie looked at him sadly. 'I know you do. I'll talk to her, I promise; I just need to find the right moment.' Her gaze travelled the room and settled on a wonky looking piece of wood that seemed to be attached to the wall in a way that defied all laws of physics. Her attention turned to her dad and she narrowed her eyes. 'What have I told you about attempting to build things?'

'I needed something to take my mind off your mother.'

Ellie raised her eyebrows so far there was a danger she would lose them in her hair. 'How about a spot of cleaning?' She wrinkled her nose.

'A shower and shave wouldn't go amiss either.' She had lost count of the times she had chastised him about the state of his flat and she was beginning to feel like a stuck record. Sometimes she felt like the parent with two children of her own the way her mum and dad carried on. But if she didn't keep him on the straight and narrow, she was afraid that her dad would sink completely.

He pouted and scuffed his slippered feet on the floor like a sullen child. Ellie dropped a couple of teabags in two clean mugs. Her father had always been a diligent man, trying his best to keep their family home in good repair on the modest budget they had, but somehow, he seemed to get everything wrong. Like the time he had boxed his glasses in with the hot water pipes in the bathroom and had to undo it all again once he realised. Or the treehouse he had built for Ellie, whose first visit had seen the ladder falling away as soon as she had scaled it. She'd been stuck up there for hours before either of her parents had realised. But he had always meant well, even when it ended in disaster.

'I'm only saying it because I care.' Ellie's tone was gentler now. 'I'm not suggesting you're not capable…' she continued, deciding that a spot of diplomacy might be the way forward, 'just that your mind might not be completely on the task in hand. It only takes a minute for your concentration to slip enough to do some real damage.' Ellie had once seen a programme on TV where a local council had decided to demolish a block of old flats by blowing them up. It had been a gracefully destructive image as the building came down in an almost perfectly symmetrical crash. The image came back to her now, only the perpetrator of the event was her dad, the crash not quite so graceful, and him running from his own block of flats chased by an angry mob of fellow residents with flaming torches and pitchforks and covered in concrete dust.

Frank Newton took a seat at the table and smiled wanly as his daughter set a mug of tea down in front of him. He looked at the shelf.

'I suppose it does look like it belongs in a museum of optical illusions,' he said.

Ellie laughed as she sat down with her own drink. 'I wouldn't go that far… although it might be worth two hundred quid on *You've Been Framed* if we can catch the moment on film when it falls on your head.'

'Watch it,' Frank said, his smile spreading a little. 'Otherwise, I might film the moment I throw it at yours.'

Chapter Five

Patrick clicked his camera as Ellie walked into the office yawning and rubbing a hand through her hair.

'You'd better not be photographing me,' Ellie warned him. She went over to her chair, where he had made himself comfortable, and slapped his feet from her desk.

'How could I miss a photo op like that?' Patrick grinned. 'Anyway, I need some compromising photos as bargaining tools when you're too famous to work at the *Echo* any longer.'

'What do you mean?' Ellie dropped her satchel on the floor and perched on the edge of her desk next to him.

'Ange says the phone lines have been going mental. Everyone wants to know about your guy on Constance Street.'

'Who's everyone?'

'Members of the public, other newspapers, women's mags. You name it.'

Ellie shrugged slightly with a bemused expression. 'I hadn't realised that one or two calls would cause such a stir. It'll all help Ben, though, so I suppose that's good. So where is Ange?' she added.

'Gone to make me a coffee.'

Ellie rolled her eyes. 'Don't encourage her, Patrick.'

'I can't help my animal magnetism,' Patrick said innocently.

Ellie folded her arms. 'So what are you doing here? Haven't you got school kids in roman togas to photograph or something?'

'Come to invite you to dinner. In fact, I've come to *order* you to dinner.'

'Patrick... I –'

He held up a hand to silence her. 'No arguing. Fiona has given me strict instructions.'

'OK, when?'

'Doing anything tonight?'

'I did have a hot date with a microwave curry but I suppose I can cancel.'

'Good girl. I'll call Fi and tell her. She's been saying all week how you've not been round for ages. The kids have been asking about you too.'

'I know...' Ellie sighed. 'I'm sorry I haven't seen them much lately, it's just that there's so much going on...'

'It's OK, you don't have to explain anything to me. We're fond of you, that's all, and we worry. You make Fiona go all weird and maternal.'

Ellie grinned. It was strange how quickly she and Patrick had become friends since she had started to work at the *Echo* only a year before, even stranger how his wife and children had taken to her too. But she wasn't complaining – since Jethro and Kasumi had left for London and most of her other friends had either got married or moved away, it was good to have a new confidante. 'It must be because I look about twelve,' she quipped.

'You laugh now but you'll be laughing harder when you're forty and everyone thinks you're twenty-five.'

'That's what everyone used to tell me when I couldn't get served in nightclubs.'

Patrick grinned at her. It was a grin she knew well.

'OK,' Ellie said, trying, but failing, to look stern. 'What do you want?'

'Not me,' Patrick replied. 'But I kinda think Fi might ask you to help out at the school fete next month.'

Ellie groaned. 'Doing what?'

'A bake sale.'

'She wants me to make cakes? My cakes are so dense they practically have their own gravity. God help anyone who buys them!'

'Don't worry, I already told her you don't do all that domestic stuff. She just needs help selling them.'

'Patrick…' Ellie said in a torn sort of whine, 'I have so much to do right now.'

'I know.' He fluttered his eyelashes at her. 'But it'll be fun and you'll make Fi so happy.'

She bit her lip for a moment, and then let out a sigh. 'Argh! I never could say no to you and Fiona. Just an hour, though, and if I get any lip from snotty nosed kids I'm allowed to shove a cake in their face.'

Patrick threw back his head and laughed. 'Deal.'

Just then, Ange kicked the door open, balancing two mugs and a tin of biscuits on a tray. 'I nicked these from the girls on reception,' she announced with a cheeky grin. 'We'd better be quick and eat them before they notice they're missing.'

Ellie laughed. 'You know there will be all-out war if you keep stealing their goodies? Rosie has already threatened to confiscate your sweet tin in retaliation.'

'Pah, she's got to find it first,' Ange said as she set the tray down. 'Sorry, Ellie, I didn't make you one as I wasn't sure what time you'd be in.'

Ellie waved away the apology. 'I just popped in to check there was nothing urgent here and then I was going to head over to Constance Street anyway.'

'Again?' Patrick raised his eyebrows.

'Ben's still there as far as I know,' Ellie said, feeling the blush in her cheeks without knowing why. 'I thought I might just write a small update.'

'The phones and emails have been going mental since that big piece,' Ange said. 'The reception girls have even had people bringing in gifts for him.'

'Really? Wow, this story seems to be catching people's imaginations,' Ellie mused.

'Jammy beggar could have his pick of girls by the sounds of it,' Patrick grinned. 'If it was me I'd tell Gemma to sling her hook and see what else was on offer.'

'Lucky it isn't you then, because that's hardly romantic,' Ellie replied.

'Romance is overrated.'

'Good for a story, though,' Ange put in as she looked between them from over the top of her mug.

'It is that,' Ellie agreed. 'What else has come in this morning?'

'The usual thrilling assortment,' Ange said as she picked up a writing pad. 'Flasher seen down in Bircheswood Park, someone stealing crates of sausages from that meat wholesaler on Millrise industrial estate, a baby born by the side of the road because they didn't get to hospital on time, a karate school celebrating its tenth anniversary… want me to go on, or are you happy to take your pick from that little lot?'

Ellie pulled her face into a comical look of pain. 'It all sounds so exciting I hardly know where to begin.' She turned to Patrick. 'Fancy coming with me on any of them?'

'The baby might be a good one. Everyone loves babies. You can keep the flasher though....' He grinned. 'Unless he and the sausage thefts are connected, in which case that would have to be worth a look.'

'Baby it is then,' Ellie laughed. 'While you drink your coffee I'm going to pop over to Constance Street and we'll go baby visiting when I get back.'

'Want to take Ben's gifts for him?' Ange asked with a mischievous wink. From under her desk she produced a cardboard box. Ellie pushed herself from her perch on the desk and peered inside it.

'Seriously?' she laughed as she held up a teddy hugging a loveheart. 'Just what every polar explorer or man camping on suburban street corner puts on their list of things essential for survival.'

'They're very good grilled over an open fire with some wild mushrooms, I'm told,' Patrick laughed.

Putting the teddy to one side, Ellie dug further into the box, producing an assortment of items from boxes of chocolates to bottles of wine to more practical things like torches and tarpaulins. 'They've really thought of everything, haven't they? I'll take this lot with me – Ben might be able to use some of it... even the teddy.'

*

The low sun slanting into the car was starting to give Ellie a headache, but once she had turned the corner into Constance Street, it was soon forgotten. The scene that confronted her made her stomach tighten. A police car was parked next to Ben's spot, two officers having an animated conversation with Annette, Lena, Sonia and Janet. Ben was standing to one side looking concerned but seemingly unable to get a word in.

'What's happening?' Ellie asked Ben breathlessly after she had parked and raced over.

'Someone has complained that I'm a nuisance. I'm breaking some sort of ancient vagrancy law, apparently,' he replied miserably.

'But you're not asking for money or anything.'

Ben shrugged. 'I think it's all a bit of a grey area. That's what the girls are discussing now.'

Ellie frowned. There was a part of her that thought Ben letting them fight his battle for him was a bit of a cop out. But then, looking across at them in full swing, she realised that he probably hadn't had much choice in the matter. Once his very own neighbourhood task force had decided they were getting involved, they well and truly got involved. Even the police officers were looking harassed and on the verge of surrender.

'People have a right to sit where they want!' Lena squeaked, looking red-faced and giving the disturbing impression of an unexploded bomb. 'If he pays his taxes, then he pays to sit on the street if the fancy takes him.'

'If he was a car he'd be allowed to park on this corner for as long as he wanted and nobody would be able to move him,' Annette added.

Ellie wasn't entirely sure about that line of argument. She could have suggested that perhaps Ben disguise himself as a Fiat Cinquecento, but instead carried on listening in silent wonder.

'But he's not a car,' one of the policemen replied, voicing Ellie's thoughts in a tone that suggested a barely disguised exasperation.

'I watch *Taggart* and I know that you have to have a warrant thingy,' Janet said with a confident nod.

'Ladies… nobody wants to see this situation get ugly and we certainly don't want it to get to *Taggart* proportions. We've simply had a complaint from a resident and we've come to investigate. The fact of the matter is that Mr Kelly shouldn't be camped out on a public road. If someone has made a complaint then Mr Kelly could be seen as behaving antisocially.'

'Antisocially?!' Janet squeaked. 'You should see the hoodies up and down that shopping precinct on their bikes. Go and round them up for being antisocial before coming here and picking on an innocent man who wants nothing more than to show a lady his love for her. Who's made the complaint? I bet it's Arthur Woodall at number fifty, isn't it? He's always bloody complaining… when he isn't pulling his y-fronts from his backside…'

'Look…' The police officer turned to Ben. 'We don't want to have to use our formal powers to make you move on, so if you would take this as a friendly warning, pack up and go home, we'll say no more about it.'

'You see, officer, I can't do that,' Ben began quietly. He took a deep breath. 'I'm sorry,' he continued, a new steel in his voice, 'but I *won't* do that. I'll wait here for Gemma as long as it takes, whether that's a day, a month, a year… and if you arrest me, then as soon as you let me out I'll just come back… so you'll have to keep arresting me and you'll have to put me in prison for a long time.' He drew himself up to his full height. Ellie could see that although he seemed unshakeable in his resolve, he was not used to flouting authority in quite this way; his quickened breathing gave it away.

The police officer began a reply but his argument was cut short.

'What if he's not here *all* the time?' Annette interrupted. 'What if he's *staying*…' she put her fingers in the air to make speech marks, 'at my house and sometimes we all stand on this street corner for a friendly neighbourhood chat? Would that be within the law?'

The policemen looked at each other.

'*Will* he be staying at your house?' the first one asked. 'Because I don't believe that will actually happen.'

'Um…' Annette faltered, uncertain whether the policeman merely wanted her to perpetuate the white lie or whether she was actually expected to come clean about the ruse. 'Yes…' she finally answered. 'Most of the time…'

He gave the tiniest shrug and a barely concealed grin at his colleague. They clearly knew that no such thing was going to happen. Whether the paperwork involved was just too much or whether they were secretly on Ben's side, they weren't saying, but the look they gave him suggested to Ellie that the latter was the case.

'If we drive past a few times and see that Mr Kelly is still here and looks to be constantly here, then we would have to caution him…' The first officer looked at Ben sternly, though Ellie was pretty sure she could see the humour in his eyes. 'And if we receive another complaint from residents then that would also lead to more formal action.'

'Don't worry, there will be no more complaints from residents,' Janet said darkly.

The policeman gave a short nod to Ben. 'Good luck, mate,' he murmured with a slight smile.

Ben bit back a grin of his own. 'Thanks.'

As the officers walked away, Annette beamed at Ben. 'Lucky we were here, isn't it?' she said in a low voice.

'Sure is,' Ben replied. 'I don't know what I'd do without you ladies. But…' He frowned at Annette. 'I can't stay at your house. What would your husband say? And I have too much equipment here to keep out of sight… Besides which, what would be the point of all this if Gemma arrives and I'm in someone's house when she gets here? There's no way I can leave this corner for longer than –'

'Don't worry, I didn't mean you would actually stay in someone's house. We'll carry on as before – but one of us will always be looking out for police cars and we'll come to warn you if we see one so you can get your equipment out of the way. We'll draw up a rota.'

'It'll be just like espionage,' Lena added breathlessly.

'Ooooh yes, like 007. You could be 006 ½, Lena,' Sonia laughed.

'You could be Q, Sonia,' Janet said.

'How long do you think you can keep this up?' Ellie interrupted in a practical tone. Was she the only one who could see how surreal this whole situation was becoming?

Ben shrugged. 'I don't know. I only know that I'm not ready to give up yet. If I get arrested, then I suppose it would be even more of a sign to Gemma that I'll do whatever it takes.'

'And I'm sure she'll be dead impressed with your criminal record too,' Ellie remarked, unable to keep the sarcasm from her tone.

His smile slipped into an expression of intense sadness. Ellie suddenly felt as though she had been privy to his innermost soul. And what she'd glimpsed wasn't a confident charmer, as he always appeared on the surface, but a lost and lonely man.

'I thought you might like to see what gifts have been arriving for you at the *Echo*'s offices,' she added in a gentler tone.

'Gifts?' Ben asked, a slightly bemused smile returning. 'For me?'

'Hang on,' she replied. 'I'll go and get the box from the car.'

Ellie jogged over to her Mini. She might not be able to bring Gemma back. She might not be able to fix whatever darkness lurked at Ben Kelly's core either, but she was sure as hell going to try and cheer him up, even if it was just for the next hour. Proving to him that most of the people of his town were rooting for him seemed like a good place to start.

*

'You're a bad influence, Ellie,' Fiona laughed as she came back to the dinner table. 'There was no way Jack and Jay were going to bed with you still here – I've had to bribe them with the park tomorrow evening. I bet they won't be asleep for hours either, even with that promise hanging over them.'

'Sorry,' Ellie smiled. 'I probably got them a bit over-excited playing *Mario Kart*.'

'Yes,' Patrick put in, 'so I know who to blame tomorrow when they can't get up for school.'

'Yes, dear,' Fiona patted his hand. 'You just pretend that it is actually you who gets them up for school and we'll all pretend to believe it.'

Ellie grinned at her as she took another sip of wine. Fiona had that air of beatific calm that all the mothers she knew seemed to have. All except her own mother, of course. She could imagine Fiona floating around the house in the morning like Mary Poppins, clicking her fingers to fill lunch boxes and singing sweetly as she did so, her deep blue eyes dancing with mischief. Come to think of it, Ellie mused, Fiona even looked a bit like Mary Poppins. And the way Fiona cooked was definitely like someone who couldn't possibly be quite real. The sublime risotto that she had just 'thrown together at the last minute' made Ellie's attempts at cooking seem more like something she had once seen growing in a Petri dish in a school science lesson.

'Oi! Patrick said with mock affront. 'I'm a very hands-on dad.'

'Yes… hands on the paper, hands on the TV remote, hands on my bottom when they shouldn't be…' Fiona replied serenely.

Patrick winked at her and crammed a leftover crust of bread into his mouth. Fiona simply rolled her eyes and sighed theatrically. She reached for the wine bottle and refilled Ellie's glass.

'Patrick says that your mum and dad still haven't made up.'

Ellie nodded. She felt entirely comfortable with Patrick taking home what she had told him during their time at work, knowing that it wouldn't also go around the *Echo*'s offices. He and Fiona shared everything.

'I can't make Mum see sense,' Ellie said.

'You'd think in the circumstances, what with her sister being so ill, she'd realise that life is too short to hold grudges,' Fiona commented as she filled her own glass.

'You would, indeed,' Ellie agreed. 'But my mother is not like normal people. If she gets angry she finds it very hard to forgive. And I think my aunt's illness is merely adding to her stress so that her judgement is more clouded than ever.'

'What about your dad? How is he coping with his exile?'

'Not very well. He's not looking after himself at all. You hear of people dying of a broken heart, and I honestly think the way he's going, that's what will happen. He's just so miserable without her. And if the broken heart doesn't get him, the dodgy attempts at home improvement will.'

'It'll get easier,' Patrick cut in, 'these things always do with time.' He reached for the bottle that Fiona had moved out of his way and grinned at his wife as he did. 'If all else fails, he could always join Ben Kelly on his corner.'

'That's not even funny,' Fiona chided. 'That's why I moved the wine – you say all the wrong things when you get squiffy.'

'It's OK,' Ellie said. 'I get Patrick's point. For the mess in my dad's flat, he might as well be living rough anyway.'

'How is *the man who can't be moved*?' Fiona asked.

Ellie stared into space for a moment as her thoughts went to Ben and what he might be doing right now. She shook herself.

'We had a bit of drama there today actually. The police tried to move him on.'

'Yes, Patrick told me. Do you think he's going to stick it out until his girlfriend comes back? And do you think she will? It's been almost a week now and he's still waiting.'

'It doesn't seem very encouraging for him,' Ellie agreed. 'I honestly don't know whether she will. But… as for Ben… I've never seen anyone so determined.'

'That'll be some sort of abandonment issue,' Patrick said, taking a swig of his drink.

'What do you mean?' Ellie turned to him.

'Because of how he lost his parents.'

'*He lost his parents?*' Ellie repeated.

'Mmmm, when he was twelve they were both killed in a house fire. He was the only one to be rescued by a neighbour.'

Ellie stared at him. 'How do you know this?'

'He told me.'

'How did *I* not know this?' Ellie squeaked.

'I suppose you just weren't listening properly. I asked him what his parents thought about him camping out. I'd have thought it was an obvious question really. It must have struck you as odd that there was no input from them? I mean, whatever age a man gets to, he never stops being a mummy's boy.'

'You more than most,' Fiona cut in.

Patrick grinned. 'The point is that you'd expect them to pop over and see how he was – at least from an emotional point of view if nothing else. Or they'd make their feelings on the situation known to someone, perhaps even the *Echo* as we're covering it. He's gone through a break-up that has driven him to some pretty extreme measures. Your mum and dad would be upset if it happened to you, right?' Patrick took another gulp of his wine as he eyed Ellie. 'Clearly I should be the reporter after all…'

Ellie suddenly felt like the room was spinning. 'This is huge,' she murmured.

'I don't think he wants that bit of his life reporting,' Patrick added, serious now.

'But an angle like that would get so much public sympathy.'

'And also rake up very painful memories,' Fiona said gently. 'I don't usually agree with Patrick but in this case I do think he's right. Best to leave that bit of the poor boy's past well alone.'

'I *should* have asked but I never thought…' Ellie said, more to herself than anyone else.

'Don't beat yourself up,' Patrick said. 'You were covering the story he wanted you to.'

'God, he's out there right now, all alone in the cold and dark…'

'Ellie…' Patrick interrupted, 'he's about as far from alone as you can get. Every female on that street is in love with him.'

'It's not the same. And they won't stay out there all night.'

'It's his choice. He knows what to expect, he's spent lots of nights out there now.'

'We can only hope this Gemma is not as big a bitch as she's making herself look right now,' Fiona added. 'Assuming that she knows about his past, which she must do, I can't believe she hasn't been to him already, if only to put him straight so that he can get on with his life if she doesn't want him.'

'I do feel guilty for my part though,' Ellie said. 'There was me thinking he was just out to grab attention when all the time he's got this awful tragedy always there with him. The whole picture makes so much more sense now.'

'Like Patrick says, you were doing your job. You were there to report on his plight with Gemma and you did that. You mustn't worry about it. You have far more pressing things in your own life.'

Ellie sighed. 'It feels like everywhere I turn at the moment there's tragedy, or at least the promise of it.'

'Life is tragedy, waiting to take bites from us whatever we do,' Fiona said. 'We just have to learn how to avoid letting it swallow us whole.'

Patrick leaned over and squeezed his wife's shoulder with a broad grin. 'Have you been at the philosophy books again? I thought you were going to kick the habit.'

'Shut up,' Fiona said, slapping his hand away. 'You know what I mean.'

Ellie didn't reply. There was very little she could do to put her own life straight at that moment, but there was, perhaps, something she could do for Ben. Somewhere in the back of her mind, a plan was forming. The more she thought about it, the more it seemed like the answer. It would need a little detective work… but being a reporter, that surely wouldn't be too difficult?

*

Ellie stood at the gate and looked up at the house. It was a regular post-war semi, neat lawns and uniform borders of new bulbs just showing their first shoots, white plastic windows and front door – nothing out of the ordinary. Her head was still pounding from all the wine she had promised herself she wouldn't drink the night before but then had. Annoyingly, Patrick had looked bright and rested when he arrived at work that morning, whereas Ellie was pretty certain she looked like road-kill. He had definitely drunk more than her too. She had considered for a moment asking him to come here with her, but then decided, for a reason that even she couldn't work out, to come alone.

Finding the address had been much easier than she had imagined – it turned out that Gemma Fox's mother had entered her into a modelling competition held by the paper the year before and her details were still on file. It was around the time that Ellie had begun work on the *Echo* and she recalled the competition being won by a sweet Romanian girl who had settled in Millrise only months before.

Collecting herself, Ellie pushed open the gate and approached the door. Her next lines had been carefully rehearsed in the car on the way over, and she smoothed her expression into one of professional amiability.

After a few moments of waiting, the door was opened by a thick-necked bald man in his late-forties to early-fifties, dressed in a shell suit that could only have come straight from the eighties. If this was Gemma's dad, then Gemma had clearly inherited her model looks from her mum. Or the milkman. The man looked Ellie up and down.

'I don't buy from door-to-door salespeople.'

'That's alright,' Ellie replied brightly. 'I'm not selling.' She was about to show her work ID when he interrupted her.

'I don't do religion either.'

'I'm from the *Millrise Echo*,' Ellie said, 'I wondered whether I could speak to Gemma Fox. Does she live here?'

All at once his expression changed and he broke into a yellow-toothed smile. 'My Gemma? Has she won something?'

'I'd prefer to talk to her, if that's OK,' Ellie said as courteously as she could manage.

The man opened the door and stepped back to indicate that Ellie could go in. Shutting the door behind her, he shouted up the stairs. 'Gem! Some reporter here for you!'

Gemma's face appeared at the top. 'What?'

The man nodded his head in Ellie's direction. 'A reporter... Here for you.'

'Shit, I'm still in my jammies.'

Gemma disappeared again, leaving Ellie and the man in awkward silence.

A few excruciating sentences about the weather later, Gemma reappeared dressed and in full make-up. Ellie had to be impressed – she had never seen anyone go from bed-head to full-on glamour in such record time. As she came down the stairs, Ellie took a moment to be equally impressed by the fact that she was the only woman she had ever seen wearing patterned leggings who actually looked really good in them. She had teamed the leggings with a figure hugging black top and her hair tumbled about her shoulders in impossibly bouncy curls. Gemma was every inch the perfect specimen of the female form, just as her photos had suggested. Ellie found herself willing the girl to be a bimbo; it was the only way that she wouldn't feel like a waste of DNA in comparison. But when she opened her mouth, it was clear there was a sharp mind behind the lip gloss and mascara.

'This is about Ben, right?' Gemma threw a glance at her dad before Ellie had time to answer. 'Dad, stick the kettle on. Me and this reporter are going to talk in the front room for a bit of privacy.'

With an idiotic grin, her dad went off to the kitchen whistling. Clearly, Ellie thought, Gemma had inherited the clever genes from someone else too.

'I wondered if anyone from the paper would come round,' Gemma said as she led Ellie into another room.

Ellie shot a quick look around to form some sort of immediate opinion about who and what she was dealing with. The room offered very little in the way of clues; as soulless and as uniform as the exterior of the house, it was decorated in lightly patterned magnolia paper, plain beige curtains and a teak dining set as inured in the 1980s as Mr Fox's shell suit. It didn't look like they were an affluent family but they didn't seem particularly badly off either. Squashed in a corner behind the table and chairs was a cream two-seater sofa. Gemma sat down without inviting Ellie to do the same, but Ellie followed and sat next to her anyway.

'You've read the newspaper coverage then?' Ellie asked.

'Yes,' she said simply.

'But you haven't been to see Ben.'

'No. I didn't want to give him false hope. I thought he would give up and go home after a night.'

'I don't think he has any intention of doing that.'

'I can't send a clearer message than I am already.' Gemma curled a lock of hair around her finger as she watched Ellie produce a notepad and pen.

'Maybe he thinks,' Ellie said, 'however misguided the belief may be, that he can change your mind.'

Gemma sniffed but didn't reply.

'You must have been fond of him once?' Ellie pressed.

'Yes… of course.'

'So what changed?'

'Things got stale. I felt so trapped in that flat with our lives of doing nothing. Ben had dreams, but they seemed a long time coming true and we had no money –'

'Money isn't everything.'

'Try telling that to someone who has none.'

'Just because there's no money now, doesn't mean it will always be so. Lots of couples start off a bit broke. Things change along the way.

What about his plans for a music school? Things will be better when that gets going.'

'You mean *if* that gets going. I had thought his band would make it… they came close and I was so excited for him, you know. His passion is music and he's always wanted to work in the industry in some way. But then it all came to nothing. I think he was more gutted than he says but his nerves let him down…'

'Performing didn't suit him – he told me that. But the music school is a very different proposition.'

Gemma didn't reply immediately. And when she did, Ellie was taken aback by her change of tone. She sounded far less certain of herself than she had when Ellie arrived. 'I suppose you think this is all my fault. I look like the villain here. It doesn't matter…'

'I hadn't meant to make you look like a villain,' Ellie said, the dry heat of the room now making her feel flustered. She was beginning to think coming here was a bad idea. Driving over she had felt so sure of how the conversation was going to go, but now, meeting Gemma, she was more confused than ever. What if Gemma was the victim here? If there even was a victim. Hundreds of relationships fizzled out, every day; what made theirs different? Did Ellie have the right to interfere in their lives this way? Perhaps some relationships were better off dead. Like her parents' for instance… She shook herself. No, she decided, she wasn't giving up on this one just yet. Not when there was a man as determined as Ben to make it work. 'If you want, now might be the time to tell your side of the story…'

Gemma paused and appraised Ellie thoughtfully. 'Maybe that's not such a bad idea. Is this just me telling you or for the paper?'

Ellie frowned. 'I suppose it's whatever you want it to be. Would you mind terribly if it went in the paper?'

'I suppose you could print some. Not all of it though.'

'Why, was he a bad boyfriend?' Ellie asked with an unexplained sense of dread.

'Oh no,' Gemma said. 'He didn't knock me about or anything.'

Ellie heaved a silent sigh of relief. 'So what's your version of events then?'

Gemma shrugged. 'He never had time for me. There was always something else to do: band practise, his bar job, volunteering at Millrise High –'

'He volunteered at the high school?' Ellie interrupted. Ben hadn't mentioned that to her.

'Yeah, he taught some of the kids guitar. They don't have a school budget for it and he agreed to help out once a week with the ones who couldn't afford private tuition.'

'Once a week doesn't sound too bad,' Ellie said. Instead of being appalled by his supposed neglect of his girlfriend, she was becoming increasingly impressed by him. 'I suppose that's his way of coping with his own tragedies in life,' she added.

'You know about his parents?' Gemma asked.

'It's my job to find things out,' Ellie replied serenely, trying not to think about how she'd actually done nothing of the sort.

Gemma seemed to consider the point for a moment. 'I felt so sorry for him when I found out. I suppose, in some ways, it was the reason we moved in together. He didn't ask for sympathy, of course, but once you know about something like that it's hard not to think about it.'

'You didn't love him?'

'No, no, that came out wrong. Of course I loved him. I adored him but… I'm not sure we were ever suited to go the distance.'

'Well…' Ellie said, scribbling on her pad, 'If you love him then surely that's worth a second chance. Nobody can know if a relationship will go the distance but if we all thought like that nobody would ever get married. I mean, look at how he's trying to show you he loves you. Not many men would do what he's doing.'

'Hmm,' Gemma mused. 'I want to go back but…'

'But what?'

'It's hard now this has all come out. I've left him there so long… Everyone will be watching and judging. They all think I'm a cow.'

'No one thinks that. And if they do then my article will put them right.'

'How do you go back to what we had after all that's happened? I just don't think we can.'

'You won't know unless you try.' Ellie chewed on the end of her pen for a moment as she regarded Gemma. 'Pretend none of the news reporting had ever happened and it was just down to you and Ben – do you think you might have given him another chance?' she asked finally.

'I honestly don't know. But the longer this goes on the harder it gets.'

'You have the power to put the brakes on it now. He's waiting, desperate for you to go to him.'

Gemma's reply was cut short by her dad who came in with two large earthenware mugs emblazoned with the name of a local haulage firm. 'Two teas, ladies,' he said as he handed them over with a huge grin.

'Ta, Dad,' Gemma said.

Ellie grimaced at the film of grease on the surface of her drink and tried not to think about the germs as she gingerly took a sip.

The man nodded before leaving them alone again.

'What if I ran that story telling your side?' Ellie asked. 'Do you think it might even the odds a little?'

Gemma gave her a small smile. It lit her face in a way that made her unbelievably pretty – like a doll Ellie had once owned. She could see why

Ben was besotted with her. And the fact that she seemed so sweet-natured had thrown Ellie a real curveball when she had arrived expecting to find a vain and shallow airhead. She was struck by guilt for all she had presumed before. And she wasn't entirely sure that opening up both sides of their relationship for scrutiny was a good thing. Still, if it got them back together then it couldn't be all that bad, could it? There were so many things in her own life she was powerless to influence so perhaps if she could do this one thing she wouldn't feel like such a monumental screw up.

'We could do a small interview now,' Gemma said. 'I have time if you do.'

'I've always got time for a story,' Ellie smiled. 'And I'll call my colleague as soon as we're finished here so he can pop round to get some shots,' she added.

Gemma beamed at her. 'Do you know when? I'll need a bit of notice to get my hair done.'

'Not yet,' Ellie said, a little taken aback by the request. 'But I expect he'll phone you first to organise a time when I've spoken to him.'

'Great. I'd better let you have my number.'

'Here, write it down on my pad,' Ellie said, handing it over. Gemma scribbled down her number and handed it back.

'Do you think he'll be upset? About me being in the paper too?'

'Ben?'

Gemma nodded.

'As long as you don't say anything dreadful about him,' Ellie smiled.

Gemma gave her a shy smile in return. 'I'll try not to.'

Ellie tapped her pen against her front teeth thoughtfully. 'What's really stopping you from going to that corner right now?'

Gemma shrugged. 'I don't know how to put everything right. If I go to him, that's it, we're back together, and I'm not ready to make that decision yet. So, you see, I can't go there at all without confusing things.' She frowned. 'Don't put that in the paper.'

'Of course I won't,' Ellie replied with a reassuring smile. 'I think you're wrong, though. I think he'd be happy just to talk it through, as long as you gave him the chance.'

'I will go to him... I want to... but...' She sighed. 'Ellie...'

'Hmmm?'

'Don't tell him about what we've discussed, will you?'

'If you don't want me to then I won't.'

'Not just yet. And thanks...'

'For what?'

'For listening to my side of the story.'

Ellie smiled. 'It's what I do.'

*

Back in the car, Ellie ended her call to Patrick and stared at the road ahead, deep in thought. She was beginning to wonder if she was getting too personally involved in this story. *Hell*, there was no *beginning* about it – she was already far too involved. But she pushed all doubts to the back of her mind, convinced that this time she was going to make a difference. Even though her head ached and her eyes were heavy, the thought raised a smile. If it had anything to do with her, Ben and Gemma would be back in their flat by Valentine's Day.

Chapter Six

Patrick leapt out of his car and bounded across the car park with a grin. The day had been bright and mild for the time of year but now, as the shadows lengthened across the tarmac, the temperature was dropping rapidly. Ellie shivered slightly as she waited for her colleague.

'How can you be that lively after last night?' Ellie frowned as he drew level. 'It's just not fair, you know. I feel like a dead dog. I'm even worse than this morning and if I don't get to my bed soon I'll collapse.'

'What can I say? I love my job so much it makes me bounce with enthusiasm!'

'Even when it involves reporting *Millrise Businessman of the Year*?'

'Especially when it involves Millrise Businessman of the Year. I can't get enough of businessmen, me.'

Ellie laughed. 'Shut up and let's get this done.'

Patrick followed her into the tiny office of *Delaney's Fresh Produce*. An earthy smell filled her nostrils – one that took her right back to visiting her granddad's allotments as a kid – and the distant clattering and whistling-along-to-the-radio of the busy warehouse beyond the front entrance met her ears. Behind a desk littered with a chaotic looking array of paperwork sat a rather more attractive man than Ellie had been expecting. Max Delaney, the proprietor, was young – not more than his early thirties – tall and slim with blond hair that dropped almost foppishly over one eye and a warm smile. He jumped up to shake hands with both of them.

'You're from the *Echo*?' he asked.

'Yes, how did you…?' Ellie began with a note of surprise in her voice.

Max Delaney grinned and nodded at Patrick's camera. 'Either I'm being scouted as a model for *Plums Weekly*, or that's for newspaper photos.'

'And we phoned to make an appointment, didn't we, Ellie…' Patrick reminded her with a half-frown.

Ellie nodded, shaking herself. She really did need to lie down in a darkened room. Something was eating at her today, and she couldn't put her finger on what it was.

'You'll have to excuse my colleague,' Patrick said with a conspiratorial grin. 'We only took her on as part of the Care in the Community initiative.' His voice dropped into a stage whisper. 'You can see that it's not really working out.'

'Oh dear,' Max laughed. 'Can I get you anything to drink… tea, coffee?'

'Coffee would be fantastic,' Patrick said.

'Not for me, thanks.' Ellie pulled her notebook from her satchel as Max disappeared into a small room behind the office. They heard the sound of a kettle being filled. Max appeared again.

'I must apologise for the mess,' he said, gesturing to the stacks of paperwork on his desk. 'I would ask my secretary to sort it but I can't… on account of not being able to persuade my girlfriend to come and work for me. I'd pay her far more than the miserable pig she works for now.' He smiled broadly. 'She seems to have some daft notion of making her own way in the world and not living off my money. She doesn't seem to get that she wouldn't be living off me if she was contributing to the business. So I run the office on my own as I haven't got round to recruiting yet. I have a few warehouse lads, but that's it. As the business grows, though, I am going to need someone…' He gave Ellie a cheeky smile. 'I don't suppose you fancy a Saturday job?'

'I think I might be the worst secretary you've ever seen…' Ellie said. 'You do a great job of running the business on such a small staff though,' she added absently, her mind not on Max Delaney's business at all.

'I love my Bonnie to bits, even though she won't work here with me,' Max said with obvious pride, his mind clearly, if only momentarily, not on his business either. 'She'd been on her own for a while before me and when she had a fella before that he was a complete waste of space. It's marvellous how strong that's made her.'

'Have you been together long?'

'Around a year.' He opened a desk drawer and rifled for a moment before producing a stained teaspoon with a look of triumph. Ellie realised she'd had a lucky escape – one questionable drink a day was quite enough. 'I'll just get those coffees and then we can settle down.'

*

'That wasn't so bad,' Patrick said as they walked back to their cars. 'I liked him; he was the sort of bloke you'd be happy to go for a pint with.'

'He wasn't like the people who usually get nominated for the businessman of the year award, that's for sure,' Ellie said.

'I wouldn't mention that to any of the other candidates,' Patrick laughed.

Ellie gave him an absent smile.

'So, come on,' Patrick said, his tone more serious, 'what's bothering you?'

Ellie glanced across at him as they walked. 'I don't know what you mean.'

'Yes you do. You've been behaving like you left your brain on a bus seat all afternoon. Something isn't right. Do I have to set Fiona on you again?'

Ellie sighed as she stopped next to her Mini. 'Did you get a chance to go and do the photos of Gemma?'

Patrick shook his head with a slightly bemused expression. 'Gemma?'

'Ben Kelly's ex.'

'Ohhh, *that* Gemma! The original Foxy Lady. Oh yes,' he grinned.

'And…' Ellie fought the impulse to ask, but it came out anyway. 'What did you think of her?'

He shrugged. 'She seemed really nice to me. Very attractive. Not my type, of course,' he added quickly, seeing Ellie's frown. 'How come you ended up going there anyway? I mean, as another angle to the story, it's inspired, but I'm surprised you didn't mention your plans to me before.'

'It wasn't exactly what I had planned. I was going to go and see if I could persuade her to take him back, and before I knew it I was doing a story on her.'

'Ellie…' Patrick said gently, 'I don't know how to ask this but… do you think you might be getting a bit… *attached* to Ben?'

'He's had a terrible time. I'm just concerned for him. I can be a journalist and a nice human being at the same time, can't I?' Ellie's tone had become somewhat defensive. Patrick opened and closed his mouth, seemingly uncertain of the correct response.

'Of course,' he said finally. He rubbed a hand across the fine stubble on his chin. 'I'm just not sure it's a great idea to play agony aunt between them.'

'I can't ignore what I know about him.'

'It's tragic, sure, but none of our business,' Patrick shot back. 'You can't fix his life, Ellie, this is between him and his girlfriend.'

'*Ex-girlfriend*,' Ellie corrected.

'Whatever. I'm saying this to you now as your friend and it's up to you whether you choose to listen or not. If the situation makes you this crazy then you should stop going over to Constance Street. Let Ange follow the story from now on.'

Ellie gave a snort and turned away from him, rifling savagely in her bag for her car keys.

'This is not the Ellie Newton I know.' Patrick laid a hand on her shoulder and pulled her around to face him again. 'Whatever this is about, you need to let go of it.'

'How can I?' Ellie stared up at him. She swallowed hard and ran a hand through her hair. 'They belong together and I can help them.'

Patrick gave his most severe frown. 'Are you sure that's not just you thinking about your mum and dad?'

'OK, you're right,' she sighed. 'Ange can follow up. I suppose all the stuff that's going on in my own life is getting to me and I'm not thinking straight.'

'Good girl,' Patrick said. 'You know it makes sense.' He held his arms open. 'Hug for the big guy?'

Ellie gave a watery smile. She felt like crying and she wasn't entirely sure why. 'Thanks,' she whispered as he folded her into his arms. She closed her eyes and hugged him back. 'Thank you, Patrick.'

*

Despite knowing that she really ought to, Ellie simply couldn't face visiting her mother or Aunt Hazel after work that night. She texted her mum with vague excuses of feeling unwell and headed home. She wanted nothing more than to curl up in front of the TV and watch something utterly mind-numbing. It was all down to stress, of course, and she was letting small things get to her far more than they ought to. What did it matter to her that Ben Kelly waited on a street corner, day after day?

Patrick was right – it was nothing to do with her other than professional interest. Looking at it logically, the longer Ben stayed there the better the story was. And that story was playing out slap bang in the middle of Millrise. When the nationals got hold of it, as they inevitably would, things would go nuts for the person who'd got the scoop. If Ellie could pull herself together, then she could continue following up instead of asking Ange. Ellie tried to focus on this as she stabbed a fork at the plastic cover of a microwaveable cottage pie, but found the idea no solace at all. Instead, she couldn't stop thinking about that glimpse into Ben's soul she had accidentally been granted the last time she'd seen him, the wounded look that had revealed the real Benvolio Kelly – a twelve-year-old boy still grieving for precious days of happiness lost. What was the point in pretending otherwise; she was hopelessly involved. The fact that she'd deliberately gone and met his girlfriend and found a friendly girl she rather liked had made things much, much worse… It had been far easier when Gemma had been an ice-maiden she could dislike from afar.

As the microwave hummed and worked its magic, Ellie wandered into her living room to retrieve her phone. The screen showed the same two messages she hadn't even had the energy to open when she'd first got home from work. One was from Patrick, asking her if she was feeling better, and the other was from Jethro:

COME TO LONDON! WE NEED TO BE DRUNK TOGETHER! YES I AM WRITING IN CAPS AND YES IT MEANS I'M SHOUTING. DON'T MAKE ME COME UP THERE AND GET YOU!!!!

Ellie couldn't help but smile. Maybe a weekend away was exactly what she needed.

When?

The answer came through straight away – Ellie wasn't surprised. Jethro was more attached to his phone than she was and rarely took long to reply to a message.

Kas is free this weekend so how about Saturday?

Saturday? Two days away. It was a bit close. But then, Ellie mused, it wasn't like she had anything else to do… apart from worry about her mum and dad and Hazel and an idiot she hardly knew camping on a street corner. Perhaps the only thing better than a bit of hedonism for making you forget your woes was a bit of totally spontaneous hedonism.

Ok, you asked for it! See you Saturday. x

*

'London will be a lovely break,' Hazel said the following evening as Ellie and her mum sat with her. 'I haven't been for years.'

'Me neither,' Miranda said, her attempt at cheeriness painfully transparent. All three continued with the charade as if by denying that there was a dying woman in the room they could somehow save her.

'How long will you be going for?' Hazel asked.

'Just overnight. I have to be back in work on Monday morning.'

Miranda sniffed and reached for the TV remote. 'We might as well turn this film off if nobody is watching it.'

'We *are* watching it,' Ellie replied, wrestling the remote from her mum's grip. 'We're just interspersing the tedious dialogue with more interesting conversation of our own.'

'So, now you're saying my film choices are boring? Next time you can choose and we'll all complain about it.'

Hazel shared a grin with Ellie. 'That's us told off.' She let the spoon fall into her empty bowl.

'Do you want some more?' Ellie asked.

'Is this your new plan to bump me off – death by ice-cream?' Hazel held out her bowl for Ellie to collect.

'That's absolutely it. A far nicer way to go.'

'Can we stop all this talk of death?' Miranda asked tartly.

'Oh, Mi, I'm only having a bit of fun,' Hazel chided.

'I don't like it,' Miranda replied.

Ellie jumped up from the sofa and when she returned a few moments later, both women were engrossed in the film again.

'Thank you,' Hazel said as Ellie handed her another tiny portion. 'I read the story about the man on Constance Street, by the way,' she added. 'I thought it was interesting.'

'Interesting as in *what a nut-job*, or interesting as in *I wish he was waiting there for me*?' Ellie asked. 'They seem to be the two main camps.'

'It's incredibly loyal. People aren't like that nowadays. Everyone moves on so quickly to the next bigger and better thing.'

Ellie paused, grappling for the right thing to say. She sensed they were on dangerous emotional ground. Before her reply had been formulated, Hazel continued.

'It's comforting to see that some people still understand promises.'

Ellie and her mum exchanged a worried glance. There was little either of them could say to Hazel's observation. The fact was that she had every reason to be bitter – and considering her current situation, more than most.

'He turned sixteen this week, you know,' Hazel added in a low voice, 'Callum, that is…' She uttered the name with a wince, as though the syllables in her mouth caused her pain.

'How did you find this out?' Miranda asked, seemingly uncertain that she wanted an answer.

'Facebook, of course.'

'I don't know why you go on there,' Ellie said, forcing a casual air. 'It's so full of pointless status updates and crap adverts that even I don't bother with it now. I mean, there are only so many photos of kittens wearing hats that you can look at without it melting your brain.'

Hazel shrugged slightly with a wan smile. 'I don't know why either. But it's sort of comforting, in a weird way, watching all that life continuing to be lived beyond my little bubble.'

'Blimey,' Ellie said, still trying but failing miserably to lighten her tone, 'that's a bit deep for a Friday evening.'

'I know,' Hazel said.

'You need to stop dwelling on the past,' Miranda said. 'Especially on that loser of an ex-husband. He's not worth it.'

'John was a good man deep down. He just wanted more than I could give him.'

'You think it's OK that he got another woman pregnant when he knew you wanted children so desperately and couldn't?'

'No,' Hazel replied slowly. 'But we both wanted children and I suppose now that I've had a lot of time to think about it…'

'What?' Miranda asked indignantly. 'You're forgiving him?'

'Mum…' Ellie cut in. 'If Hazel forgives him, I think that shows she's the better person. You can't hold grudges forever,' she added pointedly.

'Life's too short… I know that better now than ever,' Hazel agreed in a tone laced with just the merest hint of bitterness.

'Don't turn this around and make it about me and your dad,' Miranda snapped at Ellie, choosing to ignore Hazel's last statement.

'He misses you –' Ellie stopped herself mid-sentence. Her mum's eyes widened.

'You've been to see him!'

'Well of course I've bloody been to see him. He's my dad!'

'He's a liar and a fraud,' Miranda said.

'He made a mistake, Mum. Everyone makes mistakes. He made a decision and it was a bad call. He thought he was doing the right thing at the time.'

Miranda huffed. 'It lost me my house.'

'You still have your house,' Ellie reminded her, biting back her impatience.

'Alright then, he lost me my security. That mortgage was paid. We should have been enjoying a stress-free existence; instead, I have another financial millstone around my neck for God knows how many years. Until I die and beyond I expect.'

'Not *you*,' Ellie corrected. '*You and Dad*. He's still paying his contribution even though you threw him out.'

'So he should. And can we stop talking about it all now please?'

'Hazel can forgive John for going off and having a child with another woman, but you can't forgive Dad one little mistake that amounts to nothing more than a bad decision about money?' Ellie folded her arms and stared at her mum. 'You are priceless; you know that, don't you?'

'You wouldn't understand.'

Ellie rubbed a hand through her hair and shot a glance at Hazel, who merely gazed sadly at her. 'You're right, I don't.'

'I don't want you to see him,' Miranda said.

'Don't be ridiculous. You don't go to that flat and see just how much this has affected him. I can't abandon him now. You don't have to take him back, Mum, but I think you should show him just a little forgiveness. It's not like he murdered someone. It's not like he committed adultery.'

'It feels like adultery to me. It was a betrayal of my trust.'

Ellie let out an impatient sigh. 'That's even more ridiculous...' Realising that losing her temper would only steel her mother's resolve, she reined back her irritation and softened her tone. 'Ask him round for a cup of tea at least, talk things through. What harm can it do?'

Miranda shook her head with an obstinate frown. 'I can't... not yet.'

'But you'll think about it?'

'I think you should,' Hazel cut in. 'Regrets are the last thing you want to be left with when the grim reaper finally comes to call.'

Miranda paused. 'I'll think about it. But I'm not promising anything.'

*

By the time she stepped off the train at Euston on Saturday afternoon, Ellie was ready for something to take her mind off her troubled week. Leaving the platform, she scanned the crowds on the marbled concourse, looking for Jethro. And then she saw him, waiting next to the information desk, dressed in fitted jeans and a navy hoodie that brought out the blue of his eyes, hair stylishly messed and a grin full of boyish mischief. It was comforting to see that some things, including her best friend, were the same as always. Just seeing him standing there set her emotions on solid ground again. He jogged towards her and swung her round in a huge hug.

'You're so mean, leaving me alone in this scary city for months on end.'

Ellie giggled as she retrieved her overnight bag from where she had dropped it in his enthusiastic embrace. 'You had Kasumi, you numpty.'

'She's even scarier than the city.'

Ellie giggled again. 'Probably.'

'How was the train down?' he asked as they made their way to the underground.

'Smelly and loud.'

Jethro laughed. 'Oh God, sounds horrendous.'

'And now we're heading into the bowels of the earth for more of the same. We must be mad.'

Jethro stopped dead at the escalators for the tube, almost tripping up a disgruntled looking man who was actually wearing a bowler hat. 'We could get a taxi if you preferred?'

Ellie laughed. 'I'm only joking. A cab will cost us a fortune; the tube is fine.'

Jethro relaxed and began to walk again. 'Cool.'

'Don't take this the wrong way,' Ellie said as they descended the escalators, 'but somehow I didn't imagine you buying a flat in Peckham.'

He turned to her with a grin. 'I took some persuading when the estate agent first suggested it to me, to be honest. But the property prices are really affordable and the area isn't nearly as grim as its reputation. I love it there so far.'

'Maybe you can show me the sights later then.'

'Tomorrow, totally. But we haven't got much time today. Kasumi is coming by this afternoon so we can go up to the club together.'

'What about Sam? I thought they were joined at the hip these days.'

'Don't worry, the boy wonder will make an appearance. I think we're meeting him there.'

'Fantastic,' Ellie said. 'The old gang and their plus one back together.'

'Yep, watch out London!' he laughed.

'What time are we meeting Sam?'

'About seven. But we have to be drunk before we leave the flat so we have to start early.'

'Oh my God, I'm so going to regret this, aren't I?'

He grinned at her. 'Yup.'

*

Two hours and a couple of bottles of Rioja later, Ellie, Jethro and Kasumi were on the tube heading for their rendezvous with Kasumi's boyfriend.

After an emotional afternoon of catching up on old times and new developments, the three had settled into their old easy ways with each other as if they had never been apart. Kasumi was chattering away now, barely drawing breath with a drunken laugh that had steadily taken on the characteristics of a football rattle with every glug of wine. Strangely, this phenomenon had done little to diminish her attractiveness and she had drawn admiring looks from men wherever she went. Her perfectly formed lips were in a mocking pout as she teased Jethro about some misdemeanour at work, her dark eyes shining with mischief.

Ellie could feel the pleasant effects of overindulgence too, though she suspected her own drunken behaviour was gaining rather fewer admirers.

'So…' Kasumi's attention now turned to Ellie. 'What's the deal with this guy?'

'What guy?' Ellie asked with a bemused look.

'You know… the street corner guy. You mentioned him earlier.'

'I did?'

'About four times,' Jethro cut in with a sly grin.

Ellie shrugged slightly, feeling herself colour. Had she really mentioned him that often? Certainly often enough to be of note. 'He's still there,' she said, 'waiting for his girlfriend to take him back.'

Kasumi glanced up at the station sign through the window as the train slowed. Satisfied that they hadn't missed their stop, she leaned across Jethro who was sitting in between them. 'Is he hot?'

Ellie laughed. 'I suppose so…'

Jethro coughed very deliberately and Ellie covered his ears as she giggled. 'Very hot,' she said in a loud stage whisper.

'In that case I think we ought to get him on TV.'

Ellie's expression became serious. 'You mean make a programme about him?'

'Sounds like a brilliant idea to me,' Jethro said, removing Ellie's hands from his ears.

'Not a *whole* programme…' Kasumi clarified. 'But definitely something.'

'It's really that newsworthy?'

'Not *newsworthy*, exactly,' Kasumi said, 'but there's the makings of a great feature in one of our daily magazine programmes. Especially if he does last until Valentine's Day. I could talk to Catherine, our boss, see what she says.'

Kasumi was spot on, of course, and it was a brilliant idea. But Ellie couldn't bring herself to be as excited. 'Vernon, my ed, is already taking care of national coverage,' she replied doubtfully.

'Pah, nobody reads papers anymore. Television is where it's at.'

'You would say that,' Ellie smiled. 'If we're going down that road then Twitter is where it's *really* at.'

'If you're going to get pedantic,' Kasumi returned, 'then Instagram is the way to go.'

Ellie laughed. 'I never could win an argument with you.'

'Few can,' Jethro said.

Ellie glanced at him and could see from that one tiny look that he still fancied her even after all this time. But then, Ellie reflected as her gaze went back to Kasumi – exotic and beautiful – she imagined that most men would.

'You met his girlfriend, Jethro tells me,' Kasumi added.

Ellie nodded.

'And what did you think?'

'She hated her,' Jethro said in a tipsy voice.

Ellie slapped him playfully. 'Actually I rather liked her… Are you going to feature her on the programme too?'

'Steady on,' Kasumi laughed. 'Nobody's said we're featuring anybody yet. We need to run it by our Lords and Masters.' At the sound of a faint ping, she dug into her tiny handbag and pulled out her phone. 'Sam is waiting up top for us.'

*

Sam, who always reminded Ellie of a sun-freckled, strawberry-haired surfer (and was definitely batting out of his league with Kasumi, though Ellie suspected that was what her friend liked about him), kissed Kasumi and exchanged a manly sort of hip-hop hug with Jethro before he turned to Ellie. 'Great to see you again, Ellie. It's been too long.'

'I know. It's ridiculous how time flies. How are you?'

'I'm really good.'

'Ah,' Ellie said, tapping her nose, 'the world of product packaging is treating you well?'

'Extremely,' Sam laughed. 'Although it takes a certain type of person to get excited about the colouration on a box of cornflakes and I wouldn't recommend it as a career for normal people.'

'I wouldn't recommend journalism for normal people either,' Ellie returned. 'Especially in Millrise.'

'Enough of this idle chat,' Jethro said, linking his arm through Ellie's. 'We need to get to this club before I start to sober up.'

'I think the same can be said for my bird,' Sam quipped.

Kasumi smacked him on the arm. 'Oi! I am nobody's *bird*. This isn't a seventies sit-com you know!'

Sam threw back his head and laughed. 'You make it so easy for me to wind you up every time.' He pulled her into a kiss. 'If it were a seventies sit-com right now we'd be making some double entendre about spanking me in punishment.'

'How about I just throw a punch in a very twenty-first century manner?' Kasumi smiled sweetly.

'Then I'd love you all the more,' Sam said with a broad grin.

'Would that be before the stitches to your lip or after?' Ellie laughed.

'Come on, let's go,' Jethro said, tugging at Ellie's arm. 'Just don't break into a fight until after we've been in the club, you two.'

*

One minute Ellie had been in reasonable control of her faculties, and the next, she seemed to be slurring and falling into Jethro every time she tried to move. It could have been something to do with the assortment of colourful and wittily named cocktails that seemed to appear in front of her every time she emptied a glass, but Ellie had to concede that Jethro's promise to take her back to his flat legless had indeed come to successful fruition. It seemed that her companions were all pretty much in the same state, so when Jethro handed out a rather ill-advised invitation for them all to continue the drinking at his flat, everyone agreed with slurring enthusiasm.

All it needed was for one of them to still possess the faculties to get them to the taxi rank and give the driver directions and for the drunker members of the party to avoid throwing up in said taxi. Not an easy task, but one they must have managed as they found themselves sitting in Jethro's flat while he searched for more alcohol.

'Aha!' he shouted, his head stuck in a cupboard. 'Got some.'

Sam whistled while Ellie and Kasumi cheered in appreciation.

Jethro turned and took a bow as he produced a tray and placed a selection of bottles on it. He blew into some shot glasses and then set the whole lot down in the middle of his living room floor. 'What?' he asked with a grin as everyone frowned at him. 'They're a bit dusty, that's all.'

'So you couldn't wash them?' Kasumi asked.

'You could if it bothers you,' Jethro said with a smirk as he sat down next to her. He leaned back on his elbows and stretched his legs in front of him. 'But I'm staying right here.'

'The alcohol will kill any germs that might be lurking anyway,' Ellie said as she filled up her glass with a green liquid. She had no idea what it was – the label kept dancing around in front of her eyes – but she figured it would probably taste as bad as everything else on offer so it wouldn't really matter. Besides, it did look so much prettier than the others. She glanced up at her companions and shook the bottle with a silent question.

'Go on then,' Kasumi said, taking a glass from the tray and holding it out. Ellie giggled as it dribbled down the side.

'Ooops!'

'You're drunk,' Kasumi admonished.

'So are you.'

'I know,' Kasumi laughed.

'Glad we got that cleared up,' Sam raised his eyebrows as he looked at them in turn.

'At least Jethro is suitably well-oiled,' Kasumi continued. 'He is the reason why we have all performed this enormous act of self-sacrifice, after all.' She raised her glass. 'To mending broken hearts!'

The others laughed and raised theirs too. 'To mending broken hearts!' they repeated before all four downed their drinks in one.

Ellie grimaced as the alcohol hit the back of her throat. 'What is that? Tastes like bloody window cleaner.'

'I think it might be,' Jethro said, peering at the bottle.

Ellie snorted and, amidst the gales of laughter, clamped a hand to her mouth and ran for the bathroom.

Chapter Seven

'Morning.' Ellie dropped her satchel onto the floor beside her desk and switched on her PC.

Ange looked up from a letter she was reading. 'Good weekend?' Her vague expression of recognition turned into a wicked grin. 'Bloody hell, I can see you had a good weekend. You look like you've been trampled by a runaway JCB.'

'Thanks for that,' Ellie replied.

'So… how was London?'

'London was good,' Ellie said in a neutral tone.

'That's good then,' Ange replied in an equally neutral tone that Ellie recognised immediately as a gentle mocking. She looked across to see Ange raise her eyebrows questioningly.

'OK, we got absolutely trollied and I can hardly remember a thing about it,' Ellie groaned.

Ange swung round on her chair and leaned forwards with a mischievous glint in her eye. 'Ooooh, now that's my kind of weekend. Do tell me more.'

'How? I can't remember anything.'

'No drunken trysts with tall, dark strangers?'

'Sadly not. Unless you count me sleeping on the sofa of a tall, dark, completely-known-to-me boy.'

'That's too bad,' Ange said, turning back to her work, her interest waning as quickly as it had been fired up.

Ellie watched the screen intently as she logged in and waited for her desktop to appear. After a moment's silence she spoke again.

'Can I ask you a favour, Ange?'

'Fire away.'

'Ben Kelly...'

'You want me to follow up any new developments?'

'Yes, but...'

'Patrick mentioned it to me earlier.'

Ellie frowned. 'Patrick never comes in *that* early.'

'I know.'

'Did he mention anything else?'

Ange paused for a moment. Ellie guessed from the pregnant silence that a discussion had taken place and she had been the subject of it.

'Never mind,' Ellie said, more to spare Ange's embarrassment than because she didn't want to know.

'You know you can talk to me,' Ange began slowly, 'about anything that's bothering you, even if that's something at home.'

'I know I can. But there really isn't anything.'

Ange turned back to her screen without reply.

'So...' Ellie said with a forced carelessness, 'what's on the menu today?' She logged onto her desk answerphone, grabbed a notepad and began to jot down the messages. 'Hmmm, pensioner does a bungee jump for charity, escaped wallaby spotted on Ferndale Road, Holden Finn has been seen driving through the Bircheswood estate... well, that one has to be a case of mistaken identity because there's no way someone like him would be driving through that godforsaken hole... school dress up, council protests... ugh.'

Putting the pad to one side, Ellie pulled her phone from her bag. There was a missed call from Kasumi. 'She's keen,' Ellie murmured as she unlocked the screen. She turned to Ange. 'I won't disturb you if I make a quick call, will I?'

'Don't mind me.'

Ellie listened as Kasumi answered with an excited squeal, sounding thoroughly refreshed and raring to go despite having had the same weekend as Ellie.

'Catherine *loved* the story about your street corner guy,' Kasumi gushed. 'She wants to get him featured on *Every Morning*.'

'Blimey,' Ellie said in a bemused voice, 'that was quick work.'

'Oh for goodness' sake, Ellie, we've been in the office since seven-thirty; there are none of your nine a.m. middle-of-the-day starts here, you know.'

'Really?' Ellie glanced across at Ange, who was engrossed in something on her screen. As she hadn't mentioned anything to the contrary, Ellie had to assume that Ben had spent the weekend on Constance Street and the situation remained unchanged. It must have been a miserable weekend if the weather in Millrise was anything like it had been in London. Ellie knew she ought to be glad of Kasumi's enthusiasm; they had discussed TV involvement at length and how it would be fantastic to put Ellie's home town on the map, but now that Kasumi had presented it as a possibility, it filled her with unease. There was no reason for it, not really, but no matter how Ellie tried to shake it, the feeling wouldn't leave her.

'Are you thinking of coming to see him then?' Ellie asked as these thoughts whirled through her mind.

'As soon as we can. Can you give me his mobile number?'

'I don't have a number. But I'll go and see him later.'

'Brilliant!' Kasumi squeaked. 'How exciting!'

'Yeah,' Ellie replied, her voice betraying a complete lack of excitement about the whole thing. 'Does that mean you'll be coming to Millrise?'

'Oh no, it'll be a roving team. Catherine can't spare me right now. Ring me later when you've spoken to him. Ciao for now.'

Ellie ended the call. 'Ange, I'll just have to pop over and see Ben Kelly. It looks like we're getting our national coverage after all.'

Ange swung around to face her. 'Really?'

'*Every Morning* want to meet him. I need to let him know that they're coming, make sure he's OK with that.'

'Would you rather I went to see him?'

Ellie pondered Ange's offer. Perhaps it would be better if her colleague went instead. Right now, her mood was so unpredictable and irrational that she couldn't trust herself to keep things on a professional level. She wanted to go and duck her head in a vat of ice cold water to clear it. Perhaps, she mused, it was down to her wild weekend and nothing more. A good night's sleep and she would be back to her practical self.

'If you don't mind, that would be good,' she replied finally. 'I don't have much in the way of solid details but as soon as Kasumi tells me more I can let you know so you can relay them to him. Would that be alright?'

'Of course. Any excuse to go and see that parcel of deliciousness in the flesh,' Ange grinned.

'You'll get a reputation as a cougar if you carry on.'

'Yes,' Ange said airily, 'one that is well-deserved and painstakingly cultivated by me.'

*

Ange arrived back at the office long after Ellie had swept the lunchtime sandwich crumbs from her desk. Vernon was at some all-day strategy meeting or other – one of the few such duties that put Ellie off progressing to editor one day. For her, it was all about the stories, the thrill of chasing that elusive gem, the satisfaction of seeing her words on paper, and all the other bits of her job were distracting, if necessary, filler.

'Good God, half the street is out with that boy; it's like Live Aid.' Ange flopped onto her chair and dropped her bag to the floor.

'Everything was OK?'

'It depends on your idea of OK.'

Patrick bounded in. 'You've missed the riot of the century on Constance Street,' he grinned.

Ellie frowned. 'OK, what's been happening?'

'When we got there,' Patrick began, 'the street was heaving with residents all outside on the corner. Ben was talking to some bloke from the council. Charlie's Angels were going berserk and some blokes – presumably their hubbies – were arguing with them. The upshot is that the council are going to serve some sort of eviction notice on Ben and it sounds like some of the *Ben Kelly Widowers Club* instigated the whole thing.'

'So he has to move on?' Ellie asked, aware that her pulse was suddenly racing without a clue why.

'Not yet,' Ange said. 'The man from the council has to come back with a formal notice, so Ben has a bit of time yet.'

Ellie couldn't decide what she felt about this new information. 'So there's time enough for the TV crew to come and film their piece?'

'To be honest, there's time enough to get us to Valentine's Day, I think,' Patrick said. 'It takes the council weeks to do anything. I reckon if Gemma hasn't come back by then, he might as well give up anyway. If there's one day that's going to swing it, then it has to be that one.'

'I think so too,' Ange said. 'If feeling all romantic and seeing hearts and flowers everywhere isn't going to soften her towards him, nothing will.'

Ellie chewed her lip as she stared into space. There had been no word from Gemma since she had seen her at her home and had promised not to tell Ben what they had discussed. She had no idea when Gemma was planning to put him out of his misery but she hoped it would be sooner rather than later. Or had she now changed her mind? 'I'm not so sure.'

Patrick exchanged a glance with Ange. He turned back to Ellie. 'What makes you say that?'

Ellie shrugged. 'I don't know.'

'Was it something she said when you interviewed her?'

Ellie felt a stab of guilt. Gemma saw her as an ally and a friend but she didn't feel very deserving of that right now.

'Are you sure there's nothing you want to share with us about her?' Ange pressed.

Ellie opened one of her desk drawers, found half a packet of bourbons and stuffed one into her mouth so that she wouldn't have to reply. She tossed them to Patrick.

'We got some cracking photos, though,' Patrick continued, clearly sensing that a change of subject was in order.

More than anything, Ellie wanted to ask if Ben was alright. Did he look well; did he look clean and fed? How was his mood? Did he still seem optimistic? Had he asked about her? But those questions didn't seem like the right ones to ask.

'Let's have a look at the photos,' she said instead.

Patrick handed his camera over and Ellie switched it on, scrolling through the pictures of the fracas they had described. She found herself fixated on Ben, the figure at the centre of it all, analysing every detail and wondering whether he had lost as much weight as it appeared he had, what each tiny frown or shadow of stubble could mean for his wellbeing. It was ridiculous, but she couldn't stop it. After a few silent moments, she handed the camera back.

'They're great. I take it we're going for another spread on this.'

'Too bloody right we are,' Ange said. 'This is gold.'

'You talked to him about the film crew?' Ellie asked, suddenly remembering the reason Ange had gone out to him in the first place.

'Eventually, when everything had calmed down. I think his ladies were more excited than he was.' Ange laughed. 'I could hear them all on their phones making hair appointments as soon as I said the word *television*.'

'I can imagine.' Ellie put her empty cup down. 'I suppose I'd better ring Kasumi then, tell her we're good to go.'

'Ellie…' Ange said as Ellie reached for her phone.

'Yeah?'

Ange smiled slowly. 'He did ask about you, in case you were wondering.'

*

Kasumi had been beside herself with excitement at Ben's agreement to be featured and before the day had even drawn to a close had phoned Ellie with the news that a film crew had been booked. Ordinarily, Ellie would have been excited too. A story she had broken was going to find its way onto national TV and that was always good for the old CV. It seemed that Millrise was becoming a small town with a big reputation these days too, and that fact alone gave her a warm feeling if nothing else did.

But as the end of the week crept towards them, bringing Friday and the possibility that Ben's new fame could change everything, Ellie was increasingly prey to the doubts that had been plaguing her. The full-page detailed report of the stand-off between Ben and the authorities, with Patrick's emotive photos and Ange's eloquent words, was really impressive. They had been inundated with messages of support from the people of Millrise. But instead of making her proud of her newspaper and her colleagues, it filled her with a vague sense of misgiving.

After a day in which Ellie had deliberately thrown herself into as many tasks as she could manage as diversionary tactics, she found herself at home, restless and unable to unwind. She had started watching a DVD but couldn't concentrate despite its lack of demand. She had tried to work on a column Vernon had asked her for on the state of the town's roads, but got no further than three sentences before staring into space and quite forgetting what it was she had wanted to say on the state of the town's roads.

In a fit of self-directed pique, Ellie turned the computer off and went to wallow in a bath. At least that wouldn't require any actual concentration and might make her sleepy. After a good early night, she might feel more herself again.

*

The bath hadn't helped at all; it had only given Ellie a quieter space in which to reflect on the real thing that she now could not deny was the root of her unease. She stood at the window in her towelling gown, watching as the rain drew silver threads against the dark pane. Unwillingly, her mind wandered to Ben for the umpteenth time that hour. She pictured him, shivering on his cold street corner, soaked through, waiting… And why hadn't Gemma been to see him yet? What was she waiting for? And why, why, why couldn't she stop thinking about the way his lips might taste, if only they were to meet hers, the way his skin would smell, the feel of his breath on her neck…

She shook herself and went to the kitchen. Chocolate – that was what she needed to lift the stupid mood that had overtaken her. *OK, no chocolate*, she thought as a search of the cupboards revealed a distinct absence. *Sweets? There must be a forgotten pack of jelly beans somewhere.*

A minute later Ellie had abandoned her quest for sugar-fuelled solace and was sitting at the table staring into space absently tapping her phone with her thumbnail. Her gaze was drawn to the kitchen window. The rain seemed worse than it had when she last looked. It would be freezing out there.

Finally, with an impatient sigh, she got dressed, packed some things in a bag, snatched her car keys from the mantelshelf and headed out.

*

Ellie hurried along underneath a huge golfing umbrella that had been gathering dust in her car boot. Her dad had picked it up as a free gift from some men's magazine and had given it to Ellie telling her it would be useful one day. She had taken it with a polite smile with no intention of ever swapping it for the gorgeous Cath Kidston one Kasumi had given her the previous Christmas. Now, however, she silently thanked her dad as she approached Ben with a shelter that would easily fit two.

He was huddled in his raincoat, a tarpaulin draped over his head (after some discussion with Patrick about how much attention a tent would draw to his already disgruntled male neighbours he had decided this was the best way to fend off the weather), and even his usually indomitable spirit seemed thoroughly washed out in the torrential downpour now attacking him. She wasn't surprised to find that he was without his now almost constant female attendants – no one in their right mind would be out on a night like this, dreamy local hero or not.

Which made Ellie wonder what state *her* mind was in for being out with him now. At Ellie's approach, he looked up, wiping water from his eyes.

'What are you doing here?'

'Nice to see you too,' Ellie said, now close enough to hold the umbrella over both of them.

'Sorry,' Ben gave her a weak smile. 'It's great to see you, but this is a vile night for you to be following up on me.'

'I'm not working,' Ellie said. 'I'm on a mission of mercy. Hold this for a sec...' Handing the umbrella to Ben, she rifled in a huge rattan shoulder bag. 'Flask tea...' she shook a silver thermos. 'Tastes like shit but it'll be a whole lot better when we add this...' Next she produced a half-full bottle of whisky.

'That's amazing.' Ben glanced around. 'I'd offer you a seat,' he added apologetically, 'but my only spare is soaked.'

'That's OK,' Ellie said brightly. 'I have plastic rubbish sacks.' She pulled a roll of black bags out, unfolded the spare seat and laid one over it before sitting down. 'I also thought you might need this...' she said, handing a fluffy white towel over.

Ben took it with a grateful look. 'You're going to make someone an amazing wife one day,' he said as he pulled back his hood with his free hand and rubbed at his face and hair.

Ellie felt the heat rise from her neck and into her cheeks. Damn it, why did he have this ridiculous effect on her suddenly? She thanked her lucky stars that it was probably too dark for him to see her blush. For a moment they sat quietly in the deserted street, listening to the rain beat a steady rhythm on the umbrella.

'Where are your ladies?' she asked, grappling for a change of subject.

'My fair-weather friends,' he replied with a wry smile as he draped the towel around his neck. 'I don't blame them for staying home. I suppose their families would have something to say if they caught pneumonia from sitting out in this with me.'

'You're all set for the film crew tomorrow?' Ellie poured some tea into a plastic cup and added a slug of whisky, which she handed to him. She had made the tea with plenty of sugar and now the air between them was steamy and sweet with the smoky, peaty smell of whisky.

Ben took a sip and grinned. '*That* is amazing!' he said, regarding his cup with approval. 'And, no, I'm not ready for tomorrow in the slightest but I'll be here when they come.'

'It's not like you can go anywhere else, is it?' Ellie laughed. She took a sip of her own drink and grimaced as the fire of the whisky hit the back of her throat. It was a good heat though, and she felt it spread through her almost immediately. 'Aren't you sick of all this now?' she asked.

Ben stared thoughtfully across the road where the streetlights wore orange haloes in the rain. 'Yes. And I don't think Gemma is ever going to come back.' He turned to Ellie. 'You think I'm an idiot, don't you? Is that what everyone thinks?'

'Of course I don't,' Ellie replied quickly. She wondered whether this was the moment to tell him that Gemma might come back… but what if she didn't? Giving him hope where there might be none was perhaps crueller than keeping quiet about what she knew. Besides, Gemma had asked her not to. There was that small part of her, too, that wanted him to give up and forget Gemma altogether. She tried not to listen to that tiny voice, though. The whole situation was becoming a terrible mess and nobody was more aware of that than Ellie. 'Nobody does. All we get at the *Echo* are endless letters and emails from women who think it's the most romantic thing they've ever heard.'

'I bet the letters from men say I'm a prize dickhead, don't they?'

Ellie smiled. 'A few of them think it's romantic too. You've had quite a few proposals from both sexes, believe it or not.'

'Proposals?' Ben frowned. 'Like marriage?'

Ellie nodded.

'Wow, that's… freaky.'

Ellie laughed again. 'I suppose it is. But people feel like they know you when you're in the public eye, especially in the way you're in their consciousness at the moment.' Ellie paused, the irony of the words she had just spoken not lost on her. Gathering her wits, she continued. 'Lots of people live lonely or unfulfilled lives without a partner or, worse, with the wrong one. You're like a beacon of hope that, perhaps, their knight in shining armour is out there after all.'

Ben stared at her before taking another swig of his drink. 'A beacon of hope *and* a knight in shining armour. I'm very sparkly tonight, aren't I?'

Ellie giggled. 'Can we think of any more light-based proverbs to add to that list?'

'To be honest, I think that's quite enough profundity for a wet Thursday night.'

'Hmmm. And I'm not even drunk yet.'

'We'll have to remedy that. I say we finish this flask between us – get proper steaming.'

'I like the sound of that,' Ellie said. 'But only if you strike a deal with me.'

He raised his eyebrows.

'We don't talk about the *Echo* or TV or Gemma or any of this weird stuff that's happening right now. We sit here as mates and talk about stupid things like Monty Python and how many Sambucas you can drink before you pass out. I'm not Ellie Newton the reporter, I'm just Ellie tonight.'

A slow smile spread across his face. 'OK, Just Ellie. I think I can manage that.'

*

The rain had stopped and the moon made the occasional appearance from the tumbling mass of clouds. Ben plucked gently at a battered acoustic guitar and sang softly as Ellie giggled.

'Oh Ellie... You're not smelly... you're like a fragrant welly... I'd like to stay in with you and watch some telly... as long as it's not about Ben Kelly....' He grinned as Ellie snorted with new laughter.

'You're crazy.'

'Thanks.' He strummed lightly again and hummed to himself. His voice was rich and soulful. Ellie felt the hairs on her neck stand on end and a peculiar tingle in her spine.

'Your guitar looks old,' she said, trying not to think about what his singing was doing to her.

'I've had it a long time. It was the first gift that was bought for me after mum and dad died. I think it was meant to cheer me up,' he smiled sadly. 'I suppose it did, in a way. My dad played guitar, so when I played I could imagine he was still with me.'

Ellie frowned, lapsing into silence as she struggled for something to say about his family that wouldn't upset him. She wanted to ask about how he had got through such dark and tragic times, who had brought him up, what relatives he had left. But as he had not volunteered the information she wondered whether, perhaps, he didn't want to talk about it.

Ben sniffed slightly. He put the guitar back into the case and forced a bright smile as he picked up the flask and sloshed it around.

'I think that's the last of it.'

'Probably just as well,' Ellie said.

'Are you insinuating I'm drunk, Miss Newton?'

'Of course not. But I may struggle to remember my own name in half an hour.'

'Will you spill your deepest darkest secrets?' he asked with an impish grin.

'I don't have any,' Ellie countered. 'I'm thoroughly angelic.'

'You mean to tell me you're never naughty? I find that hard to believe.'

'I have to be good. I have a respectable career to think of.'

'Unlike me, who is chasing a very unrespectable career.'

'What *do* you want out of life? I mean, apart from the music school and the guitar tuition, what do you *really* want?' she asked, her voice with a slight slur to it now. The alcohol had lowered her guard and even this seemingly innocuous enquiry was a question she would never have asked otherwise.

He shrugged with a sleepy smile, gazing across the street to where the clouds broke, just for a moment, to reveal the star-strewn heavens beyond. 'What does any man want? To meet the girl of my dreams and hope she becomes my best friend, to settle down with her, to raise a little family. Maybe even have a happy, blessed life and leave the sort of memories of me that raise a smile from those left behind.' He turned to look at her. 'Have I missed anything out?'

'Wow. You should write poetry.'

'I do.' He grinned. 'It's bloody awful, that's why I work in a pub.'

Ellie gazed at him. What she was beginning to learn about the real Benvolio Kelly was having a strange and unexpected effect on her. This was perhaps the time when a sober, straight-thinking Ellie Newton would realise it was time to jump ship. But this wasn't a sober, straight-thinking Ellie Newton. This was a thoroughly mixed up soon-to-be-riddled-with-guilt Ellie Newton. 'But the pub's not forever,' she continued. 'I'm sure when you get the music school up and running it will be amazing.'

'It is my absolute dream job,' he said. 'Apart from fronting the world's biggest rock band without actually having to do any speaking at all,' he laughed. 'What about you? Do you want to achieve great things?'

'I want to do well at the *Echo*.' She clapped a hand to her mouth. 'Oops! I wasn't supposed to mention the *Echo*, was I?'

He gave a low chuckle. 'I'll let you off this once.' He took a sip from his mug. 'So… there's no significant other for you right now?'

Ellie shook her head. 'Too busy.'

'How can you be too busy for love?'

'OK…' Ellie laughed. 'I'm not too busy to be in love, just too busy to go to the sorts of places where I might meet potential love candidates.'

'Hmmm. So there's nothing between you and that photographer guy?'

'Patrick?' Ellie raised her eyebrows. 'You must be joking.'

'You always seem to get on well. I thought maybe…'

'We get on brilliantly. I also get on brilliantly with his wife.'

He smiled. 'Ah. I'm still right that if there was no Mrs Photographer you might fancy him?'

'No chance. His ego wouldn't fit in my house for a start. And he'd never get past my mum's rigorous series of potential son-in-law checks.'

'She sounds like fun.'

'Oh she is. She wants six months' worth of bank statements, psychiatric profiling, CRB checks and they have to demonstrate the ability to walk on water for at least fifteen metres. Otherwise, they don't get a look in.'

'So any guy on your radar has a lot to live up to?'

'Luckily I'm not quite so picky. So long as he can make me laugh and has a cute bum he has the job.'

Ben chuckled. 'That sounds like a good checklist. What does your mum think of that version?'

'I try not to tell her about it.'

'What does your dad think?'

'He's kind of preoccupied at the moment. It's complicated.'

'Right…'

'Do you think about your parents a lot still?' Ellie bit her lip. The question was out before she'd had time to stop it. She felt the blush rise from her neck.

'Yeah,' he said quietly.

'Sorry… I didn't mean to be insensitive.'

'It's OK. It happened. It was a long time ago, but it still feels raw, ya know? I don't think I'll ever really get over it. But I try to stay strong and get on with my life because I know that's what they would have wanted.'

Ellie stroked her thumb down the side of her mug thoughtfully. How did anyone get over something like that? He laughed and joked and was charming on the surface, but the fact that he was sitting here at all after everything he had been through was a testament to a steely resolve and a remarkable strength of character. She was suddenly gripped by the urge to pull him into a fierce hug. Instead, she took another gulp of her drink and turned her eyes to the sky.

'Looks like the rain has cleared at last.'

'Thank God for that. There was a danger I was going to evolve gills if it carried on.' His words were meant in jest, but Ellie could still hear the heartbreak in them.

'You're alright?' she asked.

'Of course. I'm the man who can't be moved.'

'That was a great headline, even if I say it myself,' Ellie said, trying to lighten the mood again.

'Yep. You can totally take the credit for that. Although a certain Irish band might have something to say on the matter.'

Ellie laughed. 'I won't tell if you don't.'

Ben made a cross over his heart. 'You can count on me.'

A huge yawn took Ellie by surprise. 'Oh God, I'm sorry. That's such an attractive look! Now you know why I'm single.'

'It's pretty late,' he said with a sympathetic smile. 'I'll be yawning myself in a minute. I'm so lucky that my luxury bedroom is just feet away. I don't envy you having to make a journey home before you can go to sleep.'

'Won't it be all soggy?' Ellie said, glancing over to a pile of kit with a frown.

'The sleeping bag is all wrapped up in a tarp, which I can also drape over me if it rains. So I should be snug enough.'

Ellie wrinkled her nose. 'It doesn't sound very snug.'

'Actually, you wouldn't believe how warm my sleeping bag is. It's designed for people who climb mountains.'

'I'll take your word for it,' Ellie replied, suddenly invaded by the image of them cocooned in the sleeping bag together. Then she slapped her forehead as she was reminded of something else, something very important. 'How bloody stupid am I? I've got the sodding car sitting down the street and I'm over the limit!' She had only planned to have one tiny drink, but she had been having such a good time she seemed to have got carried away. It was the first moment that evening the fact had even occurred to her. Ellie was furious with herself for being so remiss. Now she would have to leave the car behind and get home some other way. Her morning routine would be a nightmare; she would have to fetch it again before she went to work, not to mention the fact that she would have to avoid the film crew. The last thing she wanted was to get involved in that little circus.

Ben simply grinned. 'I guess you're keeping me company all night then.'

She looked up at him and they both suddenly became silent as their eyes locked. Ellie's breath quickened and she could feel her pulse fast in her ears, some unnamed desire fizzing up from deep inside. They inched closer, a movement barely perceptible, and though the warning bells rang in Ellie's head, she could not hear them above the voice that was urging her to move closer, closer, until she was close enough to kiss him…

The briefest of moments seemed to last an eternity, until Ben blinked and pulled away with an awkward laugh.

'Wow… things got a bit intense there for a minute.'

Ellie's gaze dropped down to her cup, a curious mix of relief and disappointment now churning her insides. 'I'll get a taxi,' she said without looking up.

'Maybe that's best,' he agreed in a quiet voice.

At that, she couldn't decide what needled her most – that he hadn't tried to persuade her to stay, or that she had wanted so desperately to kiss him.

His voice broke in on her thoughts again. 'I've had a brilliant time with you, though, Ellie… the best.'

She looked up and tried to smile. 'I suppose you're off to your luxury bedroom now?'

'I'll definitely sleep better with a bit of whisky inside me.'

'A bit?' Ellie nudged him playfully, relieved that the danger of the previous few moments seemed now to have passed. 'We've almost finished that half-bottle and I'm pretty sure I didn't have *that* much of it.'

'There was never half a bottle there when you brought it,' Ben insisted with a laugh. 'Either way it will make kipping on hard concrete that little bit more bearable.'

'God…' Ellie glanced at the pavement, the moonlight now glinting from the wet tarmac. 'I never really thought about how horrible it must be sleeping out here.'

'It's not so bad.' Ben shrugged. 'I suppose I'm perfectly qualified to work for a homelessness charity when this is all over.' He gave a rueful smile. 'Nothing beats first-hand experience.' He paused. 'Actually, that's not a bad idea. Perhaps I'll do some good with my experience when this is all over.'

Ellie regarded him steadily as questions burned her mouth. What did Gemma have? What was so special about this girl? Would he have done this for any girl? Would he have done this for Ellie?

'You should really think about that,' she said. How could she ask him these things? Especially with the moment of their near indiscretion still hanging over them. Now, more than ever, discussion of Gemma going back to him was completely off-limits. But the more she thought about his future with Gemma, the more she questioned whether that future was actually right for either of them. Perhaps that was down to feelings of her own for Ben, now bubbling to the surface despite her best efforts to keep them down. The idea made her feel slightly sick with guilt as she thought about how she had pledged to help bring them back together, how she had encouraged a doubtful Gemma to reconsider her decision. This infatuation she was developing, or whatever it was, could not happen.

Ben looked at his watch. 'It's pretty late. You'll be OK getting home alone?'

'Why, are you offering to desert your post?'

He stared at her. It had been a joke on her part, but now she could see that he was torn.

'It's OK,' she added quickly, 'I didn't mean anything by it.'

'I do feel as though I should take you home though.'

'That's terribly medieval of you, but I think I can manage it alone.'

'I didn't really think this whole street corner thing through, did I?'

Ellie fastened the lid on her flask and forced a smile. She could only wonder that it had taken him this long to realise. But she didn't say that. 'You'd better not go anywhere now. You have the whole country waiting to see you on TV. Think how disappointed Annette and her gang would be if they didn't get their five minutes of fame.'

Ben returned the smile, his as tight and forced as hers. 'I suppose you're right...' He handed her the towel. 'You know what, though, between you and me...' He paused.

'What?' Ellie prompted.

Ben sighed, his shoulders seeming to slump as he folded his arms tight across his chest. 'Between you and me, I think I'm ready to go home now.'

Chapter Eight

Ellie got up early and returned to Constance Street to pick up her car before the first light of day had even peeked above the rooftops. She got the taxi to drop her off around the corner and as she walked to her Mini, could see that Ben was still huddled in his sleeping bag. The sight forced a wistful smile. It looked as though Kasumi's assertion that TV would bring about a quick resolution was right – judging by what he had said to her the previous night, today might be the last day of Ben's adventure, whether Gemma turned up or not. She felt buoyed by the idea. She was almost as fed-up with his situation as he had seemed to be. The thought of him sitting and waiting there upset her in ways that she couldn't explain and far more, the longer it went on. Yawning, she unlocked the car and threw her bag onto the passenger seat, pulling her phone out and placing it within easy reach – pure habit, as it was unlikely anyone would be calling her at that hour. As she turned the key in the ignition, however, she noticed that there was an unread message.

You need to get your backside down to London again pronto. A fantastic new club has just opened up that I know you'll love.

Jethro. It had come through the previous night and Ellie hadn't noticed it. She dropped the phone back onto the seat and ran a hand through her hair. He would probably still be in bed anyway, so she might as well reply to him later. Somehow, despite the brilliant weekend they'd all shared recently, she didn't much feel like partying at the moment. The engine started with a dull roar as she turned the key, the steering wheel icy beneath her hands. Her mind went back to Ben, still sleeping. It would be a good idea for someone from the *Echo* to be with him when the TV crew arrived, but after last night, there was no way that could be Ellie. Reluctantly, she would have to ask Ange to go again.

*

After dividing the day's workload with her colleagues, Ellie found her own day a little on the empty side. It meant that she had a rare actual break over lunch. The film crew were with Ben, along with Patrick and Ange, and after a short burst of banter with Stavros, the gregarious Greek owner of the local deli, The Bountiful Isle – known as The Bounty – Ellie was back at her desk, her sandwich barely touched, staring at her phone. Jethro's text still glared at her, unanswered. He would think something odd was going on if she didn't reply soon. Her fingers hovered over the keyboard while she ran through excuses for why she couldn't visit in her head. But as she was doing this, the phone rang.

'Hey, sexy!' Kasumi squeaked. 'How's it going? Has your Romeo finished filming yet?'

'I don't know.'

'You're not there with them?'

'No…'

There was a pause, and then Kasumi's voice came back, quiet and serious. 'What's wrong?'

'Nothing,' Ellie replied with forced brightness.

'So why aren't you at the heart of the action? And why do you sound like there's something wrong? Is it your aunt?'

'No,' Ellie said, suddenly feeling doubly wretched as she realised how long it had been since she had seen Hazel, 'nothing like that.'

'So there *is* something wrong.'

'Not wrong, exactly…' Ellie picked at the corner of her sandwich, twisting off a small piece of the crust and rolling it between her thumb and forefinger. 'Just… awkward…'

Ellie could almost hear the frown that was furrowing her friend's forehead in her voice. 'Awkward how?'

Ellie faltered for a moment. This was a conversation she hadn't meant to start and didn't want to have. She couldn't even get her feelings straight in her own mind, let alone trying to explain them to someone else. She let out a deep sigh. 'It doesn't matter.'

'You can't give me half a story, lady, and expect me to let you off the rest. Spill.'

'It's nothing –'

'Newton! You have to tell me now.'

'OK. Don't judge me… Last night I went to see Ben. It was pouring down, I felt sorry for him, so I took an umbrella and a towel and some whisky and I thought I might just cheer him up…'

'Yeah, and?'

'And there was kind of… a moment.'

There was silence down the line. '*A moment?*' Kasumi finally asked. 'The kind of moment I think you're talking about?'

'Yeah, probably.'

'Jeez, Ellie. How long has this been going on?'

'Nothing is going on,' Ellie said with a bit more irritation than she had intended.

'But you like him? What happened last night?'

'Nothing. Not really, anyway. But it could have done.'

'You stopped it or him?'

'I think we both sort of did.'

'Jeez, Ellie,' Kasumi said again. 'Your timing is amazing. So what's the deal with Gemma?'

'He's still waiting for her. He loves her...'

'I don't know whether to be happy about that because at least my film crew is going to get their story or upset because I know how much that must be hurting you.'

'It's not hurting me. It was just a drunken moment, that's all.'

'What are you going to do?'

'Nothing. What can I do? He's waiting for his girlfriend. He loves her and that's what he wants.'

'And you're certain of that? It doesn't sound like it to me if he nearly kissed you.'

'I think it was probably more me kissing him than the other way around.'

'You *did* kiss him?' Kasumi squeaked.

'No! No, of course I didn't.'

'But you wanted to...'

'Yes... no... It doesn't matter what I wanted. What kind of heartless cow would I be if I took advantage of his current unhappiness to start some sort of sordid affair?'

'You like him, right?'

Ellie was silent, not trusting herself to reply.

'If your feelings are genuine,' Kasumi continued, 'then I don't see what's sordid about that. What are you going to do?'

'I told you, I'm going to do nothing. There's nothing I can do. I just think I should stay out of his way, that's all.'

'You're not a bit tempted to get in there while his ex is still an ex?'

'Kasumi!'

'Alright! I was joking.'

'Please don't.'

'Right.'

'I mean it, the matter is over.'

There was silence for a moment. 'Right then. I'll say no more about it,' Kasumi finally replied.

'Kas…'

Ellie never got to finish her sentence. The office door opened and Patrick breezed in with a huge grin and a tray of take-out coffees, followed by Ange.

'I'll have to call you later,' Ellie said. With a vague awareness of Kasumi's reply, she ended the call and forced a smile for the new arrivals.

'Good morning?'

'Brilliant!' Ange gushed. 'Couldn't have gone better.'

'Wait till you see tonight's paper,' Patrick added, handing a cup to Ellie.

She wasn't entirely sure she wanted to know what had happened, but without raising suspicions, she was going to have to show some sort of interest. 'Come on then – tell all.'

'Bloody brilliant it was,' said Ange. 'The residents were on top form, and Ben was so adorable he'll have the female population of Britain melting as soon as the piece goes out. Whether Gemma comes back or not, he's going to be a celebrity, you mark my words. I can only say it's a good job women can't get pregnant from watching the telly because there'd be a baby boom when this hits the air.' She flopped onto her seat and prised the lid from her cup, giving the drink a satisfied sniff before taking a sip.

Ellie mulled over what Ange had just said as she pulled the lid from her own cup. There was no doubt Ben was the sort of man who would win over the British public. Would that be enough to win Gemma back? Ellie wanted it not to matter but it did.

'Are you alright?' She looked up to see Patrick watching her closely.

'Of course,' Ellie said, shaking herself. 'I just had a bit of a late night, that's all.'

'Oh?' Ange said, winking at Patrick. 'And who was the lucky man?'

Ellie glanced between the two of them. She wondered how much opportunity they'd had, with the film crew there, to actually talk to Ben. If they had, why hadn't he mentioned that Ellie had been with him the previous night? They obviously didn't know. Was it because he felt as guilty as her, despite the fact that they had nothing to feel guilty about? Was he aware of the danger too, of how close they had been to doing something they shouldn't have done? Gemma had relinquished any claim over Ben when she left him, but in light of what he was doing on Constance Street, she was owed some sort of loyalty, or the whole event would be a hollow sham. Ben must have been aware of that as much as Ellie.

'I drank a bit too much,' Ellie replied carefully. 'Got to bed later than I had planned.'

'I need some mayo for this salad,' Ange announced, apparently unconcerned by Ellie's admission. 'Anyone want anything from the kitchen?'

'You're not on another raid, are you?' Patrick said, raising his eyebrows. 'Rosie is already on the warpath.'

'She's not going to miss a bit of mayonnaise,' Ange said, pushing herself up from her chair. 'Not if I get the bottle back in the fridge quick enough.' With a laugh, she skipped out of the room. Patrick turned to Ellie with a searching gaze. He leaned against the desk and folded his arms.

'Lena told me that your Mini was on Constance Street all night.'

Ellie almost choked on her coffee. 'What?'

'You spent the night with Ben?'

'Of course I didn't!'

'You were there last night, though.'

'I... I took some things over to him. It was raining, I wanted to help.'

'Sooooo...' Patrick began in a flippant tone that masked something more like interrogation. 'Your car stayed there all night and yet you didn't?'

'I was hardly going to shag anyone on a street corner, was I?' Ellie snapped.

'Nobody mentioned shagging. Lena was right; it was your car?'

Ellie paused. There was no point in denying it; her car was pretty distinctive – an original late seventies model, bright red with a union flag painted over the roof. 'I stayed for a drink with him and I was over the limit so I got a taxi home. I went back for my car early this morning.'

'Right. I find it weird that Ben himself didn't mention it.'

'He didn't?' Ellie shrugged, trying to look unconcerned despite the fact that her mind was racing with questions. 'Maybe he was busy with all the TV stuff. Last night wasn't that important.'

'Ellie... It's none of my business. As long as you know what you're doing.'

She was about to snap a reply when Ange returned with a triumphant grin.

'Just call me Raffles,' she said, holding aloft a half-full bottle of mayonnaise.

Ellie shot a quick glance at Patrick, but his attention was now on his camera as he scrolled through some photos. She turned to her computer screen, wondering just what else had been seen by the sharp-eyed residents of Constance Street.

*

It had been tempting to go and see Ben on the way home, but in light of the day's events, Ellie resisted. Instead, she popped into the nearest takeaway, picked up two curries, made a quick phone call to warn him she was coming, and turned the car towards her dad's flat. Not the kind of Friday night debauchery that others her age were getting ready to indulge in, but Ellie was rarely in the mood for that sort of behaviour these days anyway. She had called Hazel to be told that her aunt would rather settle down for a quiet night alone and Ellie had known from experience not to argue. The alternative: a night with her recently rather neglected dad – telly and trays of food on their laps – seemed like a very attractive proposition. At least she knew where she stood with her dad.

After buzzing at the main entrance, Ellie found the apartment door open for her.

'Hey, Dad!' she called, wandering through into the living room.

Her dad was dressed for once – neatly-shaven and groomed. The room was clean, tidy and freshly aired. Ellie had to stop herself from doing a double-take.

'Frank Newton is finally growing up,' he announced with a rueful smile as he noted her glance around in a state of amazement. 'Do you approve?'

'It's great, Dad,' Ellie replied, wondering at what point she had fallen into a parallel universe. She half expected some doppelganger of herself to appear from the living room dressed in Prada and dripping with jewellery. Not knowing what else to say, she held out a carrier bag. 'I got supper.'

'Curry?' He smiled. 'Rogan Josh if my nostrils aren't deceiving me.'

'Of course. Unless you've suddenly stopped liking that as well as freaking me out with the whole cleaning up thing.'

'Come on, let's eat and I'll explain my irrational behaviour,' he smiled. 'What have you had?' he added. 'Passanda?'

'My usual wimp's choice,' Ellie laughed.

She followed him through to the kitchen where he searched in the cupboards for plates and cutlery and Ellie opened the fridge to look for something to drink.

'Can I open this wine?' she asked.

'Aren't you driving?'

'Yes, but I can have a small one.'

She turned to see him nod vaguely. 'I might as well finish it up anyway. This time tomorrow I'll be teetotal.'

Ellie let the door close behind her and put the wine on the table. 'What's brought all this on?'

'I've come to the conclusion that your mum may never take me back so there's no point in continuing to mope about it. And if there is the slightest chance she might, moping is not going to persuade her. I'm taking a leaf out of your Constance Street man's book. I'm doing something positive.'

Ellie almost winced at the mention of Ben. 'You're not going to camp out on Constance Street with him, I hope,' she replied, rooting in a drawer for a corkscrew and trying to keep her voice neutral.

'Of course not, that would be idiotic. I just mean that he hasn't sat back and let himself fall apart. He's doing something to change his situation, however misguided it may be. So I'm going to show your mother that I'm capable of being the strong and wise man that she wants. She may not take me back, despite that, but at least I've moved on and perhaps…' He paused, and Ellie glanced up at him as she fiddled with the wrapping on the top of the wine bottle. 'Perhaps,' he continued as her head went back to her task, 'I'll find love again.'

Ellie's head flicked up and she stared at him. 'Wow! I didn't see that coming.'

He shrugged slightly. 'Neither did I.'

Ellie handed him the bottle and corkscrew. 'You can do this; I always make a mess of the cork.' She sat at the table and watched as he worked, reeling at this new development. Her mum and dad splitting up was one thing, but acceptance of it from them both? That was something she had never envisaged in her wildest dreams.

'I've looked into getting our money back,' he said, cutting in on her thoughts.

'From the travel agents?'

He looked up and nodded as the cork withdrew from the bottle with a pop.

'And?'

'I can get some of it. We'll still lose quite a lot, though.'

'What are you going to do?'

He handed Ellie a glass of wine before digging into the takeaway bag and passing her a foil carton. 'Part of me still wonders whether she'll change her mind. It seems daft to lose all that money.' He looked up hopefully from spooning rice onto his plate. 'Unless I leave it booked and you might fancy coming with me?'

'All that money was the reason she left you. And as for coming with you, Mum would disown me. Not to mention the three months I would have to take off work. I can't imagine Vernon being happy.'

He leaned forwards slightly, a new glint in his eye. 'But it's Australia! A once in a lifetime trip.'

'That you re-mortgaged the house to pay for without consulting Mum.'

'I wanted to do something amazing for us. I wanted us to share an experience that we would remember when we were old and grey. The house will still be there when we're dead and gone but the chance of adventure won't be. Was that such a crime?'

Ellie sighed. 'No. But you should have asked her. She feels as though the rug has been pulled from under her now. You know how she likes order and security. She knew where she was with the house paid for, she felt safe in the knowledge that no matter what else happened you had a home.'

'Feeling safe is boring.'

'Adventure is what *you* wanted out of life, not what Mum wanted.'

'She wanted it too, once upon a time. We'd talk about travelling the world for hours, before we had you. Used to read every travel guide and watch every programme on telly. We'd sit and say: *one day, when we have some real money…*' His expression was suddenly wistful, as if he was reliving those long forgotten moments. 'We never got the money, though. Until we had equity in the house.'

'Maybe she changed. People do that.'

'She certainly did,' he replied, his tone hardening now. 'Besides, I would have made sure that the home was safe, somehow. I would never have let us become homeless, no matter what your mum thinks.'

Ellie gazed at him thoughtfully as she swallowed a forkful of her meal. Her mind turned over possibilities for a solution. In a strange way, it was soothing to think about more practical problems for once, problems that actually had some kind of logical solution. 'Can you get the cost of one ticket back? Give Mum her money, take on the small portion of the mortgage that's left outstanding and go to Australia by yourself.'

'It's not the same alone.'

'It'll make the adventure that much bigger,' Ellie replied with a smile.

The smile he returned was a wistful one. 'I don't think so.'

'OK… so what are you going to do?'

'I thought I'd ask her to meet me. Maybe take her for dinner – neutral ground, you know? We could talk it through.'

'What makes you think she'll say yes to dinner this time?'

'Distance. The longer it's been, the more forgiving she might be.'

Ellie laughed. 'We're talking about the same woman, right?'

He paused before laughing lightly too. 'Maybe she'll be persuaded by a serenade on my banjo?'

'That banjo you can barely play? Maybe not, eh?'

'Point taken. I am going to try though.' Breaking off a hunk of naan bread, he became serious again. 'Any ideas how to approach her?'

'How should I know?'

'Well, you were always the sensible one.'

Ellie took a gulp of wine. *The sensible one.* For a fleeting moment, she was tempted to demonstrate to her dad just how sensible she was by telling him about her almighty mess of a love-life. But then another, bigger irony occurred to her. Here she was, being told by her father that the only reasonable person in their marriage was his daughter, as if she had been born solely for the purpose of one day mediating. Everyone had heard of couples who had children thinking they might save an ailing marriage. Ellie tried not to dwell on the possibility. The main problem was that any help Ellie gave her father would look to her mother like she was taking his side. One thing Ellie definitely didn't want to do was take sides with either of them.

Getting involved in mending broken relationships, she reflected ruefully, only led to heartache.

'Sorry, Dad,' she said quietly, 'but I think you're going to have to figure that one out yourself.'

*

Saturday found Ellie in a strange mood. Her phone contained unanswered text messages from Kasumi, Jethro and Patrick, but although she had read them all, she couldn't think what to say to any of them. The fact was that they all, more or less, dealt with the same subject, and it was one she was desperately trying not to think about. Instead, she wandered the shopping centre of Millrise aimlessly under the pretence of needing a new jacket, but in reality trying to keep her mind off the urge to drive to Constance Street and make a monumental idiot of herself. As she took her phone out in Top Shop for the fourth time that hour, reading the messages again, the one that caused her particular pain was Jethro. Despite what he pretended, he would be worried about her, especially if Kasumi had shared what she knew about Ellie and Ben. Ellie hoped she hadn't. Perhaps she should phone Kasumi and ask her straight not to tell Jethro. But then, wouldn't that simply attach significance to the event that wasn't merited? It would certainly attach significance to it that Kasumi would pick up and run with. Ellie decided that the best thing to do was leave well alone.

Ellie locked her phone and tapped it against her chin thoughtfully, staring at a rack of coats (although if anyone had asked her a moment later what they looked like, she wouldn't have been able to tell them a thing), wondering what to do. She could just drive past Constance Street; see if he was still there, see how quiet things were, whether Gemma had turned up...

Turning for the doors of the shop, Ellie strode out and into the grey murk of another rainy Saturday.

*

Somewhere between the shop and the car park, Ellie had managed to talk herself out of driving to Constance Street. She ended up back at home, an open recipe book propped up on the kitchen worktop in front of her, liberally splattered in flour, butter, sugar and egg. She had also managed to get some in her hair, on her nose, on her bottom, even on the ceiling (although, as she stared up at the offending blob, she couldn't help but be impressed and a little confused as to how it had got there). As she stood back and inspected the gloop in the mixing bowl, she wondered when it was going to start resembling the contents of the bowl in the photo in her recipe book.

'Bloody Nigella,' she muttered. 'I bet a team of minions does these for the book.' She peered more closely at the picture. 'Those cakes probably aren't even real…'

Her gaze travelled the rest of the worktop. The items strewn across it now – cake cases, brand new cake tins, piping bags, spatulas, various packs of edible decorations – had been hastily procured an hour before, and had cost her more money than it would have cost to simply buy a box full of cakes from the local bakery. But she had promised Patrick and Fiona (in yet another drunken *faux pas*) that as well as helping out at a charity bake sale, she would also actually bake for it, and although the results wouldn't be pretty, she felt honour-bound now to display some Dunkirk spirit and have a decent go.

And anyway, she reminded herself, this was a trial run. Trial runs always went wrong – that was what they were for. She'd take the cakes to Hazel's later and test them out. Perhaps her mum would be there too and she could get them both to try. Hazel would be polite about them but her mum certainly wouldn't. If they were disgusting Ellie would go to plan B (bash up a few Mr Kipling's to make them look like they'd come from her own oven) and the evidence of her ineptness could be buried in the nearest bin, never to see the light of day again.

Deciding that what was in the bowl was as close as she was going to get, Ellie began to slop the mixture into already laid out floral fairy cake cases. Perhaps they would look better once they were cooked and decorated, she thought. Although she failed to see how they could look much worse.

*

At Hazel's, Ellie pulled up at the kerbside and glanced across at the house. Her aunt was at the window and beckoned her in with an unsteady hand.

In the time it took Ellie to lock her car and get inside, Hazel was still making her way back to the living room from the front door that she had left open for Ellie.

'Look at the state of me,' she wheezed as she finally got enough breath to talk. 'It's ridiculous.'

Ellie dropped her satchel to the floor next to the sofa, quickly surmising that Hazel was alone in the house. 'Don't be daft. You're ill.'

She didn't reply and they lapsed into an awkward silence for a moment, only broken by the sounds of Hazel still breathing heavily.

'Shall I make you a cup of tea?' Ellie asked.

'I should be doing that for you.'

'Stop it, Hazel.'

'Sorry. You're right. No, I don't want tea, but thank you for offering.'

Ellie fiddled with the buttons of her jacket for a moment before taking it off and draping it over her arm.

'Did you want anything in particular or were you just hankering for my company?' Hazel asked.

'I thought I'd come by, see how you were doing,' Ellie said. 'Oh… and I brought these for you…' She pulled the cloth off a basket of her cakes hooked over her free arm.

'Well, they're… interesting,' Hazel said as she peered in.

Ellie frowned. What hadn't looked too disastrous when she packed them into her basket half an hour earlier, feeling pleased with her first attempt, now wasn't quite as appealing. The cakes had somehow sunk in the middle – every single one of them – causing the watery icing to pool in the cavity and the sugar flowers to slide down as if they were fat fish stranded in a whirlpool. 'I'm sure they taste better than they look,' she said with a sheepish grin.

'I sincerely hope so. You're actually going to sell these?'

'Not these particular ones. These are for practise.'

'Maybe you need a bit more practise… how about three years' worth?'

'Ha ha, very funny.' Ellie grinned, swiping the basket away from Hazel's view. 'I could just eat them all myself.'

'Good luck with that.'

'I'm sorry I haven't been over as often as I should lately,' Ellie added as she put the basket down and took a seat on the sofa. Hazel dropped into an armchair across from her. 'So how about you fill me in on what I've missed?'

'Oh, well, there's not much to tell.' Hazel forced a smile. 'I'd much rather hear about what you've been up to.'

'Apart from crimes against baking? Not a lot really. Mostly work.' Ellie's expression darkened momentarily, but it didn't escape Hazel's attention.

'I know that look,' she said. 'That's the same look your mum used to have when she was up to no good, or she didn't know how to tell me that she had cocked something up.'

Ellie couldn't help but laugh. 'Really? I can't imagine my mum cocking anything up. Practically perfect, isn't she?'

'Perfect?' Hazel raised her eyebrows. 'The scrapes I dug her out of when we were kids…'

'Go on then, tell me some of them.'

Hazel frowned. 'Where to start… how about the time when I was supposed to be looking after her while your nana and granddad went to see a solicitor about some documents and she managed to set the shed on fire. She had that look on her face when she ran in to tell me I should bring a bucket of water…' Hazel took a moment, as if reliving the scene, before she continued. 'I think it needed a bit more than water – it needed a dustpan and brush by the time I got out there. Mum and Dad gave me such a hiding for not watching her.'

'What *were* you doing?' Ellie asked. She had heard the story before, many times, but it always made her smile to hear it again.

'In my bedroom snogging Tony Todd,' she grinned.

Ellie laughed. 'You're a bad girl, Aunty.'

'Not half as bad as Miranda. The way she got through boyfriends, nobody was more surprised than me when your dad finally tamed her.'

'They really loved each other, didn't they?'

Hazel nodded. 'I think they still do. Your mum is such a stubborn cow I could slap her at times.'

Ellie was silent for a moment. 'Do you think what Dad did was wrong?' she asked finally. It was the first time since his misdemeanour that Ellie and Hazel had been alone to discuss it.

'Once I would have said yes,' Hazel replied slowly. 'Now I think there's a lot to be said for grabbing life by the scruff of the neck. There's an old song that goes: *enjoy yourself, it's later than you think.* I never understood the sentiment more than I do now.'

'Have you told Mum this?'

'What would be the point? Do you think she would take any notice?'

Ellie shrugged. 'Maybe. She's more likely to listen to you than anyone else.'

'That's a kind thing to say but sadly misguided,' Hazel laughed. 'I wish she would though. If anyone is aware of the irony of knowing what you've lost when it's too late, it's me. You'd think my pig-headed sister would learn a lesson from my experiences.'

'You couldn't have known how things would end up with John and it wasn't anyone's fault you couldn't have kids together. Would you still have married him if you had known what you know now?'

'Probably,' Hazel mused. 'I was so in love I would have followed him into an active volcano…' She looked up at Ellie and smiled. 'But I don't suppose you're that much of a sucker, are you? If I only leave one useful piece of advice for you, it's this: don't be afraid to fall in love, but handle it better than I did. Don't let anyone make you unhappy.'

Ellie nodded uncertainly. Ben made her unhappy, but not for the reasons that Hazel was thinking of. Did that mean she should do something about it? Even if the answer was yes, she didn't have a clue what. 'And you couldn't have known you would get ill like this,' she added, turning the conversation firmly back to Hazel and away from her own maudlin thoughts.

'That's true enough,' Hazel said. 'We all think we're going to somehow live forever – certainly until we're as old and wrinkled as a tortoise's dangly bits. We never imagine it can all end in the blink of an eye.' Ellie gave a strained smile as Hazel continued. 'But sometimes your body has other ideas. I feel like I was born with this time-bomb, ticking away inside me until... the point is, none of us knows. All the more reason to be happy while you can.'

The way she looked at Ellie when she said this made her feel as though she was somehow expected to mount a defence.

'I am happy.'

'Good,' Hazel replied, 'because you don't look it.'

'That's just my expression. I can't help that and it's cruel of you to bring it up.'

Hazel ignored the joke. 'You're happy in your job. There's more to life than work.'

'Why do you think I'm unhappy?'

'I see it whenever you visit these days. I don't know what's going on and it's probably none of my business but... I hope you sort out whatever it is that's bothering you soon.'

'I'm fine, I promise. I'm far too busy enjoying myself to get bogged down with the serious business of life just yet.'

Hazel looked as though she might argue, but then nodded. 'And speaking of enjoyment, how was London?'

London... Ellie's fingers twitched at the pocket of her coat as she remembered the text messages still unanswered on the phone stowed there.

'London was great.'

'I'd love to see it again, just once.'

There was no reply Ellie could give to that, and looking at Hazel's measured calm, her aunt didn't expect one. They both knew that Hazel travelling to London was about as likely as her travelling to Mars. The idea pushed a lump into Ellie's throat.

'There's no point in crying over it,' Hazel said. 'You'll just have to tell me all about your visit instead. Unless...' she gave a wicked grin, 'there are things that you *can't* tell me. I know what you and your little gang are like when you're together. Your mum did nothing but complain about it for four years.'

'What we *used* to be like.'

'No fun and games?'

'Sadly, not that sort.'

'Any sort? Come on, Ellie, I'm stuck in here day after day – the least you can do is provide me with vicarious fun when you come to visit.'

'OK...' Ellie said, 'But first we need a big bowl of ice-cream. And you *cannot* repeat any of it to my mother!'

*

Ellie deliberately chose Sunday lunchtime as an hour when she hoped Ben's almost constant entourage would be otherwise engaged with family matters. As she turned into Constance Street, she felt a quiet satisfaction that her hunch had been right. It was a dry, bright day and Ben sat alone, engrossed in a book with a mug of tomato soup half-drunk by his chair. At Ellie's approach, he folded the corner of his page and leapt from his seat, greeting her brightly.

'What brings you here? Can't stay away, huh?' He lowered his voice and gestured to the mug on the floor. 'It certainly can't be for Lena's cooking. Although...' he added ruefully, 'Lena's cooking is better than the excuse for veggie bolognaise that I managed to burn onto my billycan last night.'

Ellie smiled. She had asked herself the same question time and time again on the drive over. She wasn't sure why she had come; the only thing she was certain of was the almost irrational urge to be near him. She had tried to keep busy during the morning in an attempt to keep her mind off him, embarking on an elaborate list of activities that had included dusting off an aerobics DVD that had given her a sprained ankle the last time she used it, finally uploading three years' worth of photos from her phone to a photo printing website and a wardrobe cleansing exercise that had ended in a not remotely diminished pile of clothes that would simply have to be scooped back in once she got home.

'Billycan? Blimey, you're even picking up the lingo of a seasoned survival expert now. I think Bear Grylls might be getting a bit nervous about his TV career.'

'I doubt it,' Ben laughed. 'So what can I do for you?'

'I thought I'd come and see how everything went on Friday. I'm sorry I couldn't make it.'

'It's OK. I did wonder...' his sentence sputtered out.

'What?'

'Well... I wondered whether I had upset you. On Thursday night. And that was why you didn't come.'

'How could you have upset me?'

'I don't know. I can be a bit of an idiot when I'm drunk.'

'I thought you said you weren't drunk,' Ellie teased.

He squeezed his thumb and forefinger together and held it up. 'A teensy bit...'

'I knew it,' Ellie laughed.

'The one good thing was that I was still a bit tipsy when the film crew got here so I wasn't nervous at all. I probably looked like a prize tit, but at least I didn't care that I did.'

'I'm sure you didn't. It's airing tomorrow?'

He nodded. 'Which is good – gives me no time to back out at all.'

'It will be weird, not being able to watch it, though.'

'Oh, I'll be able to see it. Janet's son is bringing over his iPad. We can just about get onto the nearest household wifi connection from here.'

'Right…'

Ben dug his hands into his pockets as they fell silent. Ellie wished she could stop gazing into his eyes, but whenever she tried she found herself looking at his lips instead. She didn't know which was more distracting.

'At least it's sunny today,' Ellie said finally.

'Yeah. I can't tell you what a difference that makes to your resolve.' He paused. 'I know I said to you that I wanted to go home the other night but…'

'I know. The TV thing will make a huge difference, I'm sure,' Ellie replied, trying to sound as though she didn't care about what he had just said, although he couldn't have caused her more hurt if he had actually slapped her.

'And either way,' he continued, 'the thing will come to an end soon because if Gemma doesn't show then the council will move me on. I might as well stick it out now.'

'I guess so.'

They fell silent again. Ellie's gut felt like it was filled with wet cement at the idea that he had decided to carry on waiting for Gemma after all. They had both been drunk the last time she saw him but she had definitely felt some chemistry. Had she been mistaken? Of course she had, because she'd be no match for someone like Gemma. No woman would be. Why would Ben want her when he could have a supermodel whose personality was every bit as lovely as her looks? Perhaps he had been lonely. He had grasped the chance of Ellie's company with both hands but it was nothing more than a welcome distraction from the long and forlorn task he had set himself. Ellie was foolish to think it had been anything else. It was her own fault. She should have told him about the possibility of Gemma coming back to him and none of this would ever have happened.

She glanced around the street. Everywhere was quiet, save for the sounds of birds on rooftops and the occasional roar of a car from the main road a few streets away.

'What are you reading?' Ellie asked, trying to lead the conversation away from any risk of exposing her feelings any further and making an irrefutable idiot of herself. She twisted to look at the title. '*Far from the Madding Crowd*. I never had you down as a classics reader.'

He smiled. 'Hardy is a genius. What he doesn't know about the human psyche isn't worth knowing.'

Ellie shrugged slightly. 'I'm more of a *Harry Potter* girl myself.'

'I like that too. There's no reason you can't find room in your life for both.'

The conversation petered out again. The faint smell of roast chicken and potatoes hung on the air. Ellie wondered that none of the ladies had been out with any of the vegetarian bits for Ben. She wondered if the smell of cooking meat bothered him. She looked down at his soup.

'That can't be much of a meal,' she commented.

'It's just a snack. I'll be preparing a sumptuous feast later on my little stove. You're welcome to join me… as long as you're not bringing Gordon Ramsay to judge, that is.' He smiled.

'Good God, if you'd seen my attempt at baking the other day you wouldn't be saying that. I bet my cakes can trump your veggie bolognaise for rubbishness.'

'One day we might put that to the test…To be honest…' He threw a quick look around and lowered his voice. 'I think my appeal is starting to wear thin around here.'

Ellie raised her eyebrows. 'I bet they enjoyed being on the TV on Friday, though.'

'Oh they loved that. Lena got her hair done at the actual hairdressers especially.'

'So she didn't look like a fifties army cadet?'

'Oh she did. Only a really well groomed and worryingly feminine one.'

Ellie burst out laughing. 'I bet that was a sight to behold.'

'You'll be pleased to know that everyone else's hair was comfortingly normal.'

Ellie ran a self-conscious hand through her own hair, suddenly worried about what his opinion of it was. 'Was the film crew nice?' she asked, steering the dialogue into safer waters.

'Yeah, they were great. Really put us all at ease. I was amazed at how few people it took to film stuff.'

'I suppose they can't really spend loads of money sending people up and down the country all the time so they have to keep things small.'

'Of course.'

A low flying airplane roared over the rooftops and they both looked up with far more interest than such a sight would usually provoke. As it disappeared across the sky, only its ghostly vapour trail lingering, they both tried to speak at once. It ended in awkward laughter, and then more silence.

'Come on,' Ben said suddenly. 'Let me get a selfie of us together.' He yanked his phone from his pocket.

'You can't be serious?'

'Why not? I'd like something to remember my weird and wonderful camp-out when it's all over.'

'Wouldn't you be better off taking a photo of Lena's soup?' Ellie said, angling her head at the now congealing orange gloop in its clashing floral mug. Something about it vaguely resembled an impressionist painting. 'It's certainly weird if not terribly wonderful.'

'That?' He followed Ellie's gaze. 'I'd get good money at a medical institute if they wanted a new species to study. Or from a terrorist cell as a new weapon of mass destruction. Either way, after today I'd quite like to block it from my mind forever.' He waggled his phone at her. 'Just one? Would it kill you?'

Ellie shrugged.

'Great... hang on,' Ben said as he hooked an arm around her shoulder and pulled her close, his cheek resting against hers as he positioned the camera. Ellie's breath quickened with the warmth of his skin next to hers. She wondered vaguely if he could feel it. But he seemed oblivious as he grinned broadly and clicked, Ellie forcing herself to smile just at the right time. He lowered the phone to inspect the photo and just for the smallest time they stayed with faces pressed together, and Ellie squeezed her eyes closed, savouring his scent, the feel of his breath on her cheek. She longed for time to stand still so she could stay there forever, the ache of desire deep inside her. He was so close that she could...

And then he turned, slowly, to face her and she found herself locked in his gaze, swallowed by the dark warmth of his eyes. Neither moved, neither spoke, there was only the connection that neither could deny...

'Oh, it's you!' Annette hailed Ellie from across the street.

Ben leapt back as though burnt, murmuring something about finishing his soup and how the photo had turned out. Ellie spun around, trying to fight the heat that was rising to her face. Annette seemed oblivious to their discomfort as she emerged from her front door and tottered over in fluffy slippers.

'Has he told you about the telly?' Annette said as she drew level.

'He has,' Ellie said, her mind still very much on Ben's lips as she tried to pull herself together. 'It sounds like you had a good day.'

'Oh it was marvellous. I don't doubt that Gemma will be here like a shot when they show it. Ben played guitar and everything.'

'They made me do that,' Ben mumbled. 'I hope they cut it out, I felt like an idiot.'

'Oh no,' Annette gushed. 'You were wonderful. How could Gemma fail to be moved by such a beautiful song? After all, you wrote it for her.'

Ellie looked at him sharply. He had written a song for Gemma? Ellie felt as though she had been slapped across the other cheek now. She suddenly needed to get away from him, as far as possible.

'I wrote it about her when we were first together,' Ben said, glancing at Ellie with a look that seemed to hint at some internal struggle. Or perhaps Ellie was imagining it.

'It's great to see you both, but I just remembered I'm late for lunch with my mum...' Ellie excused. The longer she stayed here the greater the danger of her emotional state crumbling. 'I'd better go.'

Annette nodded amiably. Ben simply forced a pained smile.

'Thanks for dropping by to see me,' he said.

'Sure,' Ellie replied, already hurrying away. 'Anytime.'

Chapter Nine

Ellie looked at the caller ID display on the desk phone. It read NEWSROOM.

'Hello?'

'It's on the TV down here after the ad break. Get your backside here, quick,' Ange squealed from the other end of the line. Without waiting for Ellie's reply, she put the phone down.

Ellie let out a pained sigh. She would have to go down whether she liked it or not. If she didn't Ange would only phone again.

'I'm just going down to the newsroom,' she called to Vernon. He looked up with a vague nod and then returned his attention to his computer screen.

A few moments later she was standing with her arms folded watching the enormous TV.

'They had already started filming when we got there the other day,' Ange said.

'So you haven't seen it all?'

'No. Not the beginning bit. And we got a bit distracted at the end, when all the rest of the street came out to watch.'

The jangly intro music kicked in, along with a slick show of flashing images which gave way to a shot of the presenter – a twenty-something stick of a girl with huge dark eyes and impossibly buoyant hair. The music faded and the camera panned out as the girl turned to Ben and introduced him. Inset, as he explained to her the nature of his quest, was a photograph of Gemma looking unrealistically gorgeous in a skin-tight sequinned party dress and heels that would have given Ellie a nosebleed. Ellie could have been given a blank cheque book and free run of the biggest Chanel store in the world and not come out looking that good no matter how long she spent in there. In fact, every time she saw Gemma, Ellie felt oddly lacking in femininity.

Ben explained briefly the reasons he was camping on Constance Street and some of his and Gemma's history – which Ellie had heard before – and then he gestured towards Annette (the camera following to reveal her) who was standing to one side at the head of the crowd of onlookers.

'This lovely lady, along with her friends, has been looking after me brilliantly,' he said.

Annette gave a shy smile at the camera. Janet, Sonia and Lena nudged their way through the onlookers to stand next to her, followed by a couple of other women who Ellie didn't know, making it quite clear to the viewing public that they were the friends in question.

'How long do you plan to stay here?' the presenter asked. 'You can't stay indefinitely, surely?'

Ben shook his head. 'The local authority is trying to move me. But I plan to stick it out as long as I can; whatever it takes. I've come too far to quit.'

There was a little more chat about Ben's background (though the tragedy of Ben's parents was, rather tellingly, avoided) before the camera panned away again and found Annette and her neighbours. The presenter went over to interview them, and then went along the crowd randomly picking out others to ask their opinions on the situation.

Invariably, the women had faraway looks and wistful sighs in their voices, whilst the men looked thoroughly chagrined that Ben was making them look like such poor specimens of manhood, responding with curt criticisms of his behaviour and random and irrelevant comments on the state of the economy, as though it was all somehow Ben's fault.

The presenter came back to Ben. 'It's a strange thing to ask, perhaps, but have you enjoyed your time on Constance Street? With all the support you've received it looks as though it's been quite a unique experience.'

Ben smiled. 'In a strange way I have. I've made so many good friends and met some amazing people. It's funny how a situation like this can bring out the worst, but also the very best in people, and I've been lucky to find mostly the best. Along with my lovely resident friends over there,' he waved a hand towards the crowd, 'I have to thank the fantastic people at the *Millrise Echo*: Patrick and Ange who are just standing out of shot there…' The camera flicked around and from the back of the crowd Patrick held up a hand of acknowledgment. 'And a lady who is not here now but has been such an incredible support, another *Echo* journalist, Ellie Newton.'

Ellie felt the heat rise to her face as Ange nudged her affectionately.

'Is there anything else you'd like to say?' the presenter asked.

'Well, if this is my final chance to make my plea…' He gazed into the camera with an earnest expression. Ellie felt her breath hitch – it was like he was gazing directly at *her*. 'Please…' Ben said. 'Please come back. Without you I was nothing. You came into my life and made me into something… El –' Ben stopped mid-word, looking flustered. 'Gemma,' he continued, the confusion evident on his face. 'Gemma, please come and find me.'

Ellie's breath quickened. Had he just been about to say her name?

Before she knew it, she had fled the newsroom. Heading into the
nearest staff toilets, she slammed herself into a cubicle. Tears were
streaming down her face.

There was a gentle tap at the cubicle door.

'Ellie? Is that you in there?'

Ellie sniffed hard, rubbing a hand across her eyes. 'I'm OK, Ange.'

'What's the matter?'

'Nothing. There's nothing wrong,' she insisted, desperately hoping
that everyone else in the room didn't see the significance in Ben's slip
of the tongue.

There was a pause. If Ange had heard Ben almost say Ellie's name
(or had he? Ellie could barely trust her own senses anymore) then she
didn't mention it. 'So why did you run off before the report ended?'

'I felt sick.'

Another pause. 'Do you need to go home?'

Ellie flopped onto the toilet seat and put her head in her hands. Her
face would look a mess now and there was no way she could deny to
anyone she'd been crying. If she was going to avoid awkward questions,
then perhaps it was best to go home and have a good weep to get all
this nonsense out of her system.

'I think I will. Give me a minute and I'll come up to the office to
get my things.'

'OK. You're sure it's nothing more than feeling ill?'

'I'll be fine. Go up to the office and stop worrying.'

Ellie listened to Ange's footsteps, the sound of the main toilet door
creaking open, and then silence. Taking a deep breath, she unlocked
the cubicle door and pushed it open. She half expected to see Ange still
there, waiting with arms folded for an explanation. But the room was
empty. Ellie went to the sink to wash her face. The mirrors, combined

with the faintly flickering strip light in this particular bathroom, always seemed to give her face a vaguely yellow hue. It wasn't the most flattering look at the best of times, but right now, as Ellie inspected her swollen eyes, she knew her distressed appearance was not going to go unnoticed.

Remembering that she had hastily stuffed her phone in the pocket of her trousers before going down to the newsroom, she pulled it out and dialled Patrick.

'Are you in the *Echo* building right now?'

'Hello, Ellie. I'm very well, thank you.'

'Sorry, hi. Are you?'

'Yes. What's up?'

Ellie sucked in another lungful of air and ran a hand through her hair. It was taking all her strength not to cry again. 'I need to go home but my bag and coat are in the office and I can't go in there right now.'

There was silence at the other end of the line. If Patrick wanted to ask why, it seemed he had decided not to when he spoke again. 'Where are you?'

'The toilets outside the newsroom.'

'The ladies?'

'No, the blokes'!'

'Alright, sarky. Do you want me to get your stuff or not?'

'Yeah. Sorry.'

'Give me five minutes. You'll have to be outside waiting for me though. I love you to bits Ellie, but I'm not going in *there* after you.'

She left her hiding place and emerged from the toilets into the main corridor. Five minutes later Patrick raised his eyebrows.

'Bloody hell,' he said, handing her things over.

'Thanks. I'm going straight home so I'll see you tomorrow.'

'Want me to run you?'

Ellie shook her head.

'Want to go for coffee and talk about it?'

Ellie shook again.

'Want to come and see Fiona to talk about it?'

'Thanks, Patrick. I know you mean well but I just want to be alone.'

Against her will, a fresh tear tracked her face and Patrick rushed to embrace her.

'Hey, hey… This is not the sharp-tongued Newton I know. What the hell is wrong?'

Ellie pushed him gently away. 'I can't. Not here.'

Head down, she hurried away to the main entrance, leaving Patrick to stare after her with a worried frown.

*

Ellie locked the front door, turned out all the lights save a dim lamp, grabbed her duvet and pillows from the bedroom and curled up on the sofa in front of the fire. She stayed there for the remainder of the day. Old DVDs kept her company and away from the currently distressing interruptions of the outside world. Patrick sent three texts that afternoon, followed by one from Fiona, all reminding her that they were available should she need them. There was a fifth later in the day from Ange asking if she was feeling better. The sixth was from Kasumi asking whether she was happy with the TV piece. The seventh was from Jethro – some joke he had decided to forward on. There was an eighth from her mum asking why she hadn't called for days. It wasn't until she was getting ready for work the next morning, however, that she noticed the ninth.

The text was from Ange:

Have you seen the paper or the local TV news tonight?

Ellie hadn't replied to any of the other texts the previous day and although she would see Ange in an hour or so anyway it was an odd question considering that Ange had known she was home ill, so she sent a message back.

Sorry, I was asleep when you messaged yesterday. Why do you ask?

Ange's reply was almost immediate:

Gemma Fox has turned up on Constance Street.

Chapter Ten

Ellie stared at the phone. What else had she been expecting? But although it had been an obvious outcome since the start, one she had championed, she still felt numb as she read Ange's message again. Suddenly, the idea of going into work seemed like a very bad one. Everyone would be discussing Gemma's return. Ellie would be expected to write about it and talk about it and she seriously doubted she would be able to hold it together when the time came.

Ellie took a deep breath and pulled on her jacket. She still had a job to do and the occasional bad day went with the territory – right? So why was she letting this ridiculous situation and some even more ridiculous crush get in her way? Ben Kelly had made his choice and it didn't include Ellie. So it was time to stick two fingers up to him and get on with her life. This moment, right here and now, was where she made her stand. Holding her head high, she snatched her keys from the mantelshelf and strode for the door.

*

'She's asked for you specifically,' Vernon said. 'I already told her that Ange would go out to cover it but she said she'd wait until you were free.'

Ange gave Ellie an apologetic shrug before logging into her emails.

Ellie chewed on her lip, fighting the overwhelming urge to run away. With Vernon now in the loop, that was not an option. She nodded with as much professionalism as she could muster. 'It's no problem, I can rearrange my schedule. Did she say where they wanted me to meet them?'

'Constance Street.'

Ellie's stomach lurched. In light of recent events, she had already decided that if she ever had to visit the vicinity of that street again, she would take great care to drive around it and not down it. Yet Gemma had specifically asked for Ellie to cover the reunion story and to meet them at the place where everything always, with a frightening inevitability, led back to.

'Constance Street. Of course... where else?'

'So I can leave it with you? It seems only right that you report the story anyway.' Vernon shook a sachet of tomato ketchup onto his bacon and replaced the lid of his sandwich. 'I couldn't understand why Ange had taken it over in the first place.' He glanced at Ange but it seemed she hadn't been listening as her attention was fixed firmly on her PC monitor.

Ellie almost smiled. Good old Vernon – so sharp when it came to sniffing out news, but completely oblivious when hormones were flying around his office so thick anyone else would need breathing equipment to fight their way out.

'Yeah. Leave it with me,' she replied stiffly. 'I've got it covered.'

*

Just over a week before Valentine's Day and already the end of winter felt like spring. Ellie pulled up on Constance Street with the sun warming her back to see a small crowd of the regulars focused around two figures. At her approach, Annette hailed her, moving some of the others aside to reveal Ben on his usual seat with Gemma sitting on his lap looking every inch the queen holding court. Ellie shot a quick glance around. Other than two chairs, every scrap of evidence that Ben had ever lived there at all was gone. It seemed he had cleared everything away, gone with Gemma wherever they would go to make up, and then come back to his corner expressly for Ellie's benefit. She wondered whose idea that had been. As her gaze went back to them snuggled on the chair together, she tried desperately not to think about the making up part either. Her mental calculations took seconds, and as Ben seemed to realise Ellie was there, his face betrayed a certain amount of confusion and embarrassment. He sat up straight, almost throwing Gemma off-balance.

'Ellie... I didn't expect...'

Gemma stood and greeted Ellie. 'Thanks for coming. I must have forgotten to tell Ben that I'd asked for you rather than anyone else. After all...' she smiled sweetly, 'you are responsible for bringing us back together.'

Ellie made herself smile at Gemma's happy, open face. 'I'm glad to have had a part in it, but I really can't take all the credit. Perhaps you should give that to Ben for his tenacity.'

'Oh, I do,' Gemma replied, throwing him a smouldering look. 'I gave him plenty of credit last night.'

It was all Ellie could do to stop herself grimacing. The last image she needed now was of them having sex. Ben looked equally mortified at the revelation. He threw a nervous looking glance at the residents still milling around.

'Ladies, would it be OK if we do Ellie's interview and catch up with you later?'

Ellie guessed that he was no happier about what Gemma might say in their presence than she was. Annette nodded. 'We'll pop home for a bit…' She glanced at the others for approval. 'Come back later if they're still here?'

'Don't worry,' Gemma purred. 'We're going to have a reunion party soon. It might even become a celebration of something more permanent. Whatever, you'll all be invited…' She looked directly at Ellie. 'Especially you.'

'I look forward to it,' Ellie replied. As much as she would her three-yearly smear test. Even the most unobservant person would have found it hard to miss the insincerity in her voice, despite her best efforts to mask it, and her inner guilt-worm gave an especially large wriggle. Gemma simply smiled in return. The ladies dispersed, making their way back to their own houses, only Annette moving a little slower as she tried to get every last drop of gossip from the drama that would, in a few days, be a memory. Gemma ignored her. She was about to speak again when she stopped and glanced past Ellie, who followed the direction of her gaze to see Patrick striding along the street towards them. He held up a hand in greeting.

'So, the happy couple is back together,' he said. Annette beamed at him as he drew level with them. 'Hello, lovely to see you again,' he said to her. 'Where are the other angels?'

Annette giggled and flushed. 'They've just gone home for a while. I was on my way when you arrived.'

'Oh, you were going to make me a cup of tea, weren't you?' Patrick winked. 'You are a love.'

'I can do that!' Annette said brightly. 'Just give me ten minutes and I'll bring a pot out for everyone.'

Annette scurried away and Patrick pulled out his camera. 'Can we get a few photos first?'

Ellie began to wonder what Patrick was up to. She gave him a pointed look but he simply smiled amiably and began to fiddle about with the lenses on his camera. Had he guessed Ellie's distress? Was he giving her time to think, time to collect herself before she had to talk to them and dig out the details of a story that it would very likely kill her to write? Whether he was doing it consciously or not, she was grateful for the breathing space.

'Great idea, coming back to the corner where it all began,' Patrick said as he manoeuvred them into their poses. 'Who takes the credit for that bright scheme?'

'That was me,' Gemma said. 'It seemed kinda right.'

'Plus, everyone will know where to find you, eh?' Patrick said carelessly. 'You had the regional TV news here yesterday, I believe. It was a real stroke of luck that they arrived just after you did, wasn't it.'

Gemma seemed to hesitate, just for a moment. But then she regained her composure. 'Oh, I know, wasn't it? One of the neighbours must have told them I was here.'

'They got here fast from Birmingham too,' Patrick commented, not a flicker of anything but good-natured interest in his face.

'They did,' Gemma agreed, trying not to look at Ben's expression of sudden illumination.

Patrick nudged them together. 'Ben, can you just squeeze in closer… Gemma, how about looking up at him? Perfect… so are the TV crew from *Every Morning* coming back too?'

Gemma glanced at Ellie as she addressed Patrick. 'I've no idea – do you think they will?'

'So nobody has phoned them? I'd have thought they would be very keen to come back and interview you both,' Patrick replied.

'I suppose they would,' Gemma mused.

'You'll be like Will and Kate,' Patrick said. Gemma beamed at him, but Ben's face seemed to lose a shade.

Ellie stared at Patrick. What on earth was he up to?

The thread of conversation took a safer turn when Annette returned with a tray of tea things.

'You are an absolute poppet,' Patrick said, causing Annette to flush with pride. 'Mr Annette is a lucky, lucky man.'

'He is,' Ben agreed. 'I don't know what I would have done without Annette all these weeks.'

Gemma gave an earnest smile. 'Three cheers for Annette then, eh?'

Even Annette shot Gemma a faintly disbelieving look at this suggestion. When nobody obliged, Gemma linked her arm in Ben's and snuggled into him, almost as if to reinforce her ownership to anyone who doubted it.

'Are we done now?' Ben asked Patrick.

'Yep,' Patrick said to the couple, taking a mug from Annette with a jaunty nod. 'But I'll stick around for a while and drink this lovely cuppa while you do the words, eh, Ellie?'

Ellie pulled her notebook out. 'So Ben,' Ellie asked in a dull voice, 'how do you feel now that this is all over and you have the result you wanted?'

'We're totally happy,' Gemma said. 'We just want the world to know all about it.'

Ellie smoothed back a frown and resisted the urge to question whether Gemma thought Ben had suddenly developed a chronic inability to speak. 'OK... *Gemma*, how do you feel now that it's all over?'

Ben clamped his mouth shut as his girlfriend began to elaborate on her thoughts about their reunion. Ellie would have said he looked distinctly miserable if anyone had asked her. But, of course, how could a man who now had everything he'd ever wanted look miserable?

*

'She's a scheming little cow.' Patrick leaned into the open window of Ellie's Mini as she slotted the key into the ignition.

'Hold on a minute,' Ellie said, staring at him. 'That's going a bit far. What on earth makes you say that?'

'It's obvious that she arranged for the film crew to be here when she arrived for her reunion.'

'Really, do you think…?' Ellie said uncertainly. 'But I suppose they're back together now and that's the most important thing, isn't it?'

Through the car's wing mirror, Ellie could see down the street to where they had just been chatting. Ben was packing away the chairs as Gemma looked on. Annette had returned to her house half an hour previously mumbling something about vegetables that needed peeling.

Patrick turned his gaze back to her. 'You liked him a lot, didn't you?'

'I like her too.'

'Not that sort of like, though…'

Ellie gave a wan smile. 'And there was me thinking nobody had noticed.'

'I just wish I'd noticed it earlier.'

'What would you have done differently?'

'I'd have told you to stop trying to sort his life out and offer him a blowjob.'

Ellie couldn't help but laugh, her anxieties draining away with Patrick's one well-timed joke. He always knew the right thing to say.

'You know he isn't happy about all this fuss,' Patrick added.

'He was happy with it before,' Ellie replied stubbornly. She knew that he hated the attention, but she couldn't bring herself to stick up for him right now.

'That was different. He was using it to get his message across.'

Ellie glanced in the mirror again to see Ben and Gemma turn the corner of the street together and disappear from sight.

Patrick straightened up and fished in his pocket for his own car keys. 'You're going to be OK?'

'Not much choice, have I?'

'Come over, have dinner with me and Fi tonight.'

Ellie hesitated. 'I don't really think I'm in the mood for company.'

'It'll do you good…'

'No. Thanks but I'd only curdle the milk.' She forced a smile. 'I'll see you at work, OK?'

He nodded. 'You know I'll do my best to change your mind though.'

*

Ellie really needed to keep her feelings out of the reunion story in that night's edition, but it was a task that she found taxing, to say the least. It wasn't helped by the memory of the smug expression that the girl had worn earlier in the day every time Ellie had happened to shoot a furtive glance in her direction. She had an awful feeling that Patrick's suspicions were true, though Gemma had been perfectly pleasant and likeable to everyone. She tried to tell herself that it was jealousy, but the feeling wouldn't go away. She managed, finally, to pull together a flattering selection of quotes from the couple and a carefully neutral account of them together back on Constance Street where their love affair had begun.

After lunch, she clicked open an email from Patrick. He had attached an assortment of the photos he had taken that day. Ellie scrolled through them. She couldn't deny that Ben and Gemma looked good together – they looked *right*. Whatever Ellie felt about the situation, it was the way things ought to be. The admission was like a knife in the heart. Ellie got to the last photo, preparing to close the email, but then a slow smile spread across her face. Patrick had manipulated it, making Gemma's eyes pop out of her head. He had also given her a moustache and some enormous fake boobs.

Ellie hit *reply*:

You nutter! Let's hope you don't get them mixed up when you submit for copy! Thank you for cheering me up. x

Ellie shook herself. For what seemed like the hundredth time that week, she told herself that it was ridiculous pining over a man like this. She had a life of her own to live – and a complicated enough one at that. She also had a whole bunch of brilliant people in her life that she was neglecting. She pulled out her phone and sent her mum a quick text to say she'd be over during the week to visit. Next she tapped out a message to Kasumi.

What are you doing this weekend? I could come to London if you're free. x

She sent the same one to Jethro.

Locking the screen, she placed the phone back on her desk. She tried to work, but her eyes kept flicking back to her phone, waiting for a reply. It didn't take long for Kasumi to answer.

No can do, hon. I have the dreaded relatives come to inspect the homestead. Next weekend? x

Ellie tapped her phone against her chin for a moment. That was one plan scuppered. But then a second text came through from Jethro.

Fantastic! We can take you to that new club. x

Ellie pondered for a moment.

Sorry, Kasumi can't come out. So it looks like another weekend. x

A minute later Jethro replied.

I don't think she'd mind if it's just you and me. We can always try to catch up with her for lunch before you go back. x

Somehow, it didn't seem right going out without Kasumi. They were a trio – always had been. But Ellie did feel as if the time away would do her good. She sent another message to Kasumi.

I might still come and go out with Jethro on Saturday night. How about we meet you for a quick lunch on the Sunday? x

Kasumi's reply was as lightning fast as ever.

No problem! I'll see if I can rohypnol my parents and sneak off for an hour. x

A re-run of their previous weekend was just what she needed to shake this stupid state of constant moping that had settled over her of late.

Ok, Kasumi is cool with that so I'll see you on Saturday. x

Jethro was obviously waiting by his phone too as his reply was almost immediate.

Awesome! Are you coming into Euston? Let me know what tickets you book and I'll pick you up from the station. Can't wait to see you! x

Ellie gazed at the screen of her phone. She read the message again. She was going to get so drunk on Saturday night that she wouldn't even be able to remember who *she* was, let alone a man named Benvolio Kelly.

*

Miranda opened the front door and gave Ellie a quick peck on the cheek. 'I thought you'd defected or something.'

Ellie followed her into the dim hallway, peeling her coat off. There was a faint, comforting smell of freshly chopped onion and herbs that set Ellie's stomach rumbling. 'What was the *or something*?'

'I don't know… you could have joined a nunnery, run away with the circus, taken up extreme knitting…'

Ellie laughed. 'Sorry to disappoint you, but I've just been working really hard.' The heat hit Ellie as soon as they opened the door to the living room. 'Bloody hell, Mum, how high do you have your thermostat? *And* the fire is on!'

'It's my house,' Miranda replied in the manner of a moody teenager. 'And now that your dad isn't here to complain, I can have it as hot as I like.'

'Oh… so this is a protest sauna…'

'Very funny. Open that window if you're too hot.'

'If I open that window, hedgehogs in your garden will think summer has come early. I could be responsible for wiping out an entire ecosystem.' Ellie flung her coat over the arm of the sofa and stripped off her hoodie so that she was down to jeans and T-shirt.

Miranda ignored the jibe. 'Are you staying for tea?'

'What have you got?'

'Cottage pie.'

'Sounds amazing. If you have some going spare I'll gladly take it off your hands.'

'You know I always cook too much.'

'That's because you're still subconsciously taking me and Dad into account.'

'Lucky you're here, then. And as your dad isn't, it looks like you get double helpings.' The radio was murmuring quietly in the corner of the room. Miranda switched it off. 'I suppose you've seen *him* even though you haven't seen me this week?'

'Dad?'

'Who else?'

Ellie could think of a lot of *who elses*, but now wasn't the time to mention it. 'I saw him last week.' She paused, weighing her next words carefully. 'I don't suppose you've heard from him?'

'Do you want a cup of tea?' Miranda turned for the kitchen. Ellie followed her.

'That means you have.'

Miranda filled the kettle. 'Do you want that cup of tea or not?'

'*Yes, please…*' Ellie replied very deliberately. 'What did Dad say? He asked you to meet up with him?'

By the look on her mother's face, Ellie guessed that any vague hope she had that her parents might reconcile their differences was a forlorn one.

'Oh, Mum, this is getting boring now.'

'I don't know what you mean.'

Ellie flopped onto a chair. 'Why can't you just see him? He wants to explain properly. What have you got to lose by letting him? It would be an opportunity to put your side forward too.'

'Your father is already perfectly aware of my feelings. I don't need *an opportunity*.'

'So he asked and you told him no?'

'Naturally. There's no point in meeting because there is nothing to discuss that can't be discussed through solicitors.'

'You're getting divorced?' Ellie squeaked. For all her mother's stubbornness and the seemingly endless, cyclical nature of their discord, she never imagined for one moment that her parents' marriage would end in permanent separation. But her dad had alluded to it, and now her mum. Perhaps this was really going to happen after all. Ellie wasn't sure what to feel about that. She had known kids at school whose parents had split and they had consequently suffered from all sorts of issues. But Ellie was an adult now – surely a parental divorce shouldn't really affect her any more. So why did the idea make her feel so utterly bereft?

Miranda didn't reply. Instead, she pulled a pair of mugs from a high cupboard and set about making tea.

'Mum!'

When Ellie's mother turned to face her, she wore the expression of a woman who would rather burn at the stake than give an inch. In fact, Ellie mused vaguely, Joan of Arc probably looked a lot like Miranda

Newton did right now as they tied her up. 'There doesn't seem to be any point in delaying the inevitable any longer.'

'The inevitable!' Ellie almost shouted as Miranda set a mug down in front of her. 'When was this ever inevitable?'

'Since your Dad was too stubborn to see what he'd done wrong.'

'Well, it takes one stubborn old goat to know one,' Ellie muttered. She dragged her drink across the table and cupped her hands around it, staring into its depths. Right now, she didn't trust herself to look her mum in the eye.

'Pie will be another hour or so. Do you have time to stay?' Miranda joined Ellie at the table with her own drink.

'How could you do this?' Ellie asked, not moving her eyes from her mug.

'We can have chips or just some green beans with it, I don't mind either.'

Ellie's head snapped up. 'Would you just listen to yourself! Argh! You're so infuriating!' She let out a sigh. 'Does Dad know your plans to side-line him permanently?'

Miranda traced a finger down the side of her mug, catching a tea drip. 'The conversation didn't exactly get that far.'

'You put the phone down on him before he'd even said two words, didn't you?'

'Three, actually.'

'It'll destroy him, you know. He's hanging on by his fingertips now.'

'A self-made mess. We were happy and he had to go churning things up.'

'He thought you'd be as excited as him.'

'Then he clearly didn't know me, even after all these years.'

'Mum…' Ellie paused, her gaze for a moment drawn to the frosty twilight beyond the window. 'Is there a chance that this whole stand is

on principle, rather than being about what you do or don't want? You
two talked about travelling the world for as far back as I remember.'

'And we always agreed we didn't have the money. They were dreams,
Ellie, pie in the sky, the sorts of plans that every family discusses and
few ever get to make real.'

'Dad thought he could make them real for you.'

'At the expense of our security.'

'Mum... please think about this. Look at Hazel. Imagine what regrets
she has now and it's too late to do anything about them. Sometimes
security is good. But if it's at the expense of having a life, sometimes
you have to be prepared to take a risk and step into the void. You never
know, you might find you like what's there.'

'That's another thing – how can I leave my sister at a time like this
and go swanning off to Australia? Your dad has no siblings and he has
no idea what it feels like.'

'Nobody realised just how ill Hazel was when Dad first made
his plans. And I'm sure he'd wait until...' Ellie's sentence trailed off.
Everyone knew that Hazel's end was near, but to say it out loud made
it too real.

'And then do you really think I'll be in the mood to go?' Miranda
snapped. 'You always did take his side over everything.'

'I'm not even going to dignify that with a response.' Ellie took a gulp
of her tea and turned her face to the window again. The wind was getting
up. Her mind, out of sheer habit, wandered to how the weather conditions
would be affecting Ben. But then she remembered that Ben would be
indoors now, ensconced on a sofa somewhere with Gemma, and that
cruel fist of longing squeezed her heart again. She shut the feeling out.

'Hazel has spoken to her palliative care nurse and made arrangements to go to the hospice,' Miranda said, cutting in on her thoughts.

Ellie turned back to her. 'I thought she'd agreed to stay at home.'

'So did I. But I saw her earlier in the week and it seems she changed her mind.'

Ellie thought back to when she had last seen her aunt. The question of the hospice had not come up. A needle of guilt stabbed at her. Perhaps it hadn't come up because Hazel was too busy listening to Ellie's complaints, instead of Ellie listening to those of a woman whose only choices left now were the location of her death and who to leave her worldly goods to. The sad fact was that Hazel had been right – Ellie and her mum, however noble their intentions – were simply too busy with their own lives to give her the time and care she really needed. The truth stung.

'Do you want me to go and talk to her, see if I can get her to change her mind?' Ellie asked half-heartedly. If she knew anything about her aunt, it was that she could be as stubborn as Miranda. Which was very stubborn indeed. She wasn't sure there was any point trying to talk her round but it felt like the right thing to offer.

'No...' Miranda sighed. 'I don't suppose you'll budge her on this.'

Ellie regarded her mother thoughtfully for a moment. 'She'll be looked after there, at least. She'll need twenty-four-hour care soon, and much more specialised than either of us can give,' she said, trying, but failing, to make herself feel better about the idea.

'I could have done that,' Miranda said.

'Perhaps Hazel wanted to retain the little dignity she had left by not burdening you with that. Perhaps she wanted to be remembered as your big sister, and not a chore that you had to perform out of some misplaced sense of duty.'

'*Misplaced?*'

'Alright then, maybe *misplaced* was the wrong word. But we've been so busy worrying about what's best for Hazel that we've forgotten she has a will of her own. What we think is best is clearly not the same as what she thinks is best. Perhaps we ought to just accept her decision and leave it at that.'

Miranda sighed. 'They won't care for her like I would.'

'Probably not. But it's Hazel's choice.'

Miranda was silent as she stared into the distance, seemingly lost in thought. After a few moments, she drained her cup and took it to the sink. 'You never said if you wanted chips or vegetables.'

Ellie gave her a faint smile. 'That's a serious question? When have I ever chosen anything over chips?'

*

Despite her own misgivings and her mother's advice to the contrary, Ellie decided to call on her aunt the next day anyway, on her way to cover a Fattest Pig competition at a farm about five miles or so out of the town.

Hazel opened the door with a faint look of surprise. 'I didn't expect to see you at this time of the day.'

Ellie nodded and followed her inside. 'Mum told me about the hospice.'

'You're not here to bundle me in a car boot and take me away to keep me in your kitchen cupboard are you?'

Ellie smiled thinly. 'I wouldn't dare try. You might be ill but I bet you can still nag me into submission.'

'Too right I can,' Hazel laughed. She started towards the kitchen. 'Can you stay for a cup of tea or do you have to dash off now that we've sorted that out?'

Ellie resisted the impulse to look at her watch. 'Of course I can stay for tea,' she replied as breezily as she could manage. 'I can always stay for tea with you.' She dropped her satchel to the sofa as she passed and hurried towards her aunt. 'But let me make it. You should be resting.'

'Oh, I'm sick of sitting down all the time. It'll do me good to potter about a bit in the kitchen. Besides, I have no intention of cleaning it ever again now that I'm not staying here, so who cares if I leave a trail of mouldy teabags along the sink.'

'Fair enough.' Ellie watched as Hazel turned slowly back towards the kitchen, grasping the doorframe for a moment's support as she went. Sometimes, when Ellie looked at her aunt, she couldn't see the family resemblance at all. But at other times, on days like today, she could see it not in the features or colouring – Hazel, until now, had been heavier than Miranda, with darker eyes and skin – but in the determined set of her jaw and the defiance in her expression. Ellie knew then that Hazel wasn't going into the hospice because she was giving up; it was quite the opposite. She would go fighting, never becoming a chore that Ellie and Miranda might be reluctant to undertake. Hazel was far too proud for that. While she would fade, at least nobody she loved would find her passing a relief.

'Your mum will come round to the idea,' Hazel said, breaking in on Ellie's thoughts as she flicked the kettle on.

'I don't suppose she has a choice.' Ellie took a seat at the table. She had to check herself as she watched Hazel struggle around the kitchen, desperate to leap up and take over the task but mindful that she shouldn't.

'No. But she will anyway. And I actually feel like a huge burden has been lifted from my shoulders now that I've made up my mind and set things in motion.'

'When will you move?'

'As soon as my nurse has put the paperwork through and got everything sorted. It shouldn't be too long now.'

'You want some help sorting out and packing?'

Hazel lowered herself into a chair. 'I wanted to talk to you about that. There's not a lot of point in me keeping all this stuff.'

'What are you going to do with it?'

'I suppose you and Miranda might want some of it?' Hazel looked almost hopeful, as if a decline of her offer would be painful.

'Your furniture, you mean?' Ellie asked doubtfully.

'And any other bits – equipment, linens… photo albums… anything really. I'll only need a few personal belongings. As long as I have my iPad and some spare knickers I'll be happy.'

'I'll ask Mum and get some time off work. We can make a day of it – go through everything, decide what we're going to do with it all, eat copious amounts of ice-cream and giggle at photos of your ridiculous eighties perm.'

Hazel reached across the table and grasped Ellie's hand. 'I'd love that.'

Ellie smiled. 'Then, consider it a date.'

Chapter Eleven

'Hi Rosie, how's it going?' Ellie wiped a stray blob of mayonnaise from the corner of her mouth and swallowed the mouthful of sandwich she had just bitten off as she picked up the office phone. Her expression darkened as she listened to what the *Echo's* receptionist had to tell her.

'Where is she now?' Ellie asked finally.

'I've put her in one of the smaller conference rooms,' Rosie replied.

'I'll be right down.' Ellie dropped the receiver into the cradle and let out a huge breath. What did Gemma want now? Hadn't Ellie written enough stories about her? She turned to Ange, momentarily disconcerted by the fact that her colleague appeared to be Googling *Midlands witches covens*, but then shook herself. If it came to it, at least Ange might be able to put her in touch with someone who could work a good hex. Right now, knowing who was waiting downstairs for her, that almost sounded like an appealing prospect. 'Ange, I've got to pop down to one of the conference rooms to see someone. I'm expecting Patrick to phone about another Businessman of the Year nominee. If he does will you just get the details of where I have to meet him?'

Ange didn't take her eyes from the screen but gave a vague wave in her direction. 'No problem.'

Ellie made her way down to the ground floor, passing the buzzing newsroom and the classified ad department where it appeared some sort of gift presentation was taking place amid cheers and crying. She barely gave it a thought as her mind worked overtime on more immediate and pressing matters.

As she arrived at the glass-walled room, she could see that Gemma was busy on her mobile phone. Ellie pushed the door open and she looked up.

'One minute,' Gemma said, holding up a finger. She tapped out what Ellie presumed to be a message to someone before locking the screen and dropping the phone back into her bag. Ellie waited patiently, bristling slightly at Gemma's rudeness. No one was attached to her mobile more than Ellie, but when someone walked into a room to greet her she would stop whatever she was doing on it and at least greet them in return.

'Would you like to sit down?' Ellie said, smoothing her expression. She indicated a table and chairs next to a whiteboard. 'Rosie could get us coffee if you like.'

'I don't need to sit down,' Gemma said. 'It won't take long.'

'OK. What can I do for you?'

Gemma perched herself on the end of the table and rested her feet on a chair. Ellie tried not to raise her eyebrows. Perhaps Patrick was right after all – this was a very different girl to the Gemma she'd met before.

'I had an interesting conversation yesterday with someone who lives on Constance Street,' Gemma began. Then she waited, seemingly for some sort of response from Ellie, who only nodded slowly. She had a horrible feeling she knew exactly where this conversation was going but only hoped she was wrong.

When Ellie offered no reply, Gemma continued.

'I've been told that you've spent a lot of time on Constance Street over the past few weeks.'

'Of course I have. I was covering Ben's story.'

'Hmmmm, what about when you visited at night and weekends? What about when you stayed all night?'

'I have never stayed all night!'

'But you don't deny going out of work hours?'

'I'm a reporter,' Ellie replied. 'I don't have *work hours*. News breaks, I go, no matter what time of day it is.'

'Ben on that corner was hardly breaking news, was it?'

'I don't see how that's a decision you could make, to be honest.'

'It is when it involves my boyfriend!'

'He wasn't actually your boyfriend at the time.' Ellie bit back the rage that she could feel was beginning to cloud her judgement. She took a deep breath. 'You had left him.'

'We were always going to get back together, which I seem to remember sharing with you as a matter of confidence.'

'It did take you rather a long time, though, don't you think?'

Ellie chewed her lip as she looked at Gemma. *They were always going to end up back together.* Any woman whose man had put in that much effort would go back eventually. Had Ellie really misread the signs that badly?

'You were seen,' Gemma said, breaking in on Ellie's thoughts. 'All cosy under that big umbrella, drinking and laughing... You kissed him.'

'I did not!'

Gemma shook her hair out and stood up. 'Understand this...' Her gaze flitted up and down over Ellie. 'If he did kiss you he was only lonely; it didn't mean anything.'

Ellie gritted her teeth. 'He didn't kiss me. We had a drink and that was all.'

'I want to believe you, Ellie, and I'm sorry I had to come here and say this. But I wanted to make the situation clear, just in case there was any confusion. He loves *me*.'

'It is clear. I know he does, he told me so. In fact, if you recall, he pretty much told the world.'

Gemma nodded. 'Right.' She swept past Ellie towards the door of the conference room. And then she turned and smiled sweetly.

'I hope this is the end of any misunderstanding, Ellie. I like you and you've done me such a huge favour by making me see what I was missing without Ben. I would hate to have to make a formal complaint to your editor about you.'

Ellie's mouth dropped open. Replies whirled around her mind but nothing would come out. Without another word, Gemma left, letting the door slam shut behind her.

Ellie sat, her heart now pounding and her shaking legs barely able to support her. Had she just been threatened? Who had told Gemma that she and Ben had been kissing? Ellie had tried to keep her feelings hidden but had they really been that transparent? Could it be that Ellie was not only going to lose a chance of happiness, but her job too, the one she had worked so hard to get? Dragging in a deep breath, she pushed herself upright. Crying was not going to achieve anything and she was damned if she'd cry over anything Gemma Fox had done. Ben was gone now – she had to accept that – but she wasn't going to lose everything else without a fight.

In the advertising department, it looked as though the presentation was over. People were hugging a heavily pregnant woman. Ellie recognised her as someone she had exchanged a few pleasant words with down in the kitchen from time to time but she couldn't remember her name and hadn't even realised she was pregnant until now.

Ellie passed the newsroom next and could see it was still vibrant with activity. It looked as though some international scandal had broken and there was excited laughter as the staff threw around ideas for the best angles to cover it. Ellie saw all this and felt the lump rise in her throat again. The *Echo* was a small fish – a provincial paper with a tiny circulation but a huge place in the heart of the local community – it wasn't all high-flying glamour like the TV company Kasumi and Jethro worked for but it was a massively important part of Ellie's life and she loved it dearly.

Ange looked up as Ellie sat back at her desk. 'Everything alright?'

Ellie nodded before wrapping up the remnants of her lunch and throwing them into the bin. 'When is Vernon due back?'

Ange shrugged slightly. 'Not sure. He said he'd be late though. I expect you could phone and leave a message for him; he'll call back when he gets a free moment.'

Ellie considered her options. Should she speak to Vernon herself – pre-empt any complaint before it was made? But that might open up a much bigger can of worms that could have been left well alone if Gemma didn't complain. The answer was simple: she had to stay away from Ben at all costs.

'Did Patrick phone?' Ellie asked.

'No,' Ange said. 'You could text him? He's very likely stopped off at Costa for his lunch first.'

Ellie dragged her mobile across the desk. If there was one person she wanted to see right now, it was Patrick.

Where are you?

As she waited for a reply, Ellie scrolled down to check her emails.

Jethro McCoy has tagged you on Facebook.

Ellie opened the message and followed the link to her profile page. Jethro had posted a photo of a nightclub, lit up by pink and yellow fluorescent lasers and a caption that read:

Ready to dance your feet off, **Ellie Newton***? Can't wait to take you here for a night of wild debauchery. Hurry up Saturday! x*

God, in all the drama Ellie had almost forgotten about that. Right now, a rowdy nightclub was the last thing she needed. She would have to text him later. She'd still go down to see him, but suggest something a bit quieter for them to do.

Her mobile bleeped the arrival of Patrick's response.

I'm getting lunch. Want to meet me in Costa? We can go on to the hospital from there.

The hospital? I thought we were doing Businessman of the Year?

Haven't you checked your emails? There's been a mix up on the maternity unit – nearly ended up with some woman taking the wrong baby home. You want to cover it, right?

Ellie checked the rest of her list and found the email he'd been talking about. It was the sort of story that, on any other day, would have had Ellie leaping up for her coat and car keys. But today it only vaguely kindled her interest.

'Ange, have you seen this about the hospital mix up?'

Ange looked around. 'Yeah. I thought you and Patrick had it covered though.'

'I was just checking you didn't want it.'

Ange turned back to her screen. 'Not especially – knock yourself out.'

Ellie grabbed her phone and replied to Patrick.

See you in ten minutes.

*

Ellie found Patrick at his usual table. He smiled brightly as he spotted her, making space on the leather sofa he had been sprawled across as he sipped his Americano and read the first edition of the day's paper.

'Working lunch?' Ellie asked as she squeezed in alongside him.

'Of course. You want a drink?'

Ellie shook her head. 'I'm OK. How long do you think we'll be missing this afternoon?'

'Hard to say. We have to see this woman about the baby swap and take some photos at the maternity block – although I could do those by myself if you don't have time. Then we still need to get to our business guy.' He threw Ellie a questioning sideways glance. 'Why do you need to know? You don't normally worry about how long we're out.'

'I might need to see Vernon this afternoon.'

'About Gemma Fox?' Patrick looked over the rim of his cup as he took a gulp.

Ellie stared at him. 'How did you know?'

'You forget, I hear about everything on that paper.'

Ellie smiled slightly. 'Rosie told you she'd been in.'

'Yup.' Patrick pulled out his phone. 'Text message came through at 1:03 precisely. I have a very effective spy network, you know.'

'That's because all the women in that place are in love with you.'

Patrick threw back his head in a flirtatious half-laugh, half-giggle. He winked at Ellie. 'Only the silly ones. Not you, though.'

'Damn straight. I put up with you all day; I couldn't do it when I went home as well.'

'Don't try to deny it, you love being out with me.'

'I refute that allegation.'

Patrick grinned and then picked up his cup to drain the last of his drink. 'We'd better get weaving if you need to get back.'

'What exactly did Rosie tell you?'

'Just that Gemma had come to reception and asked to speak to you in private.' Patrick held her in a measured gaze. 'What did she want?'

Ellie sighed. 'To ruin my life, I think.'

Patrick set his cup down and put his arm around her. 'She doesn't seem like the type. A bit of a media whore, maybe, but harmless enough. You're not worried, are you?'

'I'd be lying if I said no. She says she'll make a formal complaint to Vernon about me if she thinks I'm after her boyfriend.'

'Bloody hell! But Vernon wouldn't swallow that? He knows you too well.'

'I don't know. Someone told her I'd been there all night and that I'd kissed him.'

Patrick raised an eyebrow. 'You kissed him?'

'Patrick! Of course I didn't.'

'Still...' Patrick sniffed as he sat back in the seat again, 'I don't think Vernon would buy it. I think you're worrying about nothing. Stay out of their way and everything will be fine.'

Ellie's gaze dropped to the floor. 'I hope you're right,' she said quietly.

*

Ellie and Patrick had spent a subdued afternoon together, Ellie lost in her own thoughts as she worked and Patrick maintaining a respectful distance to let her. He cracked his usual jokes, of course, and employed his legendary charm wherever it was called for, but he had clearly toned it down and Ellie, although she didn't say it, appreciated his muted company more than she could convey. When they returned to the office just after five, it transpired that Vernon had been in briefly, packed his things, and headed for home again. With nothing else to be done, Ellie did the same.

She spent a restless night, beating the alarm by an hour to wake the next morning, shower and dress, and head into work as early as she could.

'Ellie… my wayward protégé,' Vernon announced as she entered the office. 'I don't suppose you can spare a moment for a private chat?'

Ellie nodded, her stomach lurching. From the corner of her eye she noticed Ange throw a sharp glance in her direction.

'Good girl. We'll use a spare conference room, eh?' Vernon continued.

Ellie followed quietly as he led her downstairs, past the now sleepy newsroom and the advertising department where few of the staff had arrived yet – the ones that had yawning at their desks over freshly made cups of coffee. Vernon opened the door for Ellie and waited until she was seated before shutting it behind them. He didn't look angry as he took a seat of his own across from her, but his expression was suitably sombre.

'I think you know what this is about,' he said, folding his hands over one another on the table before him.

'Do I?' Ellie replied faintly, hoping that she was on the wrong track.

'Ben Kelly and his girlfriend…'

Ellie felt as though someone had stolen the sensation from her limbs as she waited for him to continue.

'I wanted to say how impressed I've been with the energy and enthusiasm with which you covered the story. I know things haven't been easy for you lately…'

'Oh,' Ellie replied in a daze. 'I'm not sure I follow.'

'Don't think I don't know about your little excursions out during work hours.' The shadow of a smile played about Vernon's lips. 'But I understand that you have a lot of family issues at the moment. You should have come to me and I would have been only too happy to sort something with you officially.'

Ellie chewed her lip. She had a great deal of respect for Vernon who, despite the jokes and Frank Spencer-esque mishaps, was an astute, clever man who had got to the top by keeping his wits about him and doing a brilliant job. She didn't want to lie to him. 'I'm sorry. I should have been straight with you. Do you want me to leave?'

'What? Leave the *Echo*?'

'Yes.'

'Over my dead body, Ellie Newton. You're the biggest breath of fresh air my team has had in a long time. You're keen, energetic, sharp… No, I don't want you to leave. I do, however, want you to come to me if your personal life presents problems for your work life again.' Vernon studied her thoughtfully for a moment. The slow smile that had been threatening to break emerged. 'This is awkward for me, Ellie,' he said, biting it back. 'I've become very fond of you and I know you have what it takes to take over from me one day. I want you to be squeaky clean from now on so we have no more of these conversations.'

Ellie heaved a sigh of relief. A compliment like that from Vernon would have made her delirious with joy on any other day. But today, she just prayed her legs wouldn't give way when she had to leave the conference room.

'Right...' Vernon said briskly as he pushed himself up from the chair. 'Go and find me some more cracking stories.' He turned and grinned with his hand on the door handle. 'There must be some drama or other going on in Millrise today.'

Ellie watched him go. There was some drama alright. He simply had no idea how close he had been sitting to it.

*

Ellie tried to keep busy and out of Vernon's way for the remainder of the week, though his schedule was so packed that it wasn't hard. Once Ellie had returned to her desk after their meeting, she considered writing a letter of apology to Gemma, just to clear things up once and for all. It seemed like the safest bet to prevent the complaint that hung over her.

It took many attempts – when she felt it was sincere she didn't sound sorry enough and when she sounded sorry it was transparently obvious that she didn't mean a word of it. In the end she had settled on a few stiff lines expressing sorrow for any misunderstanding and assuring Gemma that no malice was intended in her actions. Which was sort of true and didn't broach the subject of her personal feelings or opinions about Gemma at all. But then Ellie had backed out at the last moment, and thrown the letter in the bin. What she really wanted, more than anything now, was not to think about either of them.

Life carried on. Ange got herself embroiled in some juicy local witchcraft/MP/orgy scandal, and the *Ben and Gemma Show* became suspiciously quiet. During that week, Hazel and Ellie's mother had argued over the details of the hospice, sending Hazel into a spasm of coughing that had turned her blue and Miranda dashing to phone

the ambulance. Hazel had been rushed into hospital and Miranda
had been beside herself with remorse and grief. Ellie's dad had fallen
into a semi-fugue state, in which he conveniently forgot that he was
supposed to be cleaning up his act and trying to win his wife back and
had promptly regressed to his previous *distressed bachelor* lifestyle, fixing
together a flat-pack wardrobe to take his mind off things and nailing
his thumb to a back panel.

The one bright spot of the week was that Hazel had been discharged from hospital quickly and seemed better than Ellie had seen
her in many months. She had gone over with her mum and the three
of them had giggled like children as they pored over old photos,
packing each album away in boxes afterwards with a faint stab of
regret. None of them spoke of the reason; packing just seemed easier
that way. Ellie had promised to take some personal things back to her
house and put it all safely away for whichever generation came next
(if Ellie ever found time to produce offspring, Hazel teased). They
had stopped often for small portions of ice-cream or custard – just
about the only foods Hazel ever wanted to eat now – and then dived
back into the next box of mementos. Evening had turned to night
and by the time Ellie fell into her bed, tired but happy, it had gone
midnight. Sleep, however, was kept at bay by the warning that kept
sneaking back into her thoughts, the one her mum had issued in
the car on the way home.

'They say people who are dying of a terminal illness are often really
well just before it happens.'

Ellie had not known what to say in reply, and so said nothing.

By the time she stepped off the train at Euston on Saturday afternoon, Ellie was completely exhausted. But when she had expressed
her concerns about how people would cope if she went off for the

weekend again to Hazel over a lunchtime visit, Hazel had some choice swearwords for Ellie's parents and had made Ellie solemnly promise to go to London, even if the four horsemen of the apocalypse rode into Millrise on carnival floats singing *Highway to Hell*.

Jethro spotted her emerging from the direction of the train platforms and jogged over.

'How's it going? Better journey this time?'

Ellie laughed as he grabbed her overnight bag from her. 'Not really. Today I had the loudest woman in the world phoning everyone she knows to tell them about her appearance on *Dragon's Den*.'

'But did she get the money?'

'No.'

'Loser,' Jethro grinned. 'I'd want to keep that to myself.'

'I think that might be difficult, as the entire nation will see it on TV.'

'Ha ha, even bigger loser then.'

Ellie giggled as Jethro led them to the escalators.

'Got your dancing feet with you?'

Ellie hesitated.

'What?' Jethro looked sharply at her.

'You know how we were meant to go to that new club?' Ellie looked up at him as they stepped onto the escalators.

'Yeah…'

'I know it's boring, but I've had a really tough week and I would much rather do something quieter.'

'You mean go somewhere where we can actually hear each other speak, where we don't get doused in other people's sweat dripping from the ceiling and accosted at least once an hour by shifty looking people trying to sell us illegal and dangerous mind-altering substances?'

Ellie nodded.

'Well…' Jethro said, letting out a bemused breath and rubbing a hand through his thick hair. 'It'll be a novelty I suppose. Should we stop off and buy you some slippers on the way to the flat – really go to town?'

Ellie slapped his arm playfully. 'Sarky git!'

He flashed her a brilliant grin. 'I'm sure we can think of a pursuit more suited to a woman of your advanced years.'

'Oi, you're only funny for so long, you know.'

'It's strange,' he said, pretending to be thoughtful, 'but that's the last sentence every one of my ex-girlfriends uttered before they knee'd me in the nuts and nicked back all the CDs I'd nicked from them in the first place.' He scratched his head theatrically and pulled a comical face. 'Do you think that's where I'm going wrong?'

'That you're opening your mouth at all is where you're going wrong,' Ellie said, biting back laughter.

*

The sun shone kindly on them for the remainder of the afternoon, meaning that once they had dropped Ellie's bag at Jethro's flat, he could take her on the promised mini-tour of his neighbourhood that she'd been too hungover to undertake on her last visit. They wandered through Peckham Rye Park where the trees were budding with the first knots of new growth and families and couples sauntered down the paths. Jethro threw in a titbit of history or an odd fact about the place now and again, like how the common had been used as a prisoner-of-war camp for Italian prisoners during the Second World War or the dates that different sections had been opened. Ellie listened with genuine interest, glad to be thinking about things so completely unconnected to anything happening in Millrise and impressed by his knowledge and the fact that he could be bothered to retain the information at all. On the surface, Jethro always pretended to be the cool, laid-back party dude, but Ellie knew that underneath all that, he was keenly intelligent with an insatiable curiosity about the world around him. It was what made him so good at his job in television research. He was so unlike many of the men she met back home on now rare outings to nightclubs; often their primary concerns were what time the kebab shop closed or the latest football scores. It was no wonder Ellie had never found suitable boyfriend material amongst them.

They had coffee and cake at the Rye Café as Jethro told Ellie the latest goings on at his job, filled her in on the events of his huge crazy family (six sisters, three brothers, and parents who had met on an exchange trip to Finland). Then Ellie took her turn to tell Jethro about her parents' continued estrangement, Hazel's illness and who, out of the people she still knew from their course, was getting married, getting divorced, having affairs or having surprise babies.

Later, they trawled the high street, Jethro introducing Ellie to the delights of an Iranian store that sold all sorts of curiosities, a vintage shop that had her almost hyperventilating and wishing her credit card wasn't quite so full, and the most incredible chocolate shop.

Later still, as they idled away the time between the high street darkening and the bars and restaurants coming alive for the evening, Ellie beat Jethro soundly at *Mario Kart* and had a very noisy play on his drum kit, wondering how often he practised on it and quite how unpopular he was with his neighbours.

*

Jethro wandered through into his tiny kitchen in nothing but his boxers, rubbing a towel over his wet hair. Ellie looked up from a magazine she had been reading at the table.

'Good God, cover yourself up,' she laughed.

'What's the matter? Do I make you horny, baby?'

'No. You're giving me a weird hankering for spare ribs.' She frowned. 'Jesus, Jethro, don't you eat?'

'Constantly. It's not my fault I have the sort of metabolism that can set off nuclear reactions.'

'Well... it's just wrong.'

He took a seat at the table and lounged back, splaying his legs out. 'If it makes you feel better, you can wander around in your underwear too. You know, just so we're even.'

Ellie closed her magazine. 'And that's why we should always have Kasumi with us.'

'So she can join in the underwear parade too? Sounds fine by me.'

'Urgh! You're so disgusting!'

Jethro laid a hand over his heart. 'I'm mortally wounded by that remark.'

Ellie laughed and swatted the rolled up magazine over his head. 'So, where are you taking me tonight?'

'There's that tapas bar you liked the look of earlier.'

Ellie thought for a moment. 'Perfect. Can we go soon? I'm starving already and I don't think the extensive choice of Pot Noodles in your cupboards is doing it for me.'

He leapt up from his chair with a bow. 'Your wish is my command. Let us depart immediately.'

'Yeah, whatever. Just not *too* immediately, you'll start a riot if you go out in those boxers.'

*

An hour later they arrived at a cosy little tapas bar, just a couple of streets from Jethro's apartment. The exterior had a rustic look with wooden window shutters and a cobbled forecourt sheltered by potted trees strung with white fairy lights. Tables were made from the bases of huge tree trunks cut in perfect slices and polished to display the rings in all their glory, with chunky wooden chairs to accompany them. The strains of traditional Spanish music could be heard from inside.

'We could sit outside if you like?' Jethro asked. He nodded towards the patio heaters that skirted the forecourt. 'If we get a table under one of those it should be quite cosy.'

'Sounds good to me. It feels much more European to be outside, even if it is a grey February in Britain,' Ellie replied, relieved that she had brought more appropriate clothes down this time and now wore a pair of skinny jeans and a finely knitted sweater.

Jethro laughed. 'We can pretend, eh?' He pulled out a chair for Ellie with a gracious flourish. 'Not too nineteenth century for you, is it?' he grinned as Ellie took the seat with a grateful smile.

'I have no objection to a man showing me a bit of courtesy. Just don't ask me to bring up babies and stay at home darning socks by candlelight.'

'Wouldn't dream of it.'

He passed Ellie a menu and as she scanned it, she heard another voice at the table.

'Hey, Jethro.'

Ellie looked up to see a pretty red-headed girl in a white blouse and black skirt covered by an apron. She had a notepad and pen poised. Obviously the waitress, although not very Spanish, Ellie mused, as her broad cockney accent came through. Ellie noted also, with some surprise, that she seemed to know Jethro well enough to address him by his first name.

'Hi Claudia. How's it going; busy tonight?'

She flashed him a dazzling smile. 'Not for a Saturday. I'm sure it will be later though. There's something going on in town, so maybe that's why.'

'In town?' Jethro asked.

She shrugged slightly. 'I forget what Enrique said it was now. He wasn't very pleased about it though. You'll have to order extra tonight to keep him happy.'

'Don't worry.' Jethro glanced at Ellie and smiled. 'I think we can manage that. This is my friend, Ellie, by the way. She's from the Midlands. We did the same media course at uni.'

'Staying for the weekend?' Claudia asked. Her smile was courteous but Ellie detected something slightly less sincere in it than the one she had given to Jethro.

'Only tonight, then back to boring old Millrise tomorrow.'

'That's nice. So, what can I get for you guys?'

Jethro gave Ellie a questioning look. 'Have you had time to decide?'

She folded the menu and handed it to him. 'You've only just given me the bloody menu.'

'Right, I'm just going to wing it then,' Jethro grinned. Before she had time to argue, he rattled off a list of dishes to Claudia: dandelion and broad bean salad, frittata, king prawns and chorizo and other things that Ellie didn't recognise at all. For a second she thought about arguing that she was perfectly capable of ordering her own food, but then wondered what the point was. Perhaps it was more fun this way.

As he continued to order in between chatting to Claudia, Ellie found her gaze drawn to the town around them. It was vibrant with lights and chatter, as busy in the evening as it had been in the day, so much going on. Could she imagine herself living here? Perhaps this was the answer to all her problems. But then, it felt too much like running away… it was a nice dream, but a dream was all it could be when so many people at home relied on her.

'Are you OK?' Jethro asked.

She smiled brightly, shaken from her thoughts as Claudia left them.

'She fancies you.' Ellie leaned across the table with an impish grin.

'What… Claudia?'

Ellie nodded.

'No way.'

'Do you know her from somewhere else?'

'No, just here.'

'But she knows your name.'

'I come here a lot.'

Ellie leaned back with a smug look. 'Take it from me, she likes you.'

Jethro glanced back at the doors of the building that Claudia had just disappeared through. In the gloom, Ellie thought she could see him blush.

'That's crazy. Besides… I'm finished with women.'

'Really. Who's the lucky man then?'

Jethro sat back and grinned. 'I'm going to be celibate.'

Ellie threw back her head and laughed. 'I'd like to see that.'

'I can do celibate. It's not so hard.' He flexed his muscles. 'That's what God gave us right arms for.'

'You're so gross.'

'Don't tell me you don't love it.'

Ellie reached for a breadstick from a tall glass at the centre of the table and snapped it in half. The smile was still on her lips as she looked up at Jethro, grinning across at her. And then she knew what to do. She would tell him about Ben. Jethro would understand. He would know just the right thing to say to cheer her up. He would tell her exactly what she had to do to rid herself of the angst and heartache that still lingered no matter what she did to shake it.

His phone bleeped. He pulled it from his pocket and read the text message.

'Kasumi. She's having a fabulous time with her mum and dad… not.' He turned the phone screen to Ellie to reveal the photo Kasumi had sent of the front entrance of the poshest, stuffiest looking restaurant they had ever seen.

'I bet she's loving it in there,' Ellie smiled. 'How long do you think she can last without saying *bollocks* or *twat* in front of her parents?'

'I bet she's failed that challenge already. And if she doesn't Sam will do it for her.'

Ellie's eyes widened. 'Oh God! Is she taking Sam?'

'Yeah. This is the first time they've met him.'

'Bloody hell,' Ellie sat back and nibbled on the end of her breadstick. 'I think we picked the wrong night out. Is it too late to get a table at…' She peered at the phone screen again, 'the Royal Worcester? Preferably next to theirs. It'll be brilliant entertainment.'

Claudia appeared at their table again before he could reply.

'Here's your wine,' she said, glancing at Jethro and blushing slightly as she placed it on the table and laid out two glasses.

'Thanks, Claudia.' Jethro smiled up at her.

Ellie watched her walk away again. She was pretty, with a cute little wiggle when she walked. Her attention turned back to Jethro. He was watching her walk away too. Maybe he was appreciating the wiggle in her walk as well.

'I'm telling you, she fancies you,' Ellie whispered.

'And I'm telling you that I've done with girls. It all ends in disaster.'

'Completely?'

'Totally.'

Twenty rowdy minutes and half a dozen teasing text messages to Kasumi later, their food arrived. They tucked in, chatting as they ate. Ellie was aware that her own hand-flapping became more and more exaggerated and her voice grew louder the more she drank, but was unable to do much about it as the wine worked its magic. Her feelings for Ben became dulled and hazy, and that suited Ellie just fine. It was easier to tell Jethro everything when the words didn't sting quite so badly.

*

Some time just before midnight, they stumbled over the threshold of Jethro's flat. He made coffee and she fiddled with his iPod to see what music he had on there. When he returned from the kitchen, he placed their drinks on a small table and sat next to her on the sofa.

'I'm glad we went for the old ladies' option in the end,' he said.

'I wonder how Kasumi and Sam got on,' Ellie mused.

Jethro kicked off his shoes, which tumbled into a heap in the middle of the floor, and reached for his own mug. 'I wish we could have watched Sam squirm,' he laughed.

'Aren't you glad you never dated her now?' Ellie said as she tucked her feet under her on the sofa. 'That could have been you.'

'Awww, there was never any danger of Kasumi having me.' Jethro gave her a lopsided smile. Ellie thought she detected a hint of longing in it. 'It looks like I'm destined to be single forever.'

'I know that feeling,' Ellie said quietly.

He looked at her askance. 'Surely not, Ms Newton? Aren't the eligible men of Millrise queuing up for you?'

'They might be, but I seem to be having a bit of trouble locating the queue. Either that or I've accidentally come across the less-than-eligible line.'

'All men are eligible. It's just that no one has explained the rules of eligibility properly to us yet.'

'You sound like you should be on Oprah,' Ellie laughed.

'Maybe I should…' He waved a hand through the air in front of his face as if creating a headline. 'Men: The Insiders' Guide.'

Ellie sighed. 'Why do I have to want someone who doesn't want me?'

'Oh, Ellie. This Kelly guy must be a complete tool if he doesn't want you.'

Ellie smiled. 'Thanks. It's not true, but thank you for trying to make me feel better.' She put her coffee down and snuggled into him. She was tipsy, warmed by good food and drink and brilliant company, and his arms were a surprisingly nice place to be.

'What's all this?' he asked, sounding a little taken aback at her sudden intimacy.

'I don't know… you just seem like a good guy to cuddle up to right now.'

He gave her shoulder a squeeze.

They stayed like that for a moment or two, and then Jethro turned to look at her. He stroked his thumb down her cheek in a simple gesture and then, before either of them really knew what was happening, he leaned in and kissed her.

On paper, it could have been perfect. But Ellie felt not a flicker of desire or love other than something pure and platonic.

'That was just a joke… right?' she said, unable to keep the fear from her voice.

His smile was so obviously forced. 'Of course… It would be crazy, you and me…'

Oh God, Ellie thought. *This is the stupidest thing I've ever done. What am I, fifteen? I need a chaperone every time I'm left alone with a man not related to me?*

'I'm really tired,' Ellie mumbled. Would you mind if I go to bed?'

'Now?'

'Sorry. I think I might have had too much to drink; I feel a bit queasy.'

'Don't you want to finish your coffee first?'

Ellie shook her head and hurried through to the bedroom. She shut the door behind her and let out a huge breath as she leaned back against it. How could she have been such an idiot?

*

When she woke, Ellie wondered at what time during the night the Edinburgh military tattoo had moved into her head. She thought she had been what her mum would have called 'merry' the previous evening, but couldn't recall drinking all *that* much or, indeed, being *that* drunk. The way her head was pounding now, however, she must have done more damage than she thought.

She rolled over, for a moment disorientated as a strange bedroom came into view. Then she remembered that it was Jethro's room and not her own in Millrise. Her eyes roved her surroundings as she tried to pull herself together enough to sit up. His bedroom décor was surprisingly unimaginative for a man who worked in the world of media. It was painted a safe magnolia, wooden Venetian blinds at the window, with the odd framed monochrome photo hanging around the walls – stylish vistas of cities and sunsets over rivers – and a black ash wardrobe, the door of which hung open to reveal a clothes rail split into work suits at one end and hoodies, t-shirts and sweaters at the other. There were some clues that gave away the real Jethro: his drum kit crammed in a corner and a draughtsboard with a half-finished drawing, a tray of pencils and pens lying on top. The only other thing of note was a chest of drawers, the dusty surface cluttered with grooming products and electrical gadgets. It was a bedroom any teenage boy would have been proud of. Ellie sniffed at the sheets. At least he had washed those for her.

She pushed herself up, clutching at her head as it protested the change in position by giving her an extra big internal thump. It felt as though her brain and her skull were having a punch-up. Her clothes were in a tangle on the floor where she had discarded them the night before. Thank God Jethro had brought her bag in before they had left for the tapas bar, she mused as she picked up the dirty stuff with a grimace. She had fallen into bed with only her knickers on, it appeared, and the prospect of having to stay in her dirty ones whilst she hunted for spares wasn't an appealing one.

After pulling on some clean underwear, jeans and a soft, powder-blue slouchy sweatshirt, Ellie crept into the bathroom, splashed some water on her face and flicked a toothbrush around her mouth as she tried to piece together the previous night's events. Mortifyingly, she could remember *what* had happened, but couldn't quite understand her motives for any of it. What did come back to her, in startling and painful detail, was the fact that she had let Jethro kiss her. Whatever had happened, it was a bloody terrible idea. Why had she done it? The truth was in plain view but she looked away from its steely gaze. She had kissed him as a substitute for what she couldn't have.

Why wouldn't her stupid brain accept that any chance of a life with Ben was over? If it didn't see sense soon, she'd take over from her skull and beat it up herself. And why was accepting that Ben was out of her life a green light for ill-advised trysts with best friends?

Creeping into the living room, she heard the gentle breaths that signalled Jethro was still asleep on the sofa before she saw him, buried under his duvet, only the top of his head poking out. Ellie heaved a sigh of relief. She needed to wake up properly before she faced explanations. Leaving him, she padded into a kitchen the size of one of her cupboards at home to see if she could locate some coffee and aspirin.

As she searched, Jethro's voice made her jump. 'Morning.'

'God, you startled me!'

He mussed his hair and gave her a sleepy smile. 'Sorry. I heard you knocking around and wondered if you were OK.'

'You were fast asleep a minute ago.'

'Yeah. Let's just say you'd make a crap burglar.'

'Sorry. I was looking for some aspirin.'

'That, I can do.' He went to a drawer, produced a tiny white bottle and rattled it at her. 'I think I may need to join you.'

'I didn't think we'd had that much to drink.'

'Almost two bottles of wine, if I remember correctly,' he replied, handing her two tablets and a glass of water. 'Enough to make you feel like throwing up.' He narrowed his eyes as he swallowed his own. 'Were you ill after I'd gone to sleep?'

'Don't worry, I didn't chuck up over your sheets,' Ellie said.

'That's good, because being a bloke I don't have any others.'

They stood, staring at each other for a split second. Then both looked away at the same time, as if looking at each other somehow hurt. Both turned back again and tried to speak, awkward stuttering beginnings of clumsy excuses.

'You first,' Jethro said.

'No... what did you want to say?'

He shrugged. 'It wasn't that important.'

'Neither was mine.'

A heartbeat. And then they both began again. 'About last night –'
They both smiled awkwardly, explanations called to a halt.

'I know,' Jethro said. 'And it's really OK. This Ben guy has got to
you and I'm a bloke…' He gave a shrug and a sideways grin. 'One sniff
of a snog and we're there. I should be apologising, not you. We had
too much to drink. But we never tell Kasumi about this… Agreed?
She'd have a field day.'

Ellie nodded stiffly. But still she couldn't shake the fear that it was
just another thing she had managed to screw up in a long list of things
she was not supposed to be screwing up. It seemed that talking about
it now might just make things worse, though. Instead, Ellie filled the
kettle and switched it on. 'I'll make coffee, shall I?' she said with forced
brightness.

Jethro went over and clicked the kettle off again. 'Do you know
what always works for hangovers?'

'Raw eggs?'

'No,' he laughed, 'MacDonald's breakfasts. How about it?'

Ellie looked down at herself. 'I don't think you want to take me
out in public like this.'

'OK, so I'll go get some and bring it back. It's not far.'

'Sounds amazing.' Ellie smiled weakly as the guilt worm began to
nibble at her insides again.

Ten minutes later she was on the sofa, snuggled under Jethro's duvet
with the TV remote. She heard the sound of the front door slam as Jethro
went out on his quest for breakfast. With only the vaguest attention,
she scrolled through the channels and stopped at a Sunday magazine
programme that she liked for the chef who was a regular of the show.
He was on right now, demonstrating a recipe for beef stroganoff. Ellie

let the remote control fall onto the duvet and watched him handing out his food to a long table of guests. The camera panned along the row.

Then Ellie bolted up, her heart beating madly as it settled on two very familiar faces.

'What the hell...' Ellie grabbed the remote and turned the sound up.

'You like it?' the chef asked Ben with an inane grin. 'Would that be worth waiting on a street corner for?'

Ben gave a very forced smile. Ellie had never seen him look so uncomfortable. 'It's lovely,' he mumbled through a mouthful of rice. 'Although I'm a vegetarian, so I can't actually try the –'

Without waiting for the rest of Ben's sentence, the chef moved to Gemma. 'And you're the lovely lady he spent all those nights under the stars for...'

Gemma gave him a simpering smile and flicked her blonde tresses. 'I would never have gone off if Ben had been able to make food like this,' she replied breathily, doing what Ellie thought was a very bad Marilyn Monroe impersonation or a very good impression of someone with quite advanced emphysema. She leaned over to Ben and kissed him on the cheek. 'Only joking, honey.'

The chef burst into laughter. He turned to the camera with a cocky grin. 'You heard it here first: the way to a beautiful woman's heart is through her stomach. And if you'd like the recipe, you can find it on our website...'

The picture switched to a female presenter. 'Well, that certainly did look very appetising and our guests seemed to be enjoying it. We'll have more from Gemma Fox and Ben Kelly after the break.'

Hot tears stung Ellie's eyes. Was she destined to have them taunt her for the rest of her life? Was there nowhere she could go to stay away from them? Kasumi would have said she was being melodramatic but that was how it felt. Throwing back the duvet, she raced into Jethro's bedroom and began to fling her belongings into her overnight bag.

Just as she lugged the bag into the living room, Jethro came in laden with food. He stopped at the doorway and stared.

'What are you doing?'

Ellie was aware that her face was probably streaked with tears, her hair still a tangled mess and she looked like she was about to have a nervous breakdown. She certainly felt like she was.

'I've made a mess of everything and now I have to go home.'

'Hey, hey…' He pulled her into a hug. It was rather an inept hug, a bit like he was smothering a live hand grenade in the desperate hope he could keep the pin in, but a hug was a hug and right now, Ellie grasped the emotional lifeline with every ounce of strength she had.

'I'm so sorry,' she whimpered.

He pulled away to look at her. 'Is this about what happened with us last night? You've got nothing to be sorry about.'

'If I lose you on top of everything else, I really don't know what I'll do.'

'You do still want my body, don't you?'

Ellie laughed through her tears. 'Yes, but only for more hugs if it's all the same to you. I've had enough of romantic complications to last me a lifetime.' She rubbed her tears away and shook her head. 'Come on, I want to eat breakfast – that bag of junk food smells amazing.'

Chapter Twelve

By the time she emerged from her bedroom that Sunday evening, an inky dusk had fallen over the town outside her window. Ellie felt along her wall for the switch, the room flooding with light as she flicked it on. She screwed her eyes up against it. Her mouth was dry, her nose felt swollen and blocked, and her eyes weren't much better. She retrieved her phone from the floor and then stumbled into the kitchen for some more aspirin and a bottle of water from the fridge. Sitting at the kitchen table, she unscrewed the cap of her bottle as she opened the messages from earlier that day. Jethro's was brief, but full of heartfelt concern.

Hope you're ok. You know I'm only a phone call away if you need me.

Kasumi's was typical Kasumi.

WTF Ellie? Why did you bail on lunch? Jethro won't tell me. I need to know everything.

There was also a new one from Patrick.

Just remember, getting your stomach pumped in a London A&E for alcohol poisoning is not a legitimate reason to ring in sick, lol. Hope you had a good time, see you tomoz. x

Ellie let the phone fall to the table and rested her head on her folded arms. She had the most fantastic friends and family, who needed her as much as she needed them. If she was going to get her life back on track and not risk throwing these friendships away, then this obsession with Ben Kelly had to stop.

*

'I don't suppose you saw *Sunday Scullery* yesterday, being all cosmopolitan in London,' Ange said as Ellie came back into the office with her first coffee of the morning.

Ellie placed the cup on her desk and grimaced. 'As a matter of fact, I did catch some of it.' So far, after vowing that there would be no more nonsense, she had managed to keep it together as she recounted to Ange a carefully edited version of her weekend away. At least Vernon was busy at the civic hall again for the day, so that was one less pressure on her.

'So you saw our Millrise Lovebirds were on then?'

'Only the bit where they tasted the stroganoff.' Ellie really didn't want to know the rest, but had a sinking feeling that Ange was going to fill her in anyway.

'I'd love to know who they've got to do their PR because they came across like Posh and Becks.' Ange swung around on her chair and picked up her own mug.

Ellie couldn't help a small smile. Not trusting herself to reply appropriately, she turned to her computer screen to go through her emails. There was the usual assortment of requests for visits to local schools, the theatre, and an enquiry from someone whose dog could apparently howl *Rule Britannia* and wanted Ellie to go along and listen, along with administration tasks and staff bulletins. Then she opened one from a company called *Blue Pig Productions*.

Hi Ellie

I believe you are the journalist who was following the story of Ben Kelly and Gemma Fox recently. We're making a documentary about them and wondered whether we could interview you...

'Argh!' Ellie squealed. She couldn't even make it to the end of the message. She took a very deep breath and then announced to Ange that she needed to go out.

Ange gave Ellie a practical look. It was the sort of look that her mum gave when she thought Ellie was overreacting about something, although she'd never expected to see it on the face of her colleague. 'Ellie…' Ange said, 'go and get some air. Come back when you've calmed down and we'll sort whatever is bothering you.'

'I could do with some lunch anyway,' Ellie said with a sigh of resignation, realising that perhaps that practical sort of look was justified. 'I suppose I could go out to get it now and save a job later.'

'Don't come back until you're clear-headed and laden with outrageously calorific food.'

Ellie gave her a tight smile.

'Bring me back one of Stav's Cajun wrap specials, will you?'

'Yup.' Ellie pulled her coat from the stand. 'Anything else?'

'A cheerful colleague would be nice.'

Ellie turned at the office door. 'I can't guarantee that but I'll do my best.'

*

Ellie stood on the pavement outside the offices of the *Echo*. The weekend's sunshine had given way to a cold drizzle that seemed to drape over the streets like a damp blanket. Ange was right, as always; Ellie needed to be clear-headed and professional at all times no matter how she felt about things personally. A quick walk to The Bounty for her lunch in the cold air and she'd be better equipped to respond to the email from Blue Pig in a way that didn't make her sound like a bunny-boiling psychopath. Hoisting her bag onto her shoulder, she plunged her hands into her coat pockets just as her phone started to ring. Ellie took the call.

'Mum. I was thinking of coming over tonight.'

'I think you should go to see Hazel.' Her mum's voice had a desperation in it that made Ellie's stomach tighten. 'She's worse than I've ever seen her.'

Ellie chewed her lip, the fears her mother had planted the last time they had seen Hazel forcing their spiked thorns into her heart. 'Is there any word from the hospice about when she can be taken in?'

'Next couple of days, I think. When do you think you can get that time off to help finish packing?'

'I'll check with Vernon when I see him.'

'I don't think…' Miranda's breath hitched. 'I don't think she'll need to take all that much with her.'

Ellie's gut clenched a little tighter. 'Oh… she said…'

There was a stifled sob from the other end of the line.

'Mum… I'll be over as soon as I can.'

'No… no, it's OK. Come after work.'

'No way! I need to do something quickly for Ange, and then I'll call Vernon to let him know I'm going off for the rest of the day. Don't worry, he'll be OK about it and I can take the time as annual leave or something.'

'OK. Thank you,' Miranda said weakly.

'Mum…' Ellie paused. She knew her mum wasn't going to like her next suggestion, but it didn't seem right not to make it anyway. 'Don't you think you ought to let Dad be involved now? He's known Hazel for years and he thinks a lot of her.'

'He should have thought of that when he was defrauding me.'

'You make him sound like a criminal.'

'He is.'

Ellie sighed. She clearly had more chance of winning the Kentucky Derby without a horse than this argument with her mum. 'I think you're wrong about this,' she said in a low voice. 'But it's up to you. I just hope you don't come to regret it. Is Hazel happy that Dad hasn't been to see her?'

'Hazel understands how the whole affair has affected me.'

Unlike some… Ellie expected her mother to add, but she didn't. 'It's hard for me, Mum. How can you expect me to take sides between my parents?'

Miranda sniffed. 'Where are you, anyway? It sounds noisy.'

'I'm outside the offices. I was on my way to get lunch.'

'Right. Be careful, won't you?'

'Of course, Mum. Aren't I always?'

After a repeated promise to get there as soon as she could, Ellie ended the call. She barely had time to blink back the tears that had welled in her eyes when the display screen lit up again.

It was Kasumi. Ellie watched the caller ID flash for a while as she chewed her lip. She hadn't quite figured out what she was going to say to her friend, but Kasumi wasn't the sort of girl to let Ellie ignore her, even for the shortest time. Reluctantly, she took the call.

'Hey. How are you?'

'What happened at the weekend? Jethro says you were very weird.'

'Weird?' Ellie laughed awkwardly. 'I'm always weird, how is that out of the ordinary?'

'OK, weirder than normal.'

Ellie glanced up and down the street. Shoppers and workers were scurrying by, heads down against the rain that was now getting heavier. She stepped back against the wall of the building to get out of the way of the thoroughfare. 'What exactly did he tell you?'

'It wasn't what he told me, but what he left out that worries me.'

'We didn't sleep together, if that's what you're thinking,' Ellie said in a low voice.

There was a pause. 'So, what *did* you do? If that's the first denial that comes into your head then something along those lines happened.'

'We got drunk... and... he asked me not to tell you....'

'Funny, he says that he didn't think he could tell me either. What am I, suddenly, the spare wheel of this friendship?'

'God... no, Kas!'

'It feels like it. What about this Ben business?'

'Oh... so Jethro told you about that.'

'Of course. He was worried about you.' There was a static filled pause. 'So tell me why you freaked out on Sunday morning?'

'Kas... I don't know if I can understand it enough myself to explain it to anyone else right now.'

'Why don't you try?'

Ellie hesitated. Then she turned her collar up against the damp cold and started to walk, phone still clamped to her ear.

'It's not something I can talk about now. Something is happening with my aunt and I need to be there.'

'Shit... sorry, Ellie. I didn't realise...'

'It's OK. But you're right about one thing – I shouldn't have gone to stay with Jethro by myself when my head was in such a weird place. Did he sound OK?'

'You know Jethro. He's always OK.'

'You're not angry, are you?'

'No. But I don't like the idea that you feel you can't share things with me.'

'Kas, I…' Ellie's sentence trailed off as two figures ahead on the pavement caught her attention. 'Shit!'

'What now?' Kasumi asked.

'I think that's… oh, bollocks!' Ellie bowed her head and pulled her collar up as far as it would go. Veering off, she hurried to cross the road to avoid the couple walking in her direction, phone still clamped to her ear and Kasumi still talking, telling her something that got lost in the sound of revving engines and traffic hissing through the rain.

Ellie never even saw the car coming.

Chapter Thirteen

She was aware of pain in her chest and feeling like someone very large was sitting on it. As she struggled to pull air in, concerned and horrified faces appeared above her.

'She just ran out,' a woman wailed. 'I braked straight away but I couldn't stop.'

Someone else put an arm around the woman to comfort her. Ellie wanted to tell the driver that it wasn't her fault but no words would come out. She turned her head slowly to see her phone in pieces on the road, a few feet away. The sight filled her with a strange sense of panic that was greater than knowing she had just been hit by a car. If Ange had been there and was, by some extraordinary quirk of fate, suddenly blessed with the power of reading Ellie's mind, she'd have delivered some lecture about priorities and how Ellie just didn't seem to be able to grasp the concept. As these thoughts whizzed through her mind and the pain in her chest worsened, Ellie wondered vaguely if she was going to die and these strange musings were her own bizarre version of her life flashing before her. That would be about right for her. And she hoped she wasn't going to die; she had promised her mum she would be right over and Miranda would be really pissed off about being stood up.

'Someone get an ambulance,' a man's voice shouted.

Yeah, that might be an idea.

As another man made the call, the crowd around Ellie seemed to grow. But then two new faces pushed through, possibly the last two faces she wanted to see.

'Oh my God!' Gemma squeaked. To her credit, thought Ellie, she did look suitably horrified. If she was putting it on she was one amazing actress.

'Ellie!' Ben called in a choked voice. 'Oh, shit, Ellie!' He dropped to his knees, ripped off his jacket and laid it over her. 'Give me your coat,' he ordered Gemma.

Gemma stared at him. If she had looked horrified at the events unfolding in front of her, she looked appalled beyond belief at this new request. 'My coat?'

'She'll be in shock. She has to be as warm as possible.'

Gemma glanced around as others in the crowd stared at her. She sighed and was just about to comply when someone else handed Ben a duffle coat. He gave the woman a grateful smile.

'Brilliant, thanks.'

'Yeah, thanks,' Gemma huffed, her expression somewhere between mortification that she had managed to make herself look monumentally selfish in front of an audience, and relief that she got to keep her designer coat on after all.

Ben added the new coat to his own. He glanced around and saw Ellie's bag – the contents spread across the road – and her phone a few feet away.

'I'll just go and get your stuff,' he said to Ellie gently, nodding a head at her belongings. 'Gemma will stay with you, OK?'

'No…' Ellie gasped, just managing to find enough breath as the pressure on her chest worsened. 'Stay…' She could feel tears squeeze from the corners of her eyes, running a trail down her cheeks and neck until they joined the rain on the tarmac. She didn't know why she was crying. Was this what shock – real actual medical shock – was like?

'Don't try to talk,' Ben said, looking as though he was trying not to weep himself. He turned to the man who had called for the ambulance. 'How long did they say they'd be?'

'They didn't say. But the City General isn't that far – shouldn't be more than ten minutes.'

Ben put his lips to Ellie's forehead and kissed her lightly. 'Hold on,' he whispered. 'Hold on for me.'

Gemma seemed to hover, torn by indecision. The merest flicker of a sour look crossed her face as Ben kissed Ellie. But then she glanced back at the contents of the handbag strewn across the road. After a moment's hesitation, she went to collect them.

Ben looked around as two new voices joined the confusion. Ange and Rosie were racing across to them.

'What's happened?' Rosie shouted.

Their faces appeared above Ellie with everyone else's. Ellie tried to smile reassuringly but couldn't make it happen. By now, along with the pain and shock, she was feeling quite a nuisance.

'She just ran out in front of me!' The driver now sobbed uncontrollably. Ellie really did feel sorry for her. When all this was over, assuming she wasn't dying, she would have to make sure she sent her some flowers for putting her through such an ordeal. And if she *was* dying, perhaps someone could hand her paper and a pen so she could manage to write some sort of last floral request out in a shaky hand before she shuffled off.

'Has someone called the ambulance?' Ange snapped as she knelt down next to Ellie.

Ben nodded and dragged his sleeve across his eyes. 'On its way.'

Ange laid a hand on his arm and gave it a little squeeze. She turned to Ellie.

'You're going to be OK, so don't you get any ideas about having a sneaky holiday off work.'

Ellie tried to give the tiniest of nods. Her breath was coming shorter and sharper now. She wondered if someone actually *was* sitting on her chest.

Gemma appeared again and handed Ellie's bag to Ange. 'Her things,' she said quietly.

In the background, someone said the ambulance had arrived. Everything moved so fast after that. Later, when she looked back on that day, Ellie would hardly be able to remember any of it. The one thing she would always remember, with absolute clarity, was the last thing she saw before the ambulance doors closed and the sirens began: Ben, staring as if the stars had fallen from his sky as he watched her go.

*

'At least I wasn't on my phone and driving at the same time. You'd have been doing one amazing *I told you so* dance if I had been.'

'It's not funny, Ellie,' Miranda said, looking appalled at the lack of appropriate solemnity in her daughter's demeanour. 'You could have been killed. You should be banned from owning a mobile phone.'

'Then you'd complain I don't call you enough.' Ellie winced slightly as she pushed herself up. The hospital bed wasn't too bad – as beds that resembled medieval instruments of torture went – but she still struggled to be comfortable for long in any position.

'I hope this has taught you an important lesson,' Miranda replied, ignoring Ellie's jibe.

'It's taught me to send Ange out on the butty run next time.'

Her mother tutted and set about pouring a glass of water, which she didn't hand to Ellie, but proceeded to arrange alongside the grapes and chocolates on the side cabinet in some kind of bizarre hospital based feng-shui.

'Mum…' Ellie said gently. 'I'm OK. A couple of broken ribs and a bit of fluid they took off my lungs. That's nothing compared to some of the poor buggers in here.'

'It could have been worse,' Miranda sniffed.

'But it wasn't. If it makes you happy, you can be certain that I'll be more careful crossing roads from now on.'

'Honestly, anyone would think you were five.' Her mother sighed and reached for Ellie's hand. 'What am I going to do with you?'

'I don't know. I'd shrug in reply like they do in books but it hurts too much.'

'Kasumi phoned to ask how you are. She feels terrible about what happened.'

'It wasn't her fault. I just wasn't looking where I was going. I feel sorry for the poor woman who hit me. I need to send her a card or something.'

Miranda gave a sour look. 'That driver should be begging your forgiveness, not the other way around. Some people shouldn't be allowed behind the wheel of a car.'

'She came to A&E, apparently, when I was still being treated, to ask about me. So I think she was very sorry. You can't blame her.' Ellie reached over gingerly and plucked a grape from the bunch. 'So, what else did Kasumi say?'

'She's going to come up. As soon as she can get a day off work.'

'She doesn't need to do that.'

'She wants to. She was worried to death. One minute you were talking to her, the next she hears a great thump and the line goes dead.' Miranda shivered rather theatrically. 'It must have been dreadful.'

'Still, she knows everything is alright now…'

'She's bound to want to see for herself.' Miranda paused for a moment. Her gaze was drawn to the window where dusk was settling over the grounds outside, seemingly tussling with some inner dilemma. 'Who else has been to visit?' she asked finally.

'Dad won't be coming tonight, if that's what you're worried about.'

'*I've* been here since you were brought in and he hasn't turned up apart from an hour of ineffectual flapping in A&E last night,' Miranda huffed. 'Doesn't he care that his only daughter almost died yesterday?'

'I didn't almost die. And you being here all day *is* the reason he hasn't come. The nurse came in earlier and gave me a message to say he'd been to reception, asked if you were here, and then said he'd come back another time.'

Miranda raised her eyebrows. 'When was this?'

'When you went to get coffee earlier this afternoon.'

'Ridiculous. What is he, a man or a mouse?'

'A peacekeeper,' Ellie said with a wry smile. 'He obviously didn't want to cause any more stress for me than I'd already had and he knew walking in with you here would do that. He'll come tomorrow, I'm sure.'

Miranda looked at her watch. 'I should check on Hazel before I head home tonight. But I don't like leaving you like this.'

Ellie nodded. 'You can see that I'm fine now. You've been here all day and Hazel needs you far more than I do. How is she?'

'Not good. I haven't been able to spend much time with her, for obvious reasons, but I have been in contact with her nurse and they've stepped up the home visits until we can get her moved into the hospice. I don't like it but there isn't much else we can do in the circumstances.'

'Sorry…' Ellie replied, not for the first time that day feeling like a huge burden on everyone.

Miranda rose from her chair. She smoothed Ellie's bed sheets, moved the glass of water an inch closer to her daughter's grasp and kissed her on the forehead. 'Are you sure you'll be alright?'

'Of course,' Ellie said. 'If I'm not alright in here then I'll never be alright anywhere.'

'I'll be here first thing tomorrow.'

'With a bit of luck, you'll get to take me home.'

'I don't want you rushing to be discharged.'

'I'm not going to take up a bed that someone needs more, Mum. I'm sure the doctors know what they're doing. If they say I can go then I'll go.'

Miranda started walking towards the door. 'Get them to give you some more painkillers, you'll never get a wink of sleep otherwise.'

'Mum, I'm fine!'

Miranda began to say something else, but then stopped as a figure appeared at the door. 'Oh.' Her voice hardened. 'It's you. I thought you weren't coming tonight.'

'I'm sorry,' Frank said, looking in confusion from Miranda to Ellie and back again. 'They told me on the phone you'd left.'

'Dad, you are allowed to come when you like, you know,' Ellie replied, looking at her mum pointedly.

'It's just….' he began, but then shut his mouth again.

'Come and sit down. Mum has to go anyway and I need someone to help me while away the hours until bedtime.'

Miranda scowled at his back as he sidled over to the recently vacated chair. She waited at the door as he sat down. Ellie smiled at him and then looked up at her mum.

'You could always come and sit with both of us for ten minutes,' she said sweetly.

Frank's gaze was almost hopeful as Miranda hovered at the door. Then she blew out an irritated breath. 'I'll see you tomorrow, Ellie,' she said as she left them alone.

Ellie waited until Miranda was out of earshot. 'I think she's breaking,' she said when she was certain her mum had gone. 'I definitely saw a twitch of forgiveness in one of her eyelids.'

Frank smiled sadly. 'I don't think so,' he replied. 'Anyway, that's not important now. How are you? I can't believe my little girl has ended up in such a mess.'

'Cheers, Dad. You know how to make your little girl feel better.'

'I didn't mean that. Does it hurt? How on earth did it happen?'

'I had an argument with a car. You'd think I'd know by the age of twenty-seven that cars always win.'

Frank produced a vast handkerchief and blew loudly before giving her a watery smile. 'You are the most precious thing in the world to me. I couldn't bear to lose you.'

'It's lucky that I'm not going anywhere then, isn't it?'

'I bet you've had so many visitors today,' Frank said, shaking himself to a forced cheeriness.

'A few. Patrick came, of course. He ate half my biscuits and mesmerised all the nurses with his silver-fox charm.' Ellie laughed. 'Mum was impressed, as you can imagine. Ange popped in for an hour too. And, of course, Mum has been here as much as she could, though she had to go to Hazel too. I think she's well and truly frazzled now.'

'Sorry.'

'What for?'

'I should have been here.'

'You're here now, that's all I care about. I know how awkward things are.' Ellie's mind wandered, momentarily, to another man who had not visited that day. She hadn't expected him to, of course, but… When she came back to her senses, Frank was brooding on the rapidly gathering darkness outside.

'How did our family get in such a state?' he asked quietly, his eyes still trained on the window.

'Every family has their ups and downs. We'll get through it.'

He looked at her. 'Do you think so? Because right now it doesn't feel like that at all.'

'I know so, Dad. Mum will come round, I'm sure of it.'

'I wish I could be that confident. I'm losing hope every day faster than I'm losing my hair.'

Ellie leaned forward, but then checked herself as she winced. Moving with more care this time, she reached for her dad's hand. 'When she comes tomorrow, I'll talk to her again. Maybe she'll be more receptive this time.'

He looked up at her with a small smile. 'If anyone can talk her round it's you.'

Ellie's laugh turned into a cough. When she'd caught her breath again she leaned back on her pillow and stared up at the ceiling. 'Oh, Dad. If only I could have your faith in me for myself. I'm afraid the one thing I don't do right now is talk any sense.'

'I know I haven't been the best dad lately,' Frank began carefully, 'but if there's anything you ever want to confide in me…'

'I know. And you're totally forgiven for being a rubbish dad.'

It was his turn to laugh. 'Thanks for that vote of confidence.'

'Well, you did say it first.'

'I did, didn't I? In that case you're forgiven for being a clumsy daughter who almost got herself killed yesterday.'

Ellie looked back at him. '*In that case* we'll call it quits.'

*

The last time Ellie had stayed overnight in a hospital before this admission she had been wearing a romper suit and sucking on bottled milk. The noise and activity, even during the small hours of the morning, came as a complete surprise to her this time around. It didn't do much to help her sleep, either. Not that she needed noise and activity to keep her awake – the internal replaying of events on the road outside the *Echo* offices were doing a great job of that by themselves. Her recollections were hazy, to say the least, but better than they had been the previous evening when she had still been woozy from anaesthetic and painkillers. One feature of the event stood out through everything. Ben had seemed so tender, so worried, so absolutely invested in her survival. Had she imagined his look of distress as she lay there? He was bound to be distressed, she kept telling herself – after all, he had just witnessed a car knock down someone he knew. But Ellie couldn't help seeing more than that in it.

She couldn't remember falling asleep, but when the tea trolley came clanging into her room she woke with a start. It seemed a bit unnecessary to come and wake someone with tea that they didn't particularly want rather than let them sleep on, but Ellie tried to smile with as much gratitude as she could muster as the cup was deposited on her bedside cabinet.

A little later breakfast came, much in the same fashion, and Ellie did her best to pick from the stoneware plate, even though she wasn't really hungry. Once she had shuffled with surprising pain to the shower room and cleaned up, she was exhausted, but at least she felt better for being fresher. For what seemed like the hundredth time that morning, she thought about checking her phone for messages or emails, before remembering that her phone was now in pieces at the bottom of her handbag. Her mum wouldn't turn up for about an hour, so, with nothing better to do, she climbed back into bed and dozed for a while.

A little later, she was woken by a nurse who had come to administer her medications.

'Fantastic,' Ellie said with a slight smile. 'Drugs are my friend right now.'

'They certainly make hospital more bearable,' the nurse replied, plumping Ellie's pillows as Ellie took her tablets.

'They do,' Ellie agreed. 'It's just a shame they can't give you anything more fun.'

There was a tap at the door and a second nurse put her head round it.

'You're decent?' she smiled.

'I don't know who started that rumour but I refute it,' Ellie said.

'You seem brighter than yesterday,' she laughed.

'I am.'

The woman disappeared from the room, to reappear a few seconds later with an enormous bouquet of white and pink roses, delicate white carnations and lush greenery.

'These were just delivered for you.'

'They're amazing,' Ellie said. 'I have no idea who could have sent them, though.'

'Colleagues, perhaps?' the nurse asked as she produced a glass vase from the side cabinet and filled it with water from a sink across the room.

'Probably.'

'Well, your suspense needn't last, as there's a card here.' The nurse handed a small envelope to Ellie, who ripped it open.

Her breath caught in her throat as she read it.

To Ellie

I hope you make a quick recovery. I owe you a half bottle of whisky — remember? We can't drink it while you're in hospital.

Ben. X

'Ooooh, secret admirer?' the first nurse asked Ellie with a wink to her colleague. 'It is Valentine's day, after all.'

'No, just a friend,' Ellie said, realising the date had completely passed her by. She stowed the card back in the envelope, gripping it as she gazed at the floral gift. 'Just someone I helped once.'

'Must have been some favour.' The nurse moved aside Ellie's other gifts and placed the vase on the side cabinet. The sweet, fresh fragrance of roses immediately filled Ellie's head.

'I'm sure everyone gets flowers in hospital,' Ellie replied vaguely, only half with the conversation.

'You'd be surprised,' the nurse laughed. 'Some poor things can go days without visitors, let alone flowers.' She swept from the room, leaving Ellie still gazing at the vase and its contents.

'I'll leave you in peace too,' the first nurse smiled. 'Get some rest. It'll be visiting hours soon and the place will sound like a bunch of chimps having a hoedown.'

Ordinarily, Ellie would have giggled at the nurse's humorous simile. But it had hardly registered. She turned and nodded slightly as the other nurse left and the room was almost silent again, save for the footsteps, bleeps, clangs and voices in neighbouring rooms and distant corridors.

*

Ellie had plenty of time before visiting hours to think about what the surprise bouquet might mean, or not mean. Just as she thought she had got her head around it, and that nothing else could surprise her, the door of her room swung open. Gemma sashayed in, a cloud of perfume and pure sex appeal in her wake. Ellie bolted up, grimacing as pain shot through her chest. She had no reaction for this new development but to stare with a silent and rather gormless expression at Gemma's entrance.

Had she come to make peace? Had she come to gloat? Or perhaps she did have a heart after all and was genuinely concerned for Ellie's welfare. Judging by the immaculate grooming and the fact that Gemma's outfit had obviously been chosen with great care for maximum effect, she had either been up half the night getting ready, or had a crack team of personal stylists hidden in the under-stairs cupboard at home. Ellie, sitting in bed, scrubbed of make-up and hair still damp from her early morning shower, couldn't have felt any less worthy as a specimen of womanhood if she had tried.

'I hope you don't mind,' Gemma purred, 'I asked at the desk and they said you were awake and up to visitors.'

Ellie's mind raced. The nursing team must have asked Gemma who she was before letting her in, surely? What had she told them? And Ellie's mum would be due at any moment too. It was lucky that Ellie hadn't told her the full story of what had gone on between her and Gemma, or Gemma might have found herself in the next bed with handbag induced injuries.

Gemma's gaze flicked, momentarily, to the lavish bouquet by Ellie's bed. She made no comment on it. 'Ben and I were horrified when we saw what happened to you. We were on our way to do a Valentine's special feature at your offices and... well, we couldn't concentrate on it after that. It took lots of coffee for us to be able to talk to the feature writer. I even smoked a cigarette and I haven't done that in months.'

Ellie paused, wondering who had done the Valentine's story and why she hadn't heard about it. Did people at the *Echo* know more about her feelings for Ben than they were letting on? Was that the reason she hadn't been informed? She had confided in no one and, apart from Patrick and Ange making astute guesses (but even they didn't know the true extent), nobody else knew. Was her inner turmoil so obvious to others that they didn't need to be told? Did that mean follow ups had been done covertly? But they must have known she would see the article at some point.

She shook herself. She was obviously overreacting and it was a genuine case of departments not communicating fully with each other. It wouldn't be the first time – she often recalled ruefully the occasion when, as a new employee at the *Echo*, she was reporting on allegations of fraud directed at a local double glazing company owner as the advertising features department were writing a glowing report of his stratospheric business prowess. The two articles were due to go to print the same day but luckily the mistake had been picked up hours before the paper went to press. It was Ellie's piece that had been removed at the eleventh hour, and Ellie was quite certain that the decision had a lot to do with advertising revenues. It was a harsh introduction to the business, but one she had never forgotten.

'Well...' Ellie painted on a smile. 'I'm glad that you recovered enough to go ahead in the end.'

'The photos were lovely. I asked for some copies for the wall of our flat. The piece is in tonight's paper. I'm sure you'll see it.'

Ellie made a mental note to take great care *not* to see it. For the first time in her career, she vowed not to read that day's edition of her beloved newspaper.

'How are you feeling?' Gemma flicked her hair back and took a seat by the bed.

'Not too bad,' Ellie replied carefully. The question of why Gemma had come still plagued her. Ellie wished Gemma would just get it off her chest. The sooner it was aired, the sooner she could leave. 'My mum should be here soon and I should be cleared to go home later today,' she added, hoping that the information would hurry Gemma along.

'That's great.' Gemma paused. 'I bet you're wondering why I've come.'

Hallelujah! Ellie didn't reply but gave a tight smile. It was the best she could manage and she hoped it would be enough encouragement for Gemma to reveal whatever had brought her there.

'I wanted to thank you properly,' Gemma began. 'I know we've had our differences in the past, but that's all history now, right?'

Ellie gave a brief nod.

'But your help has brought me and Ben back together. That's got to be the most amazing thing that anyone could have done for us. Ben, especially, is *so* grateful…' Gemma paused, letting the emphasis of that last statement sink in. 'Bless him, he really does love me to bits and without you doing your part to help him find me again he would have had to try and mend his shattered heart with someone who would always be second best…' There was another pause while she fixed Ellie with a look that was so subtle but significant that Ellie could not fail to recognise the thinly veiled triumph. 'You know what I mean?' She smiled sweetly. Ellie wasn't fooled for a moment. She knew exactly what Gemma meant.

'I'm glad I could help,' Ellie replied stiffly. Was that it? Could Gemma now please clear off?

'Of course,' Gemma added, seemingly oblivious to the insincerity in Ellie's reply. 'You'll be the guest of honour at our wedding... After all, you made it happen.'

Ellie stared. As much as she had tried to hide her real feelings, for an instant every emotion was plainly displayed on her face. *Wedding?* They were really going to get married? Marriage was sacred, an incredible commitment that needed effort and selflessness; it was for life. Ellie had watched too many people she loved suffer from the after-effects of ill-advised matches. Why would they get married? Unless they really did love each other and Ellie was just seeing some skewed version of reality, entirely coloured by her own personal feelings and desires. Sensing Gemma watching for her reaction, she quickly gathered her wits again.

'Congratulations,' she managed to force out.

'Thank you,' Gemma said. 'He proposed to me this morning in bed. Brought a tray in first thing with a heart shaped piece of toast on it, a glass of champagne and an envelope containing a diamond ring.'

Ellie's gaze involuntarily flitted to Gemma's left hand.

'Oh,' Gemma gave an affected laugh, seeing the reaction. 'It's too big, of course.' She held up her hand to study it. 'Most rings are, because my fingers are so slender. I have to get it altered before I can wear it.'

Ellie fought the lump rising in her throat. She glanced at the flowers and then back at Gemma. What was wrong with this boy? He'd sent her flowers, along with a note with an unmistakably romantic subtext, on the same morning he'd proposed to someone else. She should have seen the signs that Ben was a fruitcake the moment she came across him camped out on the corner of Constance Street. What on earth said *emotional stability* about that behaviour? It had to call into question

Ellie's own judgement that she had even considered a relationship with him. She thought all this, and she was certain that she was right. So why did it feel as though Gemma had just taken a mallet to her heart? She gave a jerky nod.

'That's marvellous news... really marvellous...' The words almost ground out of her mouth. 'I expect someone from the *Echo* will attend to report on the day, even if I'm not available myself.'

'Oh, no,' Gemma gushed with an earnestness that made Ellie suddenly want to throw up. 'I insist it's you. You're our little good luck cupid.'

Ellie was silent for a moment. Her gaze wandered to the window. The room was high up and sky was all she could see, but the clouds that scudded across her view were heavy again with the promise of more rain. 'I hope you won't think I'm rude if I say that I'm exhausted and I could do with a rest. And my mum is due to visit soon too.'

Gemma rose gracefully from her chair and swung her jacket on. She gave Ellie a beatific smile that belied what Ellie had guessed was her true intent. She had come with this news, virtually straight from her early morning love-in with Ben. Ellie wondered if she had been the first person Gemma had run to with it, even before her own parents. The idea seemed a likely one. But the motive wasn't a desire to share her happiness with the person who had played an instrumental part in making it happen – the real reason was far less pure. Ellie could feel guilty all she wanted about the conclusion she had come to, even about the way she had dreamt of them splitting up so that Ben would be single and available to date without remorse, but no matter how she weighed it up, the unsavoury conclusion was the only one that made sense. It was gamesmanship, nothing more, nothing less. And Gemma had just scored the winning point.

'I'll send your invite to the *Echo* offices, shall I?' she called behind her as she headed for the door, shaking her glorious hair free from the confines of her jacket collar. There was no immediate reply, and Gemma didn't bother waiting for one.

*

Ellie eased herself down the pillow. Gemma had left an hour ago, the nurse on duty popping her head in shortly afterwards to announce that she had never seen Ellie's 'sister' leave. The lie had prompted a bitter smile from Ellie. She had to hand it to Gemma, she was a devious little bitch, but it got results. For the entire hour since, Ellie had been alone with her tumultuous thoughts about Ben and his unreliability. She had to conclude that he was just like every other man, and that she should learn to steer clear of them all. These thoughts were interspersed with vague musings about why her mum was so late. Visiting hours were almost over, and Miranda had been told that she didn't need to adhere to them anyway, being next of kin. She also knew that she had to be on standby to accompany Ellie home in a taxi if she was discharged that day. So where was she? Had something happened to Hazel? The door to her room had remained open since Gemma's departure, so that Ellie could easily see along the corridor, straight to the front desk of the ward. People came and went, but nobody for Ellie. She was beginning to feel something between abandonment and all-consuming worry and she didn't like it at all.

As she lay propped up on her pillows, brooding on all this, she noticed a familiar figure approach the main desk on the ward outside. Her stomach tightened. What the hell was he doing here? To tell her about the wedding too? Perhaps she had been mistaken over the signals the flowers sent. Perhaps they were just a get-well wish. By now Ellie was so mixed-up she didn't think it was wise to open her mouth to anyone at all – there was no telling what might come out.

Ben glanced down the corridor as he spoke to the nurse at the desk. Ellie turned away as he caught her eye, wishing desperately that the door to her room had been closed. Now he knew exactly where she was and that she was awake. He must have also seen the flowers displayed on the cabinet next to her bed. If she had possessed the strength at that moment, she would have hurled the damn things at him – vase, water and all.

'Ellie, are you awake?' the nurse asked as she hovered at the door.

Ellie turned her head, fighting back the tears that squeezed her throat. 'I don't feel so good.'

'You have a visitor…'

'I know. I'm too ill to see him.'

The nurse frowned. 'You want me to turn him away?'

'Yes. Visiting hours are almost over anyway, aren't they?'

'Yes, but –'

'There's no point in him coming in to see me then.'

'You want me to tell him to come back later?'

Ellie turned away again. She couldn't trust her expression not to betray the violent emotions bubbling inside her right now. The sight of Ben made her angry beyond reason and desperate with longing all at the same time. She couldn't decide whether she wanted to bury herself in his embrace or punch him in the head.

'Ellie… it's up to you…'

'No,' Ellie replied in a low voice that she fought to keep level. 'I don't want him to come later.'

As she turned back, she could see that Ben was already making his way down the corridor towards her room. He couldn't have been more than a few feet away. He shot her a puzzled glance, one that changed to obvious hurt as the nurse tactfully reworded Ellie's request.

'It's alright,' he said. 'I heard what she said.'

*

The duty consultant's ward round had arrived at Ellie's bedside sometime around midday with the conclusion that he wasn't quite happy enough with her progress to allow her to be discharged but hoped that the following day would be the one.

'Looks like it's Valentine's dinner with us then,' the nurse had quipped.

Ellie tried to return a smile, but it got stuck somewhere on its way to her face.

Not only had Gemma and Ben managed to completely destroy her life in ten traumatic minutes but now she was seriously worried about her mum's non-appearance. Ellie had tried to call the house on a borrowed mobile phone but there was no reply. There was no reply from her dad or Hazel either, and no message left with the ward staff.

Ellie had been ready to ask again when her dad tumbled into the room, breathless and dishevelled, stress etched into every line of his face. Ellie pushed herself up rather too quickly, wincing as her battered body protested.

'What's the matter?' she asked.

Frank gave her a pained stare, in his obviously distressed state all subtlety and tact forsaken. 'It's your aunt Hazel. She died this morning.'

Chapter Fourteen

'What?' Ellie repeated.

'Hazel is dead.'

Ellie shook her head. 'I heard you. I just...'

'It's hard to take in, isn't it?' He dropped into the seat by her bed and wiped a hand across his clammy forehead. 'Your mum says she was with her last night after she left you here and although she was very ill, of course, she didn't seem like she was about to fall off her perch or anything.'

Ellie ignored his unfortunate turn of phrase; she was used to her dad putting his foot in it. 'You've seen Mum?'

'I've been with her most of the day. She planned to see Hazel first thing and then come to see you. But when she let herself into Hazel's house, Hazel was already.... well, it didn't look as though she had lasted the night.'

Ellie's mind flitted back to the last time she had seen Hazel. What had they talked about? Stuff that hadn't mattered; stupid, pointless conversations to have been the last they would share. She should have treated every visit to her aunt as though it might have been her last, but somehow it hadn't seemed possible that there wouldn't be a next time. Now, there were things unsaid that could never be said.

'Are you alright, love?' Frank asked.

Ellie refocused on him. 'Sorry... it's just...'

'I know.' Frank placed his hand over hers.

Ellie had wanted to cry all day but had fought the tears back. Now, presented with something that was worth crying over, she felt only an overwhelming numbness. She stared at the window. Then she turned to her dad. Drops of water still clung to his woollen coat.

'It's raining?' she asked vaguely, not knowing what else to say.

'Ellie...' He frowned. 'Are you alright?'

She shook herself. 'Yes. Is Mum OK?'

'There's no point in lying; she's been better. I left her on the sofa asleep at her place. She had a terrible migraine from crying all day; blames herself for not being there in Hazel's last moments. She wanted to come and see you too but I said I would come. I thought it would be better for me to tell you about Hazel while your mum was in such a state.'

Ellie nodded slightly. 'Thanks, Dad.'

'Are you coming out today?' Frank asked. 'Your mum said you might be. You should stop with one of us for a few days if you are, especially now.'

Ellie wished dearly that she could go to her mum right now. Miranda would need some comfort in the days ahead. 'They won't discharge me today, but maybe tomorrow. I'll stay at Mum's.'

'You'll be good for each other,' he agreed.

'It's good that you were there for her, though.'

'It's at times like these when you realise what's important.' He patted her hand. 'It's just a shame that it took something so sad for your mum to see it. But if I can't be around for my wife in her darkest hours, no matter what has gone on before, then what kind of man would I be?'

'You'll always be the perfect man to me.'

He smiled slightly. 'I don't think your mum would agree.'

'What's going to happen now?'

'About Hazel?'

Ellie nodded.

'I'm not entirely sure,' he said, a frown furrowing his brow. 'We've never lost anyone in this way before. Hopefully there won't have to be a post-mortem and we can set everything in order quite quickly. She left very precise instructions for your mum for when the time came, so at least we have all her last wishes written down and the whereabouts of her will.'

'She wanted one of those forest burials – she told me that once.'

'I believe so. Your mum mentioned it. I think Hazel arranged it all too, bless her, when she knew the end was coming, so that's a big weight from your mum's shoulders.'

'She was alone when it happened,' Ellie murmured. 'Somebody should have been there. If I hadn't been stuck in here, maybe me or Mum would have been.'

Frank stood and curled an arm around his daughter. 'You can't think like that; that's what I keep telling your mum. At least she was at home.'

Ellie let her head fall onto his chest. It was a long time since he had held her like this. She suddenly felt twelve again, secure in the knowledge that whatever else happened in life, her daddy would always keep her safe. They stayed that way, and Ellie lost track of the minutes as she savoured the feeling. Right now, it was a place she could gladly get lost in. In two days, fate had thrown a lifetime of challenges at her. A tiny island of calm, safe in her father's arms, was the best she could hope for, and she clung to it like a shipwrecked child clinging to driftwood.

Eventually, his voice broke in on her thoughts, resonating through his chest as her ear lay against it.

'Your mum says you were fretting about not having a phone yesterday.'

She pulled away to look at him. 'It doesn't seem very important now, does it?'

'Maybe. But I could pick up a new one if you like. What model do you want?'

'It's very sweet of you, but it's OK. I'll get one when I'm out of hospital.'

'It's no bother. I bet it's driving you mad not being contactable.'

'I'm stuck in hospital. I'm fairly contactable for anyone who wants to find me,' Ellie replied. It seemed, if the evidence of the morning was anything to go by, that she had been a bit *too* contactable.

He frowned slightly.

'Sorry, Dad. I didn't mean that to come out the way it did. I can manage without a phone for a little longer.'

He kissed her on the forehead. 'I want to get one. Consider it my treat for the way you've stuck by me, even though I've been a complete pain in the neck. Besides, your mum will feel better if she can get hold of you easily over the next few days.'

Ellie sighed. 'Alright. I'll let you get one but I'm paying you back when I'm home.'

He smiled. 'We'll see about that.'

*

As soon as her dad had left (at Ellie's insistence that her mum needed him far more than she did) the tears that wouldn't come in his presence suddenly surged forwards in a tidal wave of emotion. And once Ellie started to cry she couldn't stop. She had never felt so completely undone as she did at that moment. But as the tears stuttered out and quiet exhaustion took their place, one sliver of light shone out from the darkness. The first person her mum had turned to in her hour of need was her dad. He'd said they spent most of the day together. Perhaps they were on their way to reconciliation after all.

The evening brought Patrick, and Ellie wept again as she recounted the day's events. And although she had vowed not to tell anyone else her feelings for Ben, the sheer weight of emotion forced the admission to tumble from her lips and the whole tale came out.

When she had finished, Patrick stood and inspected the flowers and Ben's note. 'As far as getting a date is concerned, sending the woman in question flowers whilst simultaneously getting engaged to someone else isn't the most conventional route.'

Ellie gave him a watery smile. 'It doesn't matter. Gemma is back now and he's all loved up. Do you think our suspicions about her are unreasonable?'

Patrick blew out a long breath. 'I've a feeling they're more than reasonable. From what I've heard, she's ringing around every radio station, newspaper, and TV show she can think of. Let's face it, he's become a ticket to fame and money.'

'Then I feel even more stupid for being so obsessed with him,' Ellie said miserably. 'How can he not see her for what she really is? And why am I dumb enough to fancy a man who can't see her for what she is?'

'You know what they say about love and its relationship with visual impairment. Though I think you'll find there's more to it than first appearances.'

'What do you mean?'

'When you see him doing his little TV stunts, he doesn't seem like a man whose garden is entirely rosy. I'd say he was a man who'd discovered the rose bushes were full of thorns and greenfly.'

Ellie looked at Patrick thoughtfully. 'Do you really believe that?'

He nodded. 'She's clearly not the girl he thought she was. Or maybe she once was but has had her head turned by the media attention.'

'But what about the whole street corner thing? He was so desperate to win her back.'

'People can change. I'm sure that nothing alters a man quite like sitting on a freezing street corner day and night waiting for someone who returns but, it turns out, for the wrong reasons. Not to mention that the alternative is a hot newspaper reporter.'

'Don't be ridiculous.'

'I'm not the one getting themselves knocked down by a car just to stay out of his way because it hurts so much to see him.'

'OK, you're being facetious now.'

Patrick flashed a lopsided grin.

'He loves Gemma,' Ellie concluded miserably.

'I'm not so sure. Tell him how you feel. I think you'll be surprised by the outcome. What have you got to lose? At worst he'll refuse you and you'll never have to see him again.'

'He's asked her to marry him!'

Patrick shook his head slowly. 'Yeah. Buggered if I know the answer to that. We're a funny breed, aren't we, us men?'

Ellie sighed. 'I've got more important things to worry about now anyway. When I'm out of here and back on my feet, I have a mum and dad to reunite, a couple of best friends to apologise to and an aunt to bury. I think I might be a bit too busy to figure out what delusions are going through Ben Kelly's head right now.'

'There's nothing like a bit of tragedy to put everything else into perspective. Do you know when your aunt's funeral is yet?'

'No. I suppose we'll have to wait until the death certificate is issued before we can even think about dates. Not that I know a lot about it. But I know that Hazel put a lot of arrangements in place herself when she first found out that she was incurable. I'll bet she's organised everything down to the last sandwich at the wake to save me and mum doing it.' She stifled a yawn.

'Uh oh, here we go. Bedtime for the lightweight, is it?'

'It's been a long day but somehow I can't see me getting much sleep tonight.' Ellie rubbed a hand gingerly along her ribs. 'Even without all the drama of today and the bloody constant noise of this place, I feel like I've been kicked in the chest by a life-size Buckaroo. It's not exactly conducive to sleep.'

'I can imagine. Want me to get you a cup of tea from the vending machine down the hall?'

Ellie wrinkled her nose. 'Have you tasted that tea? It's disgusting.'

'That may be…' Patrick reached into his coat pocket and produced a small bottle. He sloshed it around with a cheeky grin. 'But it will taste a whole lot better with a drop or two of this in it. Might help you sleep too.'

'Whisky!'

'Shhhh!' Patrick scolded, his expression resembling that of a naughty schoolboy more with every second. 'We don't want to get caught.'

'It's a good job you're already married to such a lovely woman, or you would have to marry me immediately.'

'I'm sure there's a cult we can join to make that possible. If only Fiona wouldn't hack off my balls and run them through the blender for mentioning it.'

'Easy, Tiger.' Ellie couldn't help but laugh despite herself. 'Go and get me that tea, you bad boy.'

*

Ellie closed the front door behind her with a contented sigh. Every limb felt like it was filled with lead, and her chest ached, but at least she was home. Miranda had already disappeared down the hallway with her bags. Ellie watched her go for a moment, breathing in the peculiarly personal smell of her own house. It seemed like years since she had been here even though it was only a matter of days. She thought back to the day she signed the mortgage agreement, a year ago. The day she had finally found her feet and fled her parents' house. The walls of her hallway were the first to be painted. Red, so that they almost glowed like fire in the filtered light of her Moroccan styled shade. Her mother hated the colour. It made Ellie love it all the more.

Ellie wandered down the hall to her kitchen. The door to the living room was on her right. This had been the room she decorated next. Behind that door were walls of white with one feature wall of bold red poppies, wooden floors stripped bare and varnished a rich oak and dotted with colourful rugs. Ellie smiled at the thought of it, the one room her mum could just about tolerate without grimacing. At the end of the hall was Ellie's kitchen. All the melamine units had come out of this room a few months ago and she had replaced them with shiny chrome and white like a restaurant-inspired kitchen she had once seen in an interior design magazine. She bought appliances so trendy and unnecessary that she didn't even know what some of them did herself. It was tiled halfway up the wall in a colourful mishmash of primary colours, the top half painted in the palest of yellows for a splash of warmth. Her mother hated this room too, but she bustled about in it now, trying her best not to show her irritation that Ellie had decided she wanted to go home and not stay with her after all (Ellie had secretly hoped that her absence from the maternal home would leave a space only her father could fill), and her sadness at the grief, still raw, of losing not only her sister, but her best friend.

'You can go and lie down on the sofa if you want, and I'll bring you a cup of tea.'

'I'm sick of lying down,' Ellie said as she lowered herself awkwardly onto a kitchen chair. 'I'd rather sit here as long as I can stand it. Besides, the doctors said that lying around would cause muscle wastage and that I need to be as active as I can manage. I can already feel my legs disappearing after only a couple of days in bed.' Ellie shuffled for a moment, changing position in tiny movements until she felt comfortable. 'It's just a shame bum wastage doesn't come with lying in bed too.'

Miranda flicked the kettle on and ran a finger along the worktops. 'I'll give the place a wipe down while that boils. Things soon get dusty when they're not done for a couple of days and these steel worktops show every mark.'

'Sit down, Mum.'

'I will, as soon as I've cleaned here. And I expect your bedding needs to be aired too, as you haven't been here for a couple of days. It's a good job I called in first to put the heating on or we'd have been dithering –'

'Mum!' Ellie held up a hand. 'Please… I'm sure the bedding is just fine. The heating will dry everything out and it doesn't matter if the worktops are a little dusty until tomorrow because I have no intention of cooking this evening anyway.'

Miranda was silent as she cast a critical eye over her daughter. 'You're practically skin and bone. You need to eat something.'

'Yes… but I can get a takeout.'

'Home cooked is best.'

'It is,' Ellie agreed. 'But not tonight. I don't want you stressing out and we have other things to discuss. I've got menus in that drawer…' Ellie gestured to the unit nearest the dishwasher. 'We can get it delivered, save either of us going out again in this rain.'

Miranda rummaged in the drawer and pulled out a handful of different flyers. 'Chinese, Indian, Thai...Good grief, do you collect these as a hobby or something?'

Ellie smiled. 'We seem to get them through the door every day on this street. And I keep a good selection because you never know when you might fancy a greasy kebab.'

'Hmmm.' Miranda dropped the pile onto the table and went back to the cupboard for mugs.

'So...' Ellie said as casually as she could whilst she perused an Indian menu. 'Did Dad stay over last night?'

'On the sofa,' Miranda replied, her eyes fixed firmly on the task of making drinks.

'That's one thing you can't deny, he's always good in a crisis.'

'He's terrible,' Miranda sniffed. 'He breaks out in hives at the merest sign of a blocked drain.'

'I don't mean that sort of crisis. I mean, when you're down, he comes running. You've always got a shoulder to cry on when he's around.'

Miranda didn't reply as she pulled a bottle of milk from the fridge and sniffed at it. 'Off.' She poured it down the sink. 'You have the powdered milk I bought you somewhere?'

'In that top cupboard,' Ellie said, waving a hand in the general direction of the dry goods cupboard. Pulling her new phone from her pocket, she turned it over in her hands, admiring with a small smile her dad's gift. 'He had to go and get the upgrade, didn't he? I'd have been happy for a straight replacement – this must have cost him a small fortune.'

'Probably spent our second mortgage on it,' Miranda replied.

Ellie looked up sharply. 'That was a bit below the belt.'

Miranda sighed as she placed Ellie's mug in front of her. 'I know. Ignore me.'

Ellie raised her eyebrows. 'You're *admitting* it? Bloody hell, times have changed.'

Miranda took a seat across from her. She traced a finger around the rim of her cup as she stared into its depths. 'Perhaps he hasn't been *completely* useless this week.'

'Now I've seen everything,' Ellie said with a wry smile. Miranda looked up and returned it with a small one of her own.

'I've lost my sister and almost lost my daughter in the same week. I suppose I was glad of the support when he offered it. I don't think I would have coped alone.'

At any other time, Ellie would have reminded her mother that her accident was far from a potential fatality but as Miranda was as close to singing her husband's praises as she was ever likely to be, Ellie thought better than to interrupt her current positive train of thought.

'Does this mean he's forgiven?'

Miranda chewed her lip, her attention back on the contents of her mug. 'One step at a time, eh?'

*

'She is bloody tedious,' Kasumi sighed as she sat curled on the corner of Ellie's sofa where she had been for the previous hour. She had arrived unexpected and unannounced, and Ellie was grateful she hadn't had to worry about what she'd have to say to her. As it was, they had quickly settled back to the easy banter and affection that usually characterised their friendship. Ellie was incredibly grateful for the company and that Kasumi had made the effort.

'Who?' Ellie asked.

'Claudia!' Kasumi rolled her eyes. 'Honestly, have you been listening at all?'

'Sorry. Claudia… of course. This is the same Claudia who works at the tapas bar?'

'Yes. I mean, she's sweet and everything, but it's like having a pathetically over-loyal puppy in your midst.'

Ellie gave a small smile. 'I told Jethro she liked him that night she served us at the bar. You could see it a mile off – she was practically drooling over him. He said I was being ridiculous.'

Kasumi shot her a sideways glance. 'I wish you hadn't planted that particular gem of an idea in his head. Now I'm doomed to double dates with her forever. Probably have to be bridesmaid for her and everything. I'll be vexed beyond reason if I'm forced to be godmother to their first child.'

Ellie couldn't help but laugh. 'They've only been out a couple of times. That's usually about the time when it goes tits-up.' She fixed Kasumi with an earnest look. 'I'm just glad the whole thing that happened with us didn't become something excruciating. I don't know what I'd do without you two in my life.'

'Me too,' Kasumi agreed. 'I need you and Jethro just as you are: my absolute best and very definitely not-a-couple friends.'

'We were both pretty drunk, I suppose.'

'Are you terribly unhappy without this man?'

'You mean Ben?'

Kasumi nodded.

'Yes,' Ellie said, her frankness surprising even her. 'But I suppose I'll get over it.'

'And you're sure all this business about the wedding is true?'

Ellie shrugged. 'Why wouldn't it be? They're meant for each other and whatever I thought existed between Ben and me was a lie. Just like Gemma said, he was lonely and I happened to be around.'

'What about the flowers?'

'It was nothing more than a friendly gesture.'

Kasumi screwed up her perfect nose in an expression that told Ellie she thought her theories were a cart full of steaming horse poo, but she didn't argue.

Ellie drained her wine glass and inspected it with mock solemnity. 'Ooops, looks as though we need supplies.' She began to push herself slowly up from the other corner of the sofa but Kasumi leapt to her feet.

'Stay there. I'm supposed to be nursey this weekend.'

'Is that what you told Sam you were coming up to Millrise for?'

'Oh yes. I left him with all sorts of delicious imaginings of me in uniform.'

Ellie giggled. 'You're filthy.'

Kasumi gazed down at her fondly. 'It's so lovely to see you laugh again.'

'There hasn't been much to laugh about, that's for sure.'

'Things will be better once the funeral is over.'

'I wish I could be so sure about that.'

'Hold that thought for a moment.' Kasumi disappeared into Ellie's kitchen and returned minutes later with a fresh bottle of red. 'You can't sort your life out with a clear head. Them's the rules, you know.'

'It's not my life I need to sort out.' Ellie held her glass up for Kasumi to fill.

'Oh? So yours is perfect already?'

'Mine is already beyond sorting.'

'Nobody's life is beyond my expert coaching.'

'Perhaps you can visit my mum and dad then and weave your magic there.'

Kasumi reclaimed her spot on the sofa and tucked her legs beneath her in one deft movement. Coiled in her corner, her silhouette had a certain feline grace to it. Even half-drunk, she was uncommonly beautiful. 'They're still at odds?'

Ellie sighed. 'I don't know. I think we might have made a breakthrough. It's just very sad that it took a death to get there. Although we're still nowhere near where they were before all the trouble started.'

'They'll work it out,' Kasumi commented sagely. 'They've got too many years behind them to throw it away. And they always seemed really happy before.'

'They had their ups and downs like everyone. But I think they were.'

'In that case, in their hearts they'll realise it's worth fighting for.'

Ellie smiled. 'You always were the glass half-full girl.'

Kasumi stretched out a leg and prodded Ellie playfully with her big toe. 'You're next.'

'Please no.'

'You can't tell me that you're happy sitting on your own every night.'

'Things would be far less complicated if I was sitting on my own every night.'

'Hmmm. I suppose that's true. But I have to say, it's bound to be complicated when you set your sights on the wrong men all the time.'

'I know. I've well and truly learned my lesson there. No more wrong men. In fact, no more men at all.'

'Ooooh, going for a lady next time?' Kasumi raised her eyebrows.

Ellie laughed. 'I'm concentrating on aspects of my life that I can control. Like my career.'

'In that case...' Kasumi said carelessly, 'you won't be upset if the station does another feature on Ben and Gemma to see how things are progressing now that they're back together?'

Ellie took a huge gulp of her wine. 'Of course I don't mind. Why would I?'

Chapter Fifteen

A freezing wind blasted through the long grass as the small crowd of mourners made their way along the ornamental path, following the coffin into the woods. The day was bright but there was a sharpness in the air that found its way through every seam of Ellie's clothing. She pulled her coat tighter and folded her arms against the cold. Her parents walked at her side. She cast them another furtive glance to see that Frank still had Miranda's hand firmly clasped in his and she hadn't yet brushed him off. That had to be a good sign. The service had been conducted in a bright, spacious, purpose-built wooden lodge, in a tranquil spot that overlooked views of the woodlands and the River Mersey beyond. It had taken them over an hour to drive from Millrise to the special site, but Ellie had to hand it to her aunt – as venues for funerals went, this was pretty spectacular and it was worth the journey. There were far worse places to spend the afterlife.

As the group went deeper into the woods, the swathes of wild grass gave way to trees peppered with new buds and wild spring flowers pushing their way from the undergrowth. Industrious birds flitted to and fro overhead. The air was sweet and clean here, and it was hard to believe that major towns and cities were only a few miles down the road in any direction.

Two weeks had passed since Hazel's death. They were two weeks filled with rest for Ellie and a certain amount of quiet reflection on her own life. There had been no more contact from Ben or Gemma. Ellie assumed that wedding plans were now in full swing, undoubtedly coupled with a lucrative magazine deal for exclusive photos. If Ellie had heard that Gemma had ordered a swan-shaped carriage set with diamante, commanded all her guests to wear purple and had chosen a huge pink taffeta dress with a matching pink suit for Ben, she wouldn't have been a bit surprised. As it was, she was thankful that she finally seemed to have slipped under Gemma's radar. Deep in her heart, she hadn't accepted that Ben was gone from her life, but she tried to believe that he was happy now, despite Patrick's opinions to the contrary, and she let that be her comfort. Wasn't that what people in love did? She remembered reading *Cyrano de Bergerac* at university, where Cyrano had selflessly and anonymously pledged his life to ensuring the happiness of his beloved Roxane until his dying breath. It was a noble thing, right, to let the one you love go?

The procession stopped at a clearing dotted with ornamental benches and bronze plaques. A mound of freshly-dug earth sat next to the waiting grave. Ellie blinked back the tears burning her eyes; she had to be strong for her mum who was sobbing uncontrollably now, for her dad whose expression betrayed that he felt helpless and ineffectual and completely out of his emotional depth, despite pulling Miranda into a protective hug. Ellie had to be strong for her aunt who would have been so proud to see it. She had to be strong for everyone.

She glanced around, desperately trying to take her mind off the fact that her aunt's body lay in a box just feet away. Only a small number of Hazel's friends had managed to make it to the burial site. Ellie supposed that was to be expected – it was a long drive and Hazel must have realised that when she planned it. Perhaps she didn't think it would matter who came in the end, only that her final resting place was perfect. Other than that, Hazel's ex-husband had made the effort along with his mother, which filled Ellie with a great deal of new-found respect for him.

There was also a sprinkling of distant relatives whom Ellie only ever bumped into at weddings and funerals. Later they'd chat, swap phone numbers, vow to keep in touch – empty promises that would be forgotten until the next family gathering when they'd make them all over again. Kasumi had only met Hazel a couple of times and Jethro never had, but they had both offered to come to the funeral. In the end, Ellie had reassured her friends that their gesture was appreciated but not necessary.

The vicar gave the usual funeral speeches and made some comments about the lovely setting. Ellie tried not to pay too much attention so that no single word, or even the merest nuance, could set off her tears. Instead, she focused on the buds on the trees, on the coloured dots of new spring flowers barely showing above ground, on the birds busy above them, on how life continued in the face of death. Before she knew it, the speech was over and Hazel was being lowered into the ground.

Miranda's hand was still firmly in Frank's grasp as they made their way back to the lodge. He reached for Ellie's at the other side of him, and the three of them walked back together, united as a family for the first time in months.

*

Miranda had given the envelope to Ellie shortly after they had returned to Millrise from the funeral. She had taken it without comment and left her mum and dad alone together at Miranda's house in the hope that they would build on the ceasefire they seemed to have achieved that day. On the front of the envelope Ellie's name was written in

Hazel's looping handwriting. Ellie had looked at it at least five times that evening without opening it. Somehow, it never seemed to be quite the right moment. It was almost as if it was something private, the last something of Hazel that Ellie shouldn't see. Too personal to be seen by anyone who might call, it lay now on the dressing table in her bedroom. As Ellie changed into her pyjamas just before midnight, it caught her eye again, a perfectly unremarkable white envelope that anyone could buy from any supermarket. But inside it, the thoughts of a dead woman waited.

Ellie perched on the edge of her bed and reached for it. She rubbed her side thoughtfully as she read her name again. The pain in her ribs had subsided but she had developed a strange habit of soothing them anyway. With a deep breath, she slid a thumb under the flap and opened the letter.

Dear Ellie

If you're reading this then I'm dead. That's a suitably Hollywood beginning, isn't it? There are so many things I have wanted to say to you in the past few months but I knew that you wouldn't want to hear them. Lots of them are boring old legal things that the solicitor will talk to you about. The other things are far more important.

The first is that you must let your mum and dad make their own way. You can't be responsible for them all your life. But I think you already know that.

The second is choose happiness over duty. It links in with number one, I suppose, but with a bit more emphasis. You may believe that you have to put everyone else first, or that you should sacrifice your feelings for the sake of what's proper or right. Those are admirable sentiments, but life is short and happiness fleeting. Choose to be happy, Ellie, in whatever path life offers you. Listen to your heart and follow it. You might find you've been led up a blind alley, but you might discover paradise.

Number three: always look forward, never back. Remember the pillars of salt? Look forward and don't cry over mistakes that can't be changed.

The last one (and I hope I don't think of any more after I'm dead or that might get a bit tricky) is don't take my life as a template for yours. I've seen the way you shy away from love. It doesn't always go wrong, you know, just because it did for me. Besides, I've had time to make my peace with John now and I wish him a blissful life with his boy. Bitterness is not going to bring me back and it's one hell of a burden to die with. Take a chance. What have you got to lose?

Don't cry for me. Time will dull the pain of loss, as it does for every loss. Remember me, but don't cry. You are the daughter I never had, and exactly like the one I always longed for. Show the world what you're made of and do my memory proud.

I leave my love lingering in every shadow for you, so you need never be afraid of the dark.

Be good, be strong, be glorious.
Hazel. Xxx

Ellie read the letter three more times before she folded it carefully and tucked it back into the envelope. Was that how Hazel had seen her – as someone who treated life with too much caution, someone crippled by duty and regrets, someone who was afraid of the shadows?

Ellie already knew that her aunt had left a great deal of money to her, at Miranda's insistence that she herself wanted none of it and would rather see it go to Ellie. When Miranda had told Ellie of this, the fact had hardly registered. It wasn't that Ellie didn't care or was ungrateful, but it hardly seemed a gift at all when all things were considered. Ellie flipped the envelope and traced a finger over the indents the pen had left beneath her name. Why had Hazel felt the need to write this letter? Had she written something similar for Ellie's mum? If so, Miranda hadn't mentioned it. Perhaps, if one did exist, she never would.

*

A week later, Ellie returned to her office at the *Echo*. Like most people, she had often joked that if she won the lottery she would take great and immediate pleasure in flouncing off from her desk in a blaze of glory and chartering the nearest helicopter, never to return. The reality of not being at work during the week was very different, however, and Ellie found that she craved the stimulation and excitement her job offered. Vernon had, in fact, phoned her personally and told her to take as long as she needed at home to recover both physically from the accident and emotionally from her aunt's death, but Ellie felt certain that the best thing to heal both those scars was to immerse herself in her work. She had reassured him that she felt perfectly well and reminded him that she was hardly training for the SAS, and couldn't see that driving out to talk to old ladies about their bingo winnings was going to stretch her either physically or mentally. Vernon had seemed happy with that and Ellie suspected that despite the concerns he had voiced, he was happy to have his newest recruit back again too.

The first Monday morning back in had passed pleasantly enough. Lots of colleagues popped into her office, or caught her on the stairs or in the communal kitchen to ask how she was and to express their pleasure to see her back at work. She had a page full of satisfying, if slightly uninspired leads, but she was hopeful that from the list something a little more intriguing would present itself. Ange had brought cakes in to celebrate Ellie's return, which she, Ellie and Vernon had gorged themselves on during coffee break. Patrick (whose cake-radar had obviously been switched on to full power) had turned up, seemingly from nowhere, like some gangly grey-haired locust and polished off the remainder in such an impressive manner that his hand-to-mouth movements had been a veritable blur. All in all, everything was reassuringly normal.

It was just as she was thinking that life really was back on an even keel that Rosie on main reception, who usually screened all Ellie's calls, decided to put one straight through to the office.

'Hello… is that Ellie?'

Ellie almost dropped the phone. He must have heard the sharp intake of breath as she paused, taken by surprise.

'Ben?' She wanted to add: *what the hell are you phoning me for?* But nothing else would come out.

'I know you're probably busy. I just wondered if you could spare some time to see me.'

'I am pretty snowed under. Ange is free this morning… or maybe someone from the features team –'

'No,' Ben cut in. 'It's not about a story. Can you meet me?'

'You could come to reception here…' Ellie began carefully. Neutral ground would probably be a good thing and she wasn't sure she trusted herself to act professionally away from the *Echo*.

'No,' Ben said again. 'Could you meet me after work?'

Ellie hesitated. She glanced around the office. Vernon had his head in the morning's edition of the paper and Ange was on another call.

'What's it about?'

'I can't tell you now, it's too complicated.'

'I'm really busy. It's my first day back in, you know, and I seem to
have leads coming from everywhere, not to mention all the unanswered
emails and general odds and ends...' Ellie was aware that she was
babbling but couldn't seem to stop.

'I know. And I wouldn't ask unless it was important.'

Ellie chewed her lip for a moment. 'OK,' she said finally, mentally
smacking herself for not being stronger-willed and letting curiosity get
the better of her. 'Where?'

'Can you come to The Horseshoes?'

'The pub on Blackshore Lane?'

'Yeah. Would that be OK?'

'I won't finish work until after six.'

'That's OK. About half past?'

'OK.' She paused again. There was another question. He had not
volunteered the information so maybe he didn't think it was important.
Perhaps it wasn't. But she found herself asking it anyway. 'Is Gemma
coming?'

His pause held even more weight than hers. 'No,' he replied finally.
'It's just me.'

*

The Horseshoes had once been a typical example of what Ellie referred
to as an 'old man's pub,' complete with nicotine-stained ceilings, dark
wooden furniture sticky with the spilt drinks of ages past, and lamps
dotted around the walls giving off a dirty glow. A few years ago it had
been bought for a bargain price by a local music promoter. It retained
the essence of the pub it once was – the old furniture was still in place

and the jovial, low-key atmosphere remained – but now it had been thoroughly cleaned and decorated, modernised by adding touches of cutting edge art, an impressive sound system and a stage for music and comedy gigs. Ellie had been in once or twice with Kasumi to see local bands, but since her friend had moved to London there hadn't been a lot of time or the right company for her to venture in again.

Ben was standing by the bar when Ellie arrived. It was very early by pub standards and apart from two women whose table was sur-rounded by shopping bags and a few bar staff the place was empty. He gave an awkward smile as he saw Ellie approach. Straightaway she could see he wasn't the relaxed Ben she knew – he was taut, anxious… almost afraid.

'I wasn't sure you'd come,' Ben said.

'Why wouldn't I? I said I would.'

'I know. I just thought you might get called to a story or something.'

'The news in Millrise isn't usually *that* pressing,' Ellie said, trying to put him at ease.

It seemed to work as his expression relaxed slightly. But then he frowned again. 'Last time I saw you… when I came to the hospital…'

'I wasn't feeling my best. I had just been knocked down by a car.'

His head bobbed in a tiny nod. 'Yeah… I just wondered… Well, I went to the offices to see if I could get your phone number at home. I wanted to see if you were OK. They wouldn't give it to me, of course – not that I thought they would, but I wanted to try anyway. Then I saw your photographer…'

'Patrick?'

'Yeah. I asked him if he'd take a message to you. I just wanted to talk to you for five minutes, clear the air – y'know? But he said it wasn't a good time.'

Ellie mulled this information over for a brief moment. Patrick had said nothing to her about seeing Ben or him wanting to get a message to her. She guessed he had been trying, in his own misguided way, to protect her. She also guessed that Ben's version of his conversation with Patrick was a diplomatically edited one; it was far more likely he had told Ben to piss off. Whatever Patrick's motives for keeping the episode from her, she would have to discuss it with him when she saw him again.

She glanced towards the bar to see a skinny young man hovering nearby, clearly waiting to see if they needed service. 'Perhaps we should get a drink and sit somewhere quiet?'

'Yeah… of course.' He turned and motioned to the youth behind the bar.

'What can I get you?' the barman asked.

'I'll have a coke,' Ellie said.

'Coke for me too,' Ben added. He pulled a crumpled five pound note from his pocket.

'I'll get them,' Ellie said.

'I can at least get you one drink…' Ben began to argue, but Ellie shook her head firmly.

'Are you working right now?'

Ben glanced at the barman, who seemed to be oblivious to their conversation as he spooned ice into their glasses. 'Not right now…' he said in a low voice. 'You know, because I didn't go in for ages the boss said he needed to cover my shifts but –'

'Exactly,' said Ellie. 'I'm not coming over all women's lib, I just figure you have rent and stuff to pay with very little coming in.'

'My guitar lessons are starting up again and this time I'll be doing paid ones too. I can stretch to a couple of cokes,' he replied, looking almost offended.

'I know you can. But I'm getting these.'

As the barman placed their drinks before them, Ellie whipped a note from her purse and thrust it at him before Ben could get a chance to argue.

Ben collected both glasses and followed Ellie to a table in a snug enclosed by coloured glass. Somehow, the partition screening it from the rest of the pub made it seem more private.

'I haven't been in here for ages.' Ellie shrugged her coat off as she scooted along the leather bench seat. Ben sat opposite and gave her a small smile.

'Me neither, as it happens. I used to play a lot here with the band.'

'What were they called?'

He grinned, more like his old self for a moment. 'Sherlock.'

Ellie nodded slowly. 'Sherlock… hmmm, well that's…'

'A terrible name!' he laughed. 'I know. It was Jamie's idea. None of us could be bothered to argue with him.'

'He's the lead singer then?'

'Yeah. How did you guess?'

'Because lead singers always get what they want.'

Ellie took a sip of her coke, letting her eyes wander beyond the confines of the snug for a moment. It seemed that whatever Ben had brought her here to talk about was causing him great concern, and the brief ease they had just shared was now replaced by anxiety and doubt again.

'So… how's it going with you and Gemma?' Ellie didn't want to talk about Gemma, but she felt the need to ignite some sort of conversation and wondered whether this would be the safe ground he needed to put him at ease again. Instead, he looked as though he had just been stung by a psychopathic wasp.

'OK...' he said carefully.

Ellie took another sip of her drink and waited. Her job had taught her how to be patient when she was interviewing, give people space to think and choose their words. Eventually, she always found, the words did come and they were more honest for it.

Finally, he dipped his gaze to his drink and spoke quietly. 'What would you say if I told you that things aren't quite how I hoped they would be?'

'Between you two?'

'Yes,' he said without looking up. He sighed and rubbed a hand over his hair.

'Is all the publicity bothering you?'

'A bit. But there's something else too.'

Ellie waited silently again. He looked up and she gave her most encouraging smile.

'When I was little,' he continued, 'my dad used to play Echo and the Bunnymen all the time. You know them, right?'

'Yeah, an eighties band,' Ellie replied, doing her best to hide the look of absolute mystification as to where this new conversational thread was going.

'So I grew up loving them. I mean, I was obsessed. It was weird, of course, because none of my friends got it. But I loved them. I collected all their CDs, I kept a scrapbook with articles about them, my dad was made up that I was such a fan and brought me things like t-shirts all the time. I even learned to play guitar because I wanted to be just like Will Sergeant. It was so perfect and I thought they would always be my favourite, number one band. Especially when I lost my parents, because then the band was like a link between me and my dad, something to keep his memory fresh. But then I got older and I suppose I changed.

One day I heard the Arctic Monkeys. My love for the Bunnymen was like a warm lamp that comforted me but this new thing was like an electric shock that jolted me into life. I never thought that any other band could move me like the Bunnymen did, and certainly not make me feel so much more alive.'

He pulled his coke towards him and sloshed the ice around in the glass. When he didn't speak for a moment, Ellie filled the silence.

'I'm not sure I understand.'

He sighed. 'I'm not sure I do either. This probably isn't the best analogy but I'm struggling to find another way to tell you.'

'Tell me what?'

'When I first met Gemma, I thought it would always be her. I couldn't imagine how anyone could compare; she was my warm glow, a constant, someone who would always be a part of my life. But then maybe she changed, or maybe I grew up, but something *did* change. And she left me. I felt all at sea, like my anchor had been ripped up and I had been cast adrift. All I wanted was for things to go back to the way they had been. And I thought that getting her back was the most important thing in the world. But while I was busy with that something else happened: my Arctic Monkeys moment. Someone else suddenly turned up and rocked my world just when it was at its most shaky. And now everything is upside-down and I don't know what is right anymore.'

Ellie stared at him. She was aware of her heart beating in her ears. Was it faster than usual? 'What exactly are you trying to tell me?'

'It's you, Ellie.'

'I'm what?'

'I can't stop thinking about you. All the time. It feels so different than it did with Gemma that I don't know what it means. I don't know whether it means I'm in love with you and I never was with her or the other way around.'

Ellie sat back. Tears burned at the back of her eyes. 'Well that's comforting,' she snapped. 'Why are you telling me this? I can't help you decide who you want and I don't see why I should just fall into your arms if you do decide it's me.'

'I'm not explaining myself very well. I didn't mean to offend you.'

Ellie opened her mouth to reply, but then closed it again.

He gave a shaky laugh. 'Aren't you going to say something? Anything?'

'I don't know what to say.'

'Say you think it's going to be OK.'

Her voice softened. She wanted to say that, more than anything. But it would be a lie. 'I can't. Because I'm not sure it will be.'

'But you like me too? I thought… when we were together that time I thought…'

'Oh God, Ben, you'd have to be blind to miss it. Of course I do. But you're engaged.'

He stared at her. 'What?'

'You asked Gemma to marry you. Why would you do that if you didn't know how you felt?'

He shook his head. 'I did *what*? Where did you hear that?'

'How can it matter who told me?' Ellie said, struggling to keep her voice level. 'All that matters is you did.'

'I didn't!'

Ellie stopped dead, the next sentence stuck in her throat.

'I haven't asked Gemma to marry me,' Ben repeated.

'But she told me…'

'*She* told you that? When?'

'She came to see me in hospital.'

Ben's jaw twitched. He seemed to be grinding his teeth as he stared out beyond the snug to where the barman was wiping down the counter. 'She never said she'd been to see you,' he said finally.

'So… you're not getting married?'

'Ellie… you have to believe that I would never do something that stupid. I don't even know if I love her anymore; why would I propose?'

'But you're sure of your feelings for me?' Ellie said quietly, holding him now in a steady gaze. She waited, breath held, almost afraid of his answer. What if he said no? Even worse, what if he said yes? How could she give herself to a man who changed like the direction of wheat blown by the wind? Even if he thought he loved her now, how could she be certain that wouldn't change? How could she know that years down the road, she would not find herself alone, just like Hazel? He went to the ends of the earth to get Gemma back and now he was ready to throw their relationship away without a backwards glance. How could she give her heart to a man like this?

'I… yes. I think so.'

In his dark eyes she could see the scars of all he had ever lost. Love was there too – intense, painful, unmistakeable love – and all her doubts of his intentions dissipated. She had never wanted him more than she did right now. She could kiss all that pain away and she would love every moment. She could keep him safe, be his warm lamp. It would be too easy to let it happen. But that didn't make it right. Hate was a strong word but it was pretty close to what she felt about Gemma right now, especially if Ben was telling the truth and she had made up the whole proposal. But didn't that simply mean that Gemma loved Ben too – despite what it looked like – so much that she was willing to go to any lengths to keep him? And if that were true, then how could Ellie look at herself in the mirror again if she stole him away?

He reached across for her hand. Ellie tugged it from his grasp, the tears she had been fighting squeezing their way out.

'But what about Constance Street, the campaign...'

'I thought it was important at the time. I know you probably think I made myself look a complete idiot. I thought I loved Gemma but... now I think I was in love with the *idea* of being in love with Gemma. And then it all got out of hand – all the publicity and the interest – until it became this huge runaway cart that kept getting faster and faster and then I couldn't get off, even if I wanted to. Does that make any sense?'

Ellie shook her head slowly. 'I suppose so. But it doesn't change anything. What will it look like to the world if you dump Gemma now and start a relationship with me?'

'I don't care about that. I already look like a tit in front of the world so what do I care what it thinks of me? All that matters is what's in my heart. And what's in my heart, filling it completely, is you.'

Ellie sighed. A few weeks ago she would have given anything to hear him say that. But she was learning that she couldn't always have what she wanted. 'What would it do to Gemma to have that sort of public humiliation?' she asked gently.

He was quiet for a moment, the pain and guilt evident in every line of his face. 'I didn't mean for this to happen. But you can't help who you fall in love with.'

'You said that to me once before... remember? But that time you weren't talking about me.'

'I know...' He looked down and traced a ring on the table. 'It's all such a bloody mess.'

'I'm sorry, Ben. You have no idea how much I wish it could be different.'

'When I saw you get hit by that car, I thought…' He rubbed a shaky hand over his hair. 'The thought of losing you hurt more than I ever thought possible. I hadn't realised until then just how much I needed you.'

'Gemma needs *you*.'

'I don't think she does, not really…'

Ellie stared into the depths of her drink. 'We can't…'

'That's it? That's your answer?'

She looked up. 'Yes.' She slid from the booth, afraid to look at him in case she changed her mind.

'Please…' Ben reached for her arm. 'I can't just let you go.'

'You have to.'

Ellie left the pub before he could answer. She didn't dare look back.

*

'I don't know what to think.' Ellie shook her head as Patrick and Fiona watched her from across the dining table. Fiona had outdone herself with the most perfect Thai green curry but despite the exquisite aromas fragrancing the air of their dining room, Ellie wasn't all that hungry. She had struggled valiantly to seem enthusiastic over her meal – equally, she had done her best to appear engaged in their small talk but, inevitably, the pair guessed quickly that things weren't rosy in the Ellie Newton garden.

'I'm sorry I didn't tell you Ben had been to the offices,' Patrick said.

'It's OK,' Ellie sighed. 'I know you were only looking out for me. But I do wish you had.'

'What would you have done differently if you'd known his intentions? Would you have even agreed to meet him?'

'I don't know. But I suppose I would have had more time to think about it.'

'And your answer would have been different in the end?' Fiona asked.

Ellie raked tracks through the rice on her plate with her fork. 'I don't know,' she said slowly. 'How can I be the person who causes that much heartache?'

'I think it might be a little late for that,' Patrick said.

'What do you think about the proposal?' Ellie asked. 'Do you think he's telling the truth that Gemma made it up?'

'It seems like a very elaborate scheme if he's not.'

'But can I trust him?'

'How can you trust anyone?' Fiona said. Patrick raised his eyebrows and she smiled sweetly at him. 'You know what I mean. No matter how well you think you know someone, you never truly do. And it doesn't matter how two people feel about each other in the here and now, because nothing in life is certain either. Even for us, husband dearest.'

'It's comforting to know that my future with you is so solid,' Patrick laughed.

'As long as you stop leaving the toilet seat up I'll keep you for a while. At least until you're old and even greyer than you are now; then I'm afraid I'll be on the lookout for a younger model.' Fiona gave him a dazzling smile before taking a gulp of her wine.

'That's not enough for me,' Ellie said. 'I can't build a relationship on that.'

'Then you'll be alone forever,' Fiona replied, the smile gone. 'Nobody can say that they'll never end up alone. Isn't it better to grab a slice of happiness while it's on offer than to turn your back on the whole cake?'

'It's not that simple.'

'Yes it is.' Fiona filled Ellie's wine glass. 'It really is.'

'So...' Ellie replied, 'you would have said yes to Ben. Despite the risks, you would have said yes?'

Fiona glanced at Patrick. He gave an encouraging nod. She turned back to Ellie, who was watching them carefully and wondering what plan they were cooking up.

'Did Patrick ever tell you about how we got together?'

Ellie shook her head as she shot her friend a questioning look. He smiled slightly.

'When I was nineteen I met this boy...' Fiona filled her own glass before continuing. 'He was gorgeous. I remember seeing him down at the outside pool, all lithe and limber in his swim shorts. He looked my way and I melted. Needless to say I did my utmost to make sure I made an impact and by the end of the afternoon he had my phone number. We dated for two years. I was head over heels and when he asked me to marry him, I said yes – no hesitation. His name was Mark...' She paused. 'You thought I was going to say Patrick, didn't you?'

Ellie smiled. 'I sort of guessed. You're going to tell me that sadly Mark wasn't the one, but after him you met Patrick and everything is now lovely.'

'Almost. But Mark *was* the one... even when Patrick came to cover a story at the rest home I was working in. He was cute, this photographer, and he was persistent. But I was engaged and in love with someone else.' She reached for her husband's hand and gave it a squeeze. 'However, my cheeky photographer kept turning up. One lunch break he took me for coffee and before I knew it, we were kissing. I went home with my head in a whirl. I loved Mark, but this was something new... I can't explain it but being with Patrick felt right too. I didn't know what to do. It carried on for months. I let Mark believe that we had a future together because I didn't want to hurt him. But I was falling for Patrick hard too and no matter how many times I thought about breaking it off with him, when I saw him I couldn't.'

'And you knew about Mark?' Ellie asked Patrick.

He nodded. 'Judge me if you like but I did. I'm not proud, but I was crazy about Fiona and I just hoped she would pick me in the end. It was all I could do.'

'Mark had a right to know,' Ellie insisted, a trace of disbelief in her tone. She had thought she knew Patrick, his morals and standards, and had always judged him and Fiona to be two of the most upstanding, considerate people she had ever met. Right now, they were blowing her beliefs about them out of the water. It was just another in a long list of beliefs being blown away of late. The idea made Ellie distinctly uncomfortable. One minute you know exactly how the little world you have constructed around you works, the next, it's like a parallel universe has opened up in its place.

'He did,' Patrick agreed.

'What we're trying to say,' Fiona cut in, 'is that love isn't clear cut and sometimes it isn't kind.'

'I know all that,' Ellie replied, unable to hide the irritation that crept into her voice. 'I'm not a kid.'

'Nobody said you were. But sometimes things that seem so wrong when they begin turn out to be absolutely right. I can't imagine now being in love with anyone but Patrick, despite how I believed I felt about Mark.'

'You should have told Mark as soon as you had doubts.'

'Yes, I should. But I didn't. People get things wrong, Ellie. All the time. It doesn't mean they're bad or cruel, just human.'

'You think I should give Ben a chance?'

'That's up to you.'

'But how can I do this without hurting someone?'

'You can't – not really. But you have to accept that someone will get hurt no matter what you do and learn to live with the consequences of whatever choice you make.'

Ellie let the fork drop and pushed her plate away, staring at the opposite wall miserably.

Patrick glanced at Fiona before he spoke. 'Ellie…' he began carefully, 'I don't want to overstep the mark, but perhaps you should meet him again for another chat, now that you've had time to think things over. When I told him to leave you alone, perhaps I should have kept my nose out after all. See, I *still* get things wrong all the time.'

'I could get this very wrong.'

'You could.' Patrick leaned forwards across the table. 'I can't say I'm right or wrong, and I don't have the kind of intuition that women are always boasting about…' He threw a sideways glance at Fiona, who slapped his arm playfully. 'But I saw something in his eyes whenever he looked at you. And I recognise that look because I've given enough of them in my time, mostly to my wife. I don't think he'll ever be happy if he thinks he's lost you and I don't think any relationship with Gemma would survive now anyway.'

'Don't forget,' Fiona added, 'he has a hell of a lot to lose too. Coming to you like that, he's put at risk everything he worked so hard to get back and more besides. He and Gemma are now high profile and people are watching them. He must know the stick he'd get if he did leave her for you, and yet he was still willing to follow his heart and do that. Ellie, I'm with Patrick – I think he's genuine and I think it's you he needs.'

'I know all that…' Ellie chewed her nail for a moment as she stared into her wine glass. 'It doesn't make things any easier to work out though.'

Chapter Sixteen

'You be careful… don't carry that!' Frank raced over and grabbed the box from Ellie.

'Dad, stop stressing. It's not heavy.'

'That's not the point. If your lung gets another hole it'll be my fault.'

Ellie giggled. 'The doctor said I should avoid bungee jumping and long haul flights for a while. Unless you tie an elastic band around my feet and hurl me from a jumbo jet I should be OK.'

'It's not funny,' Frank chided.

'Sorry, but it is a little bit.'

Ellie's dad frowned, but then he broke into a small smile. 'If you end up back in hospital your mum will kill me.'

'She should have come over to help then.'

'Steady on! It's a miracle me and my out-of-tune banjo are being let back into the house; I don't want to push it.'

'It's about time if you ask me.'

He narrowed his eyes. 'Does your mum know you're helping me to pack?'

'Not exactly… but I thought someone ought to.'

'You're a bad girl, Ellie Newton.'

'What she doesn't know won't hurt her,' Ellie laughed as she reached up to kiss him on the cheek. 'I'm so glad you two worked it out.'

'I don't think it was anything I did. I suspect your aunt should take the credit.'

'She wrote mum a letter?'

He put down the box and stared at her. 'I have no idea. Your mum just said it was because of Hazel that she was taking me back. I don't know what she did or said but whatever it was, I'm in her debt.' He bent for the box again. 'I'll just take this out to the car.'

Ellie watched him go with a smile. Her parents had finally worked out a fragile truce, but it was a truce at least. Things would soon be as they should be. On top of that, work was going well and Jethro seemed to have forgotten all about their little transgression since he had fallen madly in love with Claudia, so things between her and her two best friends were back to normal. Ellie was more relieved at that outcome than she could say. Even though the loss of Hazel was still raw, there had been closure with the funeral and time had begun to dull the pain of grief. Ellie hadn't felt this contented in a long time, but it was tempered by a sadness that she couldn't seem to shake, no matter how positive she tried to be for the future. The fear that she had let her one chance of true happiness slip through her fingers continued to nag her. But Ben had not tried to contact her again since their last meeting in the pub. Ellie had to assume that he had given up.

Frank came back in rubbing his hands together. 'It's lovely out there but still a bit nippy in the shade. Shouldn't be long before the weather warms up though.' He peered at Ellie more closely. 'Are you alright?'

Ellie shook herself and smiled. 'Of course I am.'

'You looked a million miles away.'

'I was just wondering how a flat with hardly any furniture in it can still take so long to pack up.'

'I'm not this rubbish naturally, you know, it takes years of practise.'

Ellie grinned and handed him a roll of newspaper-wrapped cutlery, which he tucked into a nearby box. 'Come on, we'll be here all weekend if we don't get a move on.'

*

Ellie padded through to her bedroom, rubbing her hair dry as she did. Despite pretending to her dad that she was well enough to help him, the day had exhausted her more than she cared to admit and her chest ached now too. As soon as she had reached home she had run herself a hot bath and spent a good half hour soaking and mulling over the things she and her dad had talked about. There was the money Hazel had bequeathed to her; Ellie's dad had given her a long and detailed list of financial options which she had stopped listening to after thirty seconds, only nodding sagely whenever he drew breath. Ellie had then offered some towards repaying her parents' second mortgage and had received a new lecture from her horrified father that she wasn't to go around offering her money to all and sundry when she needed it to secure her future. She had thought about pointing out that her dad should have taken his own financial advice back when he had re-mortgaged his home to go on a huge holiday but decided that he had her best interests at heart and she was just too pleased that her parents were finally making things up to be annoyed at his well-intentioned but misguided counsel. He'd even asked her about her love life and she'd lied through her teeth and told him she was far too busy at work to think about a relationship with anyone. He'd kissed the top of her head and told her that he worried about her and she deserved the very best man and he hoped she would find him soon.

Perching on the edge of her bed, she reached for a comb and began to drag it through her damp hair. It was then that her eye was drawn to the jewellery box. It was a beautiful thing, made of rosewood carved with an intricate elephant motif, which Kasumi had bought for her whilst on holiday in Bali the previous year. Placing the comb back on the dressing table, she pulled it onto the bed beside her and opened the lid. The interior of the box was separated into two parts – the first a tray that lay directly beneath the lid, split into smaller compartments that were now filled with trinkets and keepsakes. Ellie lifted this out to reveal a large space underneath. At the bottom, alongside Ellie's birth certificate and passport, lay Hazel's letter.

The words were already inked into Ellie's memory, but she read it again, slowly, pausing to reflect on every sentence. What had Hazel been trying to tell her? She wasn't being deliberately obtuse – her aunt's literal meaning was explicit enough – but Ellie couldn't help a growing conviction that a deeper message lay between the lines. Was Ellie afraid of love? It wasn't a problem she'd ever thought she had before. But her mind went back to Ben, and to conversations shared with Patrick and Fiona and Kasumi and Jethro and even her dad, in his advice imparted to her in his own ham-fisted way, and she kept coming back to the same conclusion. Ben had shown great courage to admit he had been wrong about Gemma, to bare his soul to Ellie in the way he had done, especially when the mistake would be such a public one. Perhaps he deserved a chance. Ellie certainly hadn't given him one.

It was all too late now, of course. Ellie folded the letter away and placed it back in the box. There was a bottle of white wine in the fridge and a problem that did not seem to right itself no matter how many different ways Ellie turned it over in her mind. It seemed like a pretty good partnership, all things considered. She pulled the belt to her bathrobe tight and went to find the corkscrew.

*

It was a Saturday morning when Ellie found herself alone – her mum and dad on a weekend away to Buxton to cement their newly-mended relationship, Kasumi in Paris, Jethro presumably in bed with Claudia, and Ellie figured Patrick and Fiona had seen enough of her recently to last a lifetime. She had woken in the early hours for no reason at all, unable to go back to sleep. Later in the morning, rattling around, alone and restless in the house, the pull of Ben's corner was just too strong to ignore. Before she could stop herself, she was in her car and on the way there.

Ellie had never seen Constance Street so quiet. Other than the occasional car passing by and the chatter of the sparrows on rooftops there was little else to suggest that she was not the last person on earth. The lively group of women who had greeted her at most of her visits, back when this whole episode in her life had begun, had disappeared back to their lives. It was as if the last few weeks had been some strange dream. It was still early – perhaps Ben was spooned around Gemma in bed right now. Gemma would be breathing in his scent, content in the warmth of his strong embrace. It was Gemma who would wake him with a gentle kiss and nudge him playfully out of bed to make her coffee and toast. Gemma would creep behind him as he showered and kiss every inch of his broad, perfectly sculpted back. And it was her fault. She, Ellie, was the one who had walked away.

The new wave of despair at her loss was almost more than Ellie could bear; an ache that seemed to pierce her very soul. There were plenty of fish in the sea, as people had so often told her, but suddenly faced with the reality of it, the thought of that was terrifying. Ellie hadn't meant to fall in love, but now that she had, she didn't want to give her heart to anyone else. It was more than that; she didn't feel capable of giving it to anyone else. Ben had stolen it completely, and now she faced a future without him.

Taking a deep breath, Ellie took one last look up and down the street. There was no point in staying here now and it was too painful anyway. Head down, she started to walk back towards her car.

'I thought it was you,' Annette called as she crossed the road. Ellie swung around at the sound of her voice. 'What brings you round these parts? I'd have thought a quiet street like ours would be terribly boring now that Ben has moved on.'

Ellie painted on a bright smile. 'I was just passing, you know.'

'An odd place to just pass and get out of your car. Didn't you stop by the other day too? I could have sworn it was your car but by the time I'd got my slippers on to come out it had gone.'

'How have you been?' Ellie asked in a bid to steer Annette away from a potentially awkward conversation. 'Are the men of the street happier now that everything is quiet?'

Annette laughed. 'Just a bit. They can be slobbish and lazy again with nobody making them look bad.' She rested her hands on her hips as she squinted at Ellie in the sun that was now skimming the rooftops in a golden blaze. 'Have you heard from Ben since Gemma came back?'

'I've seen as much of him as you have on TV,' Ellie lied.

Annette studied her for a moment. 'You know, I thought at the time he was a little bit sweet on you. If she hadn't come back... well, who knows?'

'Me? Don't be daft.'

Ellie mused on Annette's observations. No wonder Gemma had gone out of her way to stake her claim over him. Annette didn't seem like the most tactful of women – it was likely that she had said something very similar to this in passing to Gemma that had sparked the whole campaign of lies in the first place.

'I was just about to make a cup of tea if you wanted to pop in for one,' Annette said, angling her head at the house across the road.

Ellie gave her watch a theatrical examination. 'I really have to get on. Thanks anyway, though.'

'Shame... I keep hoping that Ben and Gemma will pop round. They said they would keep in touch, but you know what youngsters are like.'

Ellie bit back a smile. 'I'm sure they will when they get a moment.'

Annette looked doubtful but nodded.

'It was lovely to see you again, Annette. Perhaps next time I can get that drink.'

'Oooh, that would be lovely.' Annette clapped her hands together. 'I'll keep a look out for you.' She turned with an airy wave and made her way back across the street. Ellie watched her go, took one last look around, and started back to her car.

When Annette had asserted she had seen Ellie's distinctive Mini parked on Constance Street before that day, she had been right. In fact, Ellie had been back there half a dozen times since her last disastrous meeting with Ben. She wasn't even sure why. Perhaps she was searching for answers, and Constance Street seemed as good a place as any to start. A small part of her wanted to see him, sitting on his corner, flask at the ready, a smile and a song on his lips. If she closed her eyes and wished really hard, she could almost smell his scent on the breeze, but it only seemed to happen in this spot.

Then, she spun around as she heard her name called.

Ben was jogging towards her, weighed down with a rucksack and a pair of folded seats.

'Wait!'

Ellie began to walk back to him, her heart pounding madly and barely able to breathe. Here he was, just when she felt at her most vulnerable, just when she felt that the slightest thing might break her. Even with all the uncertainty, despite everything she had said to him and promised herself, she still needed him like she needed air.

'What are you doing here?' she asked, glancing at his paraphernalia as he drew near.

'I was just about to set up camp.'

'Here?' Ellie asked more sharply than she had meant to. 'What's happened?'

Ben smiled tensely. 'I thought I might have to wait for someone.'

'Gemma's moved out again?' she asked in confusion.

'Yes…' he said quietly, 'but this time I asked her to.'

'Then what…' Ellie's sentence trailed off. She frowned as she looked at the chairs and the rucksack again. Poking out from between the folded seats was a piece of card. 'If you've asked her to move out, then why are you here?'

Ben pulled out the card and turned it to show her.

HAVE YOU SEEN THIS GIRL? PLEASE TELL HER BEN IS WAITING HERE FOR HER.

Next to the message, the photo of them that Ben had taken on his phone had been cropped so that only Ellie's image remained.

Ellie looked up at him. 'I don't understand.'

Ben shrugged. 'Neither do I. Since I last saw you I've done nothing but think about everything you said. I asked myself time and time again what I was doing, why I was making such a bloody mess of everything. But every time I looked at Gemma, sitting on our sofa watching TV or lying in our bed asleep, I wanted it to be you. That has to mean something… right?'

'I don't know…'

'I can't give up on you. I can't spend the rest of my life regretting how I let you go without a fight. I can't just throw away something that could be so special.'

'*Something special?*' Ellie repeated in a daze.

'Ellie… I don't know that I deserve this and I don't know how you feel since we last spoke but… ever since Gemma came back.…' He paused, as if uncertain of how to choose his next words. 'Being with you…' Ben said slowly, 'it made me feel something new, something I had never felt before. It was exciting and new and terrifying but familiar and comfortable and the only place I want to be. All at the same time. I know I didn't explain my feelings properly last time we met. I don't know if I'll do a much better job this time. I only know that I have to try again. I'm going to be honest with you, I have no idea if it's love but… it feels right, more right than anything I've ever felt. All I can think about is being near you, all the time. I can't concentrate on anything knowing that we're under the same sky but not together. You have to believe me, I would never have asked Gemma to marry me feeling like this; I swear it on the souls of my parents.'

He paused, studying her.

'I don't know what to say.'

'Say you feel the same.'

Ellie suddenly felt as if the world was spinning so fast it would tip her off. She stared at him.

'I need to think.'

He started again, breathless, his words tumbling out. 'You left the pub that day and it felt like my whole world had come crashing down around me. I didn't know what to do. I handled things badly and I knew I'd hurt you and I never want to do that. I thought that staying out of your life was the best thing… that it was what you wanted. So I forced myself to do that, but I can't anymore.'

Ellie shook her head. 'What about Gemma?'

'I was never what she wanted. She will be pissed off, and she might kick up a stink for a while, but this is for the best.'

'And you're sure that *we're* right for each other?'

He nodded. 'As sure as I can be about anything in this life.'

Ellie glanced across the street. She thought she saw a curtain twitch over in Annette's house but she couldn't be certain.

'But I didn't know what to do about it,' Ben continued. 'So I thought I'd wait for you, back at the place where we first met. I knew if you felt the same, you'd find your way back to me.'

Ellie remained silent as he held her in a pleading gaze. Against her will, a lone tear tracked her cheek. Ben reached with a gentle thumb to wipe it away.

'Don't cry… I never meant to upset you…'

Ellie shook her head. She knew she was supposed to say something but nothing would come out. Her tears only began to fall faster now and there was nothing she could do to stop them. Ben let his chairs fall to the floor with a clatter and pulled her into his arms.

'Oh Ellie… I never want to see you cry.'

His warm embrace was something she had dreamed of. Finally, things felt right. Finally, she knew what she had to do. And she sure as hell wouldn't lose him again. She leaned her head against his chest and closed her eyes. He stroked a hand over her hair.

'I'm sorry,' he whispered, 'I shouldn't have come here like this. I thought…' His sentence trailed to nothing.

Ellie looked up at him. 'I know,' she smiled through her tears. 'But I'm glad you came.'

'You are?'

'Yes.'

'So you're willing to give me a chance?'

'Yes.'

His smile was so wide Ellie thought it would burst from his face. He pulled her into the kiss she felt she had been waiting her whole life for.

'You have no idea how happy that makes me... I don't know what I would have done if you'd said no.'

Ellie gazed up at him. 'Me neither.'

They kissed again, and then she leaned against his chest and closed her eyes with a contented sigh, knowing, after all, that this was where she belonged.

A Letter from Tilly

I want to say a huge thank you for choosing to read *Worth Waiting For*. If you enjoyed it and want to keep up to date with all my latest releases, just sign up at the following link. Your email address will never be shared and you can unsubscribe at any time.

www.bookouture.com/tilly-tennant

I'm so excited to share Ellie and Ben's story with you. Some of you may know that it had a previous life as *The Man Who Can't be Moved*. It's been wonderful to immerse myself in their world once more, making the story better than ever and seeing it transformed with a new cover and title for new readers. I'm so proud to share this new version with you.

I hope you loved *Worth Waiting For* as much as I loved writing it, and if so I would be very grateful if you could write a review. I'd love to hear what you think, and it makes such a difference helping new readers to discover one of my books for the first time.

I love hearing from my readers – you can get in touch on my Facebook page, through Twitter, Goodreads or my website.

Thank you so much!
Tilly

tillytennant

@TillyTenWriter

www.tillytennant.com

Acknowledgements

If, as you turn the last page of this book, you think to yourself, *I'd love to read that all over again*, spare a thought for my long-suffering friend and erstwhile agent, Peta Nightingale. She had to read this book more times than she probably cares to remember, and always found a spark of something that made her go back and do it again. If you turn the final page and think, *That was a cracking book*, then that's down to her too. She trawled through all the previous drafts, waving her magic wand so that you would see only the final sparkly one.

And while I have your attention, I have many others to thank too. Firstly, my ever-patient family and friends, who never complain when I turn from a Mogwai to a Gremlin if they dare disturb my work time! I have to thank all the wonderful book bloggers, readers, and people of social media, who are endlessly encouraging and supportive. The same can be said for my fantastic author friends, in particular Mel, Holly, Jack, Jaimie and Emma, and so many others too numerous to list here but just as important. I have to shout out to my editor at Bookouture, Cara Chimirri, who has worked so hard and so enthusiastically to get *Worth Waiting For* polished up for a new lease of life. It's been an absolute pleasure to work with her and I'm looking forward to our future projects with a great deal of excitement! As always, I have to thank lots of others at Bookouture, including Alexandra Holmes, Kim Nash, Noelle Holten, Sarah Hardy and Alex Crow.

I'd also like to give a special mention to Philippa Milnes-Smith at The Soho Agency for being such a great caretaker of my early books.

Finally, I have to say, in the words of Abba, thank you for the music. It was sitting on a train listening to a fantastic song on my iPod that inspired this story.

SEE
7/2/22

CPSIA information can be obtained
at www.ICGtesting.com
Printed in the USA
LVHW042227151120
671787LV00044B/1285